Praise for Rose Young and
Roses, Wine & Murder
"★ ★ ★ ★ ★ - 5 stars Readers' Favorite"

"The story combines aspects from different genres — thriller, historical, mystery, and crime fiction — and pulls the reader into an intriguing world. *Roses, Wine & Murder* has a beautiful setting, a gripping plot, and readers can't resist the wonderful pacing. It's one of the most entertaining books I have read this year."

- Arya Fomonyuy, *Readers' Favorite*

"The brilliantly woven canvas upon which Rose tells her story has it all from pirates to poisonous plants! I implore all of you to curl up on the couch with a warm cup of tea or a nice glass of wine, clear your mind, and escape into *Roses, Wine & Murder*."

- Terrie Scott, Editor and Author of *Shattered Rose*

"The picturesque setting, coupled with the gripping plot, with wine dinners, poisonous plants, and a gritty investigation make this story a memorable one. ...An exciting read, intelligently plotted, and accomplished to a masterly finish. A must-read from one of today's best storytellers."

- Divine Zape, Reviewer

"*Roses, Wine & Murder - In the Ci*̣ ̣*Steeples* has a little of everything for readers; New England ṿ̣ ̣ ̣ ̣ ̣ ̣ ̣ ̣ ̣ ̣ ̣ ̣iing, mystery, intrigue, friendship, crazy escapadẹ̣ ̣ ̣ ̣ ̣ ̣ ̣ ̣ ̣reading."

- Trudi LoPreto, Reviewer

"Georgi anḍ ̣ ̣ ̣ ̣ ̣ ̣ ̣ ̣ ̣ ̣ ̣ ̣ ̣ ̣pair, playing well off each other with complemenṭ ̣ ̣ ̣ ̣ ̣ ̣ ̣. There's a sharp wit, humor, and intelligence in Young's writi̤ ̣ ̣ ̣ ̣will easily charm you. ...A fun ride, funny and compelling, with a complex mystery of threads that slowly come together in a satisfying conclusion."

- Liz Konkel, Reviewer

Roses, Wine & Murder

In the City of Steeples

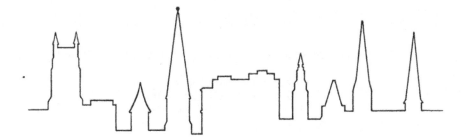

A Novel by
Rose Young

Roses, Wine & Murder - In the City of Steeples
By Rose Young

Revised Edition 2021

Best Books Publishing, 103 South Main Street, #324
Colchester, CT 06415

Printed in the United States of America

This is a work of fiction. Names, characters, businesses, organizations, places, events, and incidents portrayed in this novel either are products of the author's imagination or are used fictitiously. Any resemblance to actual persons, living or dead, events, or locales are entirely coincidental.

The Cataloging-in-Publication Data is on file with the Library of Congress.

ISBN 978-0-9988817-0-6 (e-book)
ISBN 978-0-9988817-1-3 (print)
ISBN 978-0-9988817-4-4 (audiobook)

Book Cover Design & Steeple Illustration: Cindy Samul
www.CindySamulIllustrator.com

Foreword

Rarely does a manuscript cross my desk that is as entertaining and intriguing as Rose Young's *Roses, Wine & Murder*. From the onset, the reader is swept into a madcap adventure with a murder mystery to solve. Steeped in New England history and the enticing world of vineyards and wine tasting, this kaleidoscope of colorful characters and locations mesmerizes the reader.

The brilliantly woven canvas upon which Rose tells her story has it all from pirates to poisonous plants! I implore all of you to curl up on the couch with a warm cup of tea or a nice glass of wine, clear your mind, and escape into *Roses, Wine & Murder*.

Terrie M. Scott
Editor

Terrie M. Scott has been an editor for over thirty years, with a MFA from the College Conservatory of Music, UC. She is also a decorated Army veteran and author herself.

Dedicated to:
My Inspirations

I dedicate this book to the hardworking men and women that make a little city pulse with vitality. I thank those who work in flower gardens and vineyards to create beauty and wine. They are an industrious community who made this book possible. My adopted city, New London, wonderfully inspired me, as does much of Southeastern Connecticut. In my research, I walk and drive the streets, take the trains and ferries, and find myself enamored by the rich history and architecture of the city of steeples and wine growing regions.

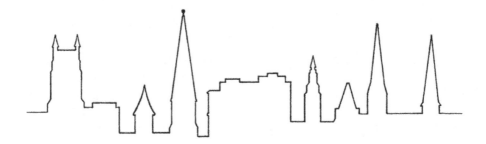

Roses, Wine & Murder
In the City of Steeples

FACTS:

All historical, viticulture, and gardening references in this novel are real.

The Connecticut vineyards can be found on the Connecticut Wine Trail.

There are more than 200 vineyards on Long Island, and several inspired this story.

There are thousands of vineyards, large and small, worldwide; all strive to make the best wine possible from their soil and climate, a.k.a. terroir. Wines graded upwards of ninety points are most desirable to wine connoisseurs and sommeliers.

The United States Coast Guard Academy, founded in 1876, is in New London, Connecticut. Presidents of the United States give a commencement speech periodically to the graduates.

New London, Connecticut, is a small city with a population of 27,000 people. The harbor became the base for military and naval operations during the Revolutionary War and Benedict Arnold attacked and burned New London in 1781. In the 1800s, New London became wealthy, as it was one of the world's three busiest whaling ports. These fortunes funded wonderful architecture and multiple churches with grand steeples throughout the city.

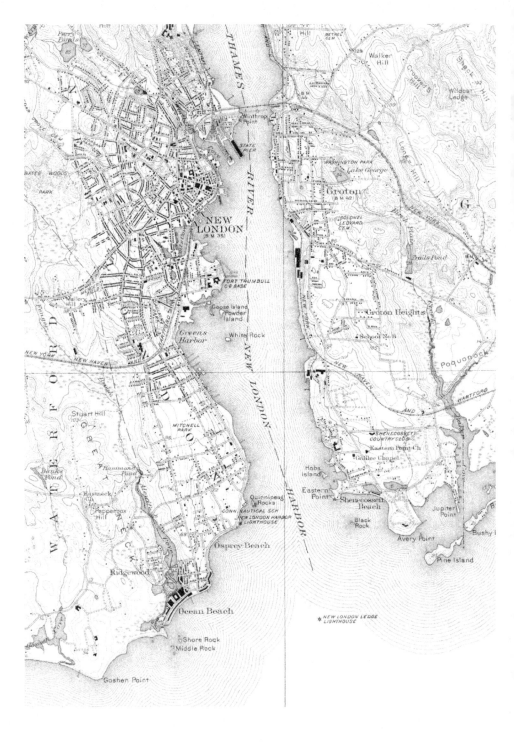

Prologue

The glowing orb on a black iron streetlamp failed to illuminate a quiet scene under the looming statue of Christopher Columbus. In the dark shadows of a small city garden, a black-clad figure crawled through the shrubbery. He desperately searched among the plants for a prized possession he lost in a scuffle. It was vital that he remain undetected, so his irritation grew with the interruption of passing headlights. Forced to stop his rummaging, due to the traffic, he proceeded silently toward his next destination.

Remaining in the shadows, the mysterious agent slipped into the alleyway of the posh Harlow Towers condominiums. Compact gear clung to his muscular form as he scaled with purpose and dexterity the grated ironwork of the Towers' parking garage. Its architects unwittingly provided perfect hand and foot holds for him to reach the third-floor roof. From his backpack, the undercover operator took a rope and small grappling hook and adroitly launched it onto a railing on a balcony far above.

With the ability of a mountaineer, he plied the rope, hand over fist, and ascended to the eighth-floor penthouse. Retrieving and packing his gear, he opened the unlocked balcony door.

Scanning the plush interior with a small flashlight, he moved toward the bedroom. Luggage was laid out on the bed. His gloved hands skimmed through, in, and under the clothes. Dissatisfied, he moved to the office.

A magnificent ebony desk was in the center of a contemporary room. The desk surface lacked a computer, hard drive, or laptop. To free his hands, he

3

placed the flashlight between his teeth. He opened the drawers of the desk, probing every crevice. His hands slid through papers; lifting them carefully, he scanned the words. Grunting in annoyance, he searched under the drawers.

Shining the light across the room on an opposite wall, he observed a panoramic picture of a vineyard. Recognizing a probability, the raider removed the large art photo. As suspected, a wall safe was behind it.

Retrieving a vial of chalk dust from a pocket, he brushed it on the surface of the safe's touch pad. Turning a knob on his flashlight, it now beamed ultra-violet. The numbered pips shone in the UV light. Four keys were prominently white.

Utilizing a digital device, he entered the numbers, and it calculated all possible combinations. He changed the numbers to read-out letters to attain any obvious word codes. One stood out. He entered 9463, and the safe clicked. The man snickered to himself, "*Quello che un buffone*" (What a buffoon)!

It spelled WINE. Pulling the handle, the door swung open, and he adjusted his flashlight to illuminate the safe's interior.

The intruder looked for a memory stick, CD, or SD card; seeing none, he groaned with impatience. He leafed through papers and found a jeweler's receipt and business contract. The contract was with his employer's Long Island vineyard partner. He slipped the papers into his backpack. He shut the safe, locked it, and replaced the artwork.

Swiftly, he removed his black garb attached by Velcro. The prowler donned a gray running suit. He stuffed the removed apparel into his backpack, placed a baseball cap on his head, and left via the penthouse elevator. He arrived at the ground floor parking garage and strolled onto Bank Street. A party of inebriated revelers wandered past him as he quite casually entered his silver sedan.

The thief drove to another building on Bank Street. The Vinho Verde Wine Bar was his next mark. After picking the lock, he slipped into the basement's delivery entrance. Standing inside the dimly lit surroundings, the trespasser observed the tall stone walls and ancient timber supports. The cellar was full of wine cases stacked into narrow rows. On his right, he spied a wooden staircase. Mounting it two treads at a time, he found a small office at the top.

He turned on the lone desktop computer and searched for the files he desired. Just as he suspected, the files had to be kept separate from the wine bar business and must be on a private laptop or memory stick. But where? Who had them?

After searching the premises, he had nothing more to accomplish at the Vinho Verde. Making his way down the stairs, he grabbed two bottles of French Cabernet Sauvignon before slipping into the night. A grin emerged as he clutched the fine vintage. *"Piccola ricompensa per i miei sforzi"* (Small reward for my efforts).

Chapter 1

Roxanne found herself disappointed with the president of the United States. His decision to give the commencement speech at the Coast Guard Academy in New London had uprooted her vacation plans. Her husband Sam, Fire Chief Samson, was part of the Homeland Security team and had to be available for the commander in chief's arrival in six days' time.

Roxanne expected to be tootling around in their vintage Buick, enjoying the sunny weather. Instead, she tended her garden at the Columbus Circle site for the New London Beautification Committee.

Carrying a hose from her truck, she attached it to the ground spigot and watered the small city plot. Grateful for shade, she admired the arching branches and mottled bark of the old London plane tree. Its fingered boughs reached over her and toward the Columbus statue, erected in 1928. Its broad canopy partly covered her quaint garden, a green oasis surrounded by pavement and the sporadic traffic of Bank Street whizzing by.

Silently appreciating a momentary lull, Roxanne noticed an odd sensation. It was a subtle sense of being watched. She looked around at the adjoining streets and buildings. Seeing nothing unusual, she continued watering.

Unexpectedly, disharmony grabbed her attention. Broken stems, squashed plants: a portion of the garden was in disarray! Sounds of dismay left her lips. "Ugh, those darn drunks! They trampled my flowers again." Crouching, Roxanne placed the hose on the ground to water the shrubs alongside the statue. Suddenly, she recoiled in horror and landed on her backside.

Motionless and staring at her through the evergreen shrubs were two glassy,

7

wide eyes! Backing away on all fours, her body shook and shivered. The lifeless eyes made her jump to her feet. Roxanne cried loudly, "Oh, for God's sake! I can't believe this!" His ashen-gray face was stiff as the stone he lay against.

Alarmed, she pressed her hands against her chest. Her heart was racing. A ripple of shock and nausea traveled through her body. Roxanne took a deep breath, trying desperately to shake off the feelings.

She glanced at him briefly and saw his body was oddly propped against the statue of Columbus. "Oh my," she whispered, "he's a handsome, well-dressed man!"

Roxanne envisioned what was to come next. She whined to herself, "Why couldn't we have just been away on our vacation?" Her husband would soon feel the same. His crew would be the first responders on the scene.

Shaking her head, she raised her eyes to the statue of Christopher Columbus and made the call to 911. The operator asked, "Nature of your emergency?"

"There's a man not breathing here at Columbus Circle on Bank Street. He appears to be dead!"

Fire Chief Samson heard the dispatch over the station's PA system: "Unconscious man at Columbus Circle on Bank Street. Engine Company One, rescue squad and ambulance responding."

Then his cell phone rang, displaying his wife's caller ID.

"Sam," she whispered, "a man seems to be dead here in my Columbus garden!"

"Oh, that was your call?" He felt deeply concerned for her.

"Yes, dear, I do mean dead! Please come quickly!"

The responders swooped in as Roxanne held onto her yellow brimmed hat. The stiff morning breeze off the water of Long Island Sound added another element of drama to Columbus Circle. She stood out amid all the dark uniformed police officers, rescue, and ambulance crews in her bright pink T-shirt and work jeans. Concerned for the man, she watched as her husband's crew trudged through the flowers to attend to him.

The emergency responders all knew her well, being the chief's wife. She was a quick-witted, petite blonde woman with a stylish pageboy haircut.

Roxanne saw her months-long work being destroyed. One of the younger men eyed her knowingly. "Sorry, Roxanne, we have big feet in these boots."

She murmured, "It's okay, Sebastian, I understand."

She took pride in the gardens she and her committee friends maintained. A dozen gardeners formed the New London Beautification Committee (NLBC) to enhance the town they loved and lived in. Containers and gardens full of colorful flowers were grown in high-volume traffic and tourist areas. Funds and water were provided by the city of New London, and these enthusiastic volunteers worked diligently to deliver beautiful cityscapes.

Roxanne was asked to stand by so the detectives could interview her about her discovery. As she waited, she spotted some of her NLBC friends arriving. They had responded to her text, "DEAD MAN IN GARDEN." The group huddled, beyond the police setback, by the corner bistro. They were assessing the situation and the damage being done to the garden.

Tessa, the NLBC leader, gave Roxanne a shrug, shook her head, and raised her hands in disbelief. Separated by the police cruiser that cordoned off the scene, they watched Roxanne in the thick of the activity.

An officer grabbed from the trunk of his cruiser a bright yellow roll of crime scene tape. In a swift motion, he stretched it around and through the flower garden.

"Oh no!" she lamented silently, sighed, and looked at her friends. They felt for her, the man, and the garden. Roxanne hung her head, and surrendered, "I give up."

Just then, Detective Dan Morrison approached her. "Hello, Roxanne. I see you've found yourself in the middle of a police case instead of hearing about it on the home scanner."

With a tone of, 'why me?' she answered, "Detective, you know it's not my plan."

He had known Roxanne and Chief Samson for many years. Morrison noticed Roxanne stayed out of the limelight, supporting her husband's position as fire chief. They frequently met at town functions, parades, and barbecues, and she was always available for interesting conversation.

They stood on the concrete sidewalk across from the large shade tree she had been admiring earlier. Morrison inquired in a low-key friendly tone, "Roxanne, I need to know exactly what you did when you arrived here this morning."

"It was eight a.m. when I pulled up in my truck and parked it where you see it," she said, pointing at the parking area by the bistro in the Harlow Towers building. "I took my hose and hooked it up there," she explained and showed him the green access box that was flush with the lawn.

"I pulled the hose across the bed behind the Columbus statue and noticed some flowers were trampled. I walked between the hostas to lay down the hose. It was then I saw him in the hedge just two feet away. We were eye to eye, Dan! Ohh, it gives me the shivers!" she shuddered. "Good gosh almighty! What a dreadful way to start a day."

"Yes," the detective agreed, nodding thoughtfully, "but Roxanne, what if you had not come by? Who knows when he would have been found if it weren't for you? He's completely hidden by these hedges."

"Yeah, better now than later," she said dryly, then wrinkled her nose and added, "excuse me but, he's not good fertilizer." Morrison knew full well she had a sense of humor, which she used to deflect her true feelings in tense situations.

"Do you know who he is?" she asked, becoming serious again.

"There is no ID," Morrison answered, "so he was probably robbed. He's clean-shaven and wearing an expensive suit and shoes. So right now, he's a John Doe."

"Oh my," she murmured and offered an idea. "Maybe his family is looking for him, and they'll call you."

"We'll see, Roxanne. I'll be in touch with you as needed. Thank you and have a better day."

"I will," she assured him. "I've decided to go to the Ocean Beach garden site and let the sea breeze blow these images away." She waved her hat over her head and grimaced, "Detective, this is too much for me. Do you get used to this?"

"You never become used to it, Roxanne," he shook his head. "I'll see you later." Detective Morrison moved on to join his forensic team.

Roxanne approached her husband and stood by him, watching the scene. Sam spoke softly to her and stated the obvious, "Aren't we a pair? Instead of having a relaxing vacation, we are knee-deep in a murder."

"Are you sure it's a murder?" she whispered. "Maybe he was drunk and choked on something or had a heart attack. Too often there are homeless people around here. Maybe one of them robbed him after he was dead."

Sam glanced at his wife swiftly. "Good thought process and in most cases, that would be a correct assumption, but probably not in this case."

Gasping, her hand moved up to her mouth in disbelief. "Are you sure it's a murder?"

"I believe so, dear," he answered, "since it appears someone has beaten him up and stuffed his mouth with a plant."

"What?" Stunned by the comment, she gave him a disturbed look. "If the beating didn't kill him, maybe the plant did."

"Yeah, he probably suffocated," Sam replied.

"Oh no," Roxanne said quietly. "What I mean is that the shrub he's lying in is poisonous, and if eaten, it is absolutely fatal."

"What?" Sam exclaimed under his breath. "Come with me. We have to report this to Detective Morrison."

chapter 2

The area around Columbus Circle was crowded with police cars, fire trucks, ambulance, and several SUVs. Roxanne trailed after her husband toward the detective. Sam's height was six feet two and appeared even taller dressed in his chief's uniform and cap. He was a robust man who enjoyed cooking and eating and hosted many firehouse barbecues and special fundraisers. Sam was good natured, yet commanding and direct when the job required it. He'd been a firefighter for over twenty-five years and wasn't planning on retiring soon.

With Sam by her side, Roxanne found herself feeling less nervous among the mayhem at the crime scene. They approached Detective Morrison.

"Detective, something else has come up."

"Yes, sir," Morrison turned from the two cops he was working with on the site.

"Roxanne, tell him what you told me," her husband invited.

"Well, Sam told me the man had his mouth stuffed with a plant," she offered. "Do you know which one it was?"

"Roxanne, I'm not sure it matters. Why? Are you missing some?" A glint of whimsy shone in his eyes.

"Dan," she whispered, "we've known each other long enough for me to say I'm not kidding around right now." His face became completely serious. "Yes, Roxanne, it was the same as the shrub he was found in."

"That, my friend," she asserted, "is Taxus baccata."

"Which is?" he probed tentatively.

13

Roxanne excitedly added, "It's extremely poisonous, Detective. Assuming the person who killed him knew how toxic it is, they really wanted him dead."

Morrison's interest changed. "Well, I'll be! Please, come with me. I'd like you to identify a sample we took from his mouth." From the back of one of the forensic team vehicles, Morrison retrieved a baggie and showed her the contents.

"Yes, that's it. That's the yew," she affirmed.

"Can you tell me the botanical name again?" he asked.

"Sure, it's Taxus baccata."

A little sheepishly, the detective asked, "Look, would you write that down for me here? Your Latin is better than mine."

As she wrote, he commended her. "Roxanne, you just saved me a step. This isn't just a brawl gone wrong. It appears we may have criminal intent to murder. Thank you for bringing this to my attention. And Chief, I'll see you this afternoon at our meeting with Homeland."

Detective Morrison moved toward his team to give them further instructions regarding the plant material.

Roxanne looked up at Sam as he leaned down and whispered, "Well, dear, after all these years…welcome to your first day on my job!"

She gave him a wry sideways look from her five-foot-two small frame and countered in a low tone, "Let's get this straight, Sam. This is your first day on my job!" He chuckled momentarily and then stopped, suddenly aware of his team and the leftover onlookers.

***

Strategically positioned away from the crime scene, the hawk-eyed killer observed the commotion through a pair of binoculars. "*Che peccato! Grande scarola!* (What a shame! Big money!)"

chapter 3

On the way to her next garden project, Roxanne took the scenic route along Pequot Avenue. She drove along the shore of the Thames River and Long Island Sound, passing large, lovely homes built after the hurricane of 1938. They lined the shoreline approaching Neptune Beach. She turned into Ocean Beach Park, which recently celebrated its seventy-fifth anniversary as a historic waterfront destination. She loved the beauty of this multiuse park.

The half-mile long, crescent-shaped sandy shore faced the sound. Its boardwalk's broad view included the popular red brick Ledge Lighthouse. Beachgoers could watch a constant parade of sailboats, tugboats, and ships pass in and out of the Thames River, some ferrying folks to Block Island, Rhode Island, and Fishers Island and Long Island, New York.

Roxanne occasionally saw the fabulous black navy submarines glide by. These nuclear whales skimmed through dark, silent waters, gathering data in the great oceans of the world. Arriving in Long Island Sound from a six-month mission, only then did Roxanne or anyone see the submarine's large black sail emerge twenty feet or more above the water.

With fanfare, several bright red tugboats and the Navy's Coastal Riverine Force escorted the great submarine. Often, she saw the naval crew on the hull deck waving proudly to people on the shore. This unannounced parade continued toward their families waiting at the Groton Naval Submarine Base.

Grabbing her tool bag and bucket, Roxanne strolled past huge potted concrete containers that her gardening buddies had planted. They were brimming with yellow flowering bidens, trailing heart-shaped potato vines, and magenta petunias. A tall canna lily with tropical burgundy leaves was the centerpiece. These colorful cheerleaders welcomed Roxanne and helped to erase the finality of death she witnessed at Columbus Circle.

Once at the edge of the boardwalk, she gazed out to the water, noticing the chop formed by the stiff breeze. The rhythm of the white foam rising and falling encouraged her to take in a deep breath of salty air. Her body responded and relaxed. She moved again toward the garden plot she planned to maintain.

Roxanne approached the garden by the large multipurpose banquet hall. Concession stands and arcades were on the ground floor, while the second level housed a few offices, the bar, and grand meeting rooms for weddings, dances, and parties. Roxanne had texted Tessa, the gardening leader of the NLBC, and expected her to arrive soon.

Determined to distract herself, Roxanne pulled a few tools from her bag and went to work deadheading, pruning, and weeding. She barely noticed the boardwalkers, sunbathers, shell collectors, and family outings gathering in numbers. She trimmed daylilies called 'Happy Returns,' appreciating their sunny yellow cups and the irony of their name.

Under the canopy of the boardwalk's shade, a few folks read their favorite book, newspaper, or e-book. Little did Roxanne know, someone was watching.

Once he knew she would be occupied for a while, he pursued his mission. The parking lot had filled up fast, and Roxanne's extended cab truck was now surrounded by cars and vans. The mystery man slipped the slim jim tool down the window of her truck door and quickly unlocked it.

Once in the truck, the man's gloved hands slid along the seat's crevices and into the compartments. He looked behind the seat and in the extended cab area. No purse, no little thing to hold what he was looking for. Disgruntled, he quickly left the cab of the truck without being noticed and knew what he had to do next.

Roxanne, feeling hot and sweaty, stepped back to assess her gardening work while lifting her water bottle to her mouth. She observed the backdrop of tall zebra grasses swaying in the wind, making a hissing sound. In front of them were shrubs of dark burgundy-leaved weigelas called Wine & Roses and pink flowering spireas called Anthony Waterer. They were accentuated by drifts of sweet flava daylilies, lemon-colored yarrow, pale pink poppies, blue elf delphiniums, multi-colored lantanas, and hot pink petunias.

There were several eye-candy vignettes like these that combined foliage and flower delights. Finally, Tessa came along, excited to ask Roxanne about the man found in the Columbus garden.

Delicately, Tessa leaned in and looked over her glasses at Roxanne as she asked, "Do you think he was a homeless man? You remember the guy they found two years ago near the Gold Star Bridge? Poor soul was a skeleton, picked clean by the birds. It's a shame no one knew he was in there. Only when the state crew came along to do the yearly mowing were those bones finally discovered."

Roxanne shook her head slightly, reassuring her friend, "No, this man was dressed very well, clean-shaven, and had good shoes. I thought he might have drunk too much and been mugged. But when they said he had a plant stuffed in his mouth, I thought right away that he was in the YEW!"

Tessa gasped, as her hand went to her mouth. "You don't say?" she whispered.

"Can you believe it?" exclaimed Roxanne. "So Detective Morrison has called it a homicide until the medical examiner tells him more."

"Oh, the yew is deadly," Tessa agreed. "They say a victim never has the chance to describe their symptoms because it acts so fast." She shifted in her gardening boots, kept her voice low, yet emphatically expressed with her hands, "So many plants we work with are poisonous: the lantana berries, the angel's trumpet, the morning glory, the castor-oil plant. We are surrounded by a veritable garden of death! Harmless to handle but deadly if consumed!"

Leaning toward Roxanne, she said, "It's a good thing no one knows what we know." Her eyes shifted from side to side to see if anyone had heard her.

Roxanne beheld her excitable friend. She was always good-humored with twinkly eyes and a 'get it done' spirit. She was wearing her green fatigues, floral T-shirt, pink boots, and a tool belt for her hand pruners, a sure sign of a serious gardener.

Roxanne laughed and added, "You know that famous line of yours that you quoted to Betsy's husband when she passed out in the heat? 'We work till we drop.' Well now someone's dead from a plant in our garden, dear me!"

Tessa huffed, "Well, no one could have imagined that happening! Don't tell Ed at the city! He'll have us pulling out all the plants that are suspects."

"Oh, Ed doesn't care," Roxanne replied. "He hears so many wonderful praises about our Beautification Committee. He'll plug his ears so not to hear that a man had a toxic plant from our garden in his mouth. Maybe there's a chance some drunk mugged him and wanted to keep him quiet. You know a drunk will do pretty much anything stupid."

Tessa nodded, "Yes, and let's keep the poisonous plant list to ourselves. We don't need to put a spotlight on all those plants I mentioned."

"No worries," teased Roxanne. "I'll put it in my next blog post on our NLBC garden site." She watched Tessa's face become horrified, then corrected herself. "Don't worry, Tessa, the secret life of plants is safe with me."

Tessa gave Roxanne's arm a soft punch as they laughed. A group of women strolled by on the boardwalk. "Tessa, I'm going to stretch my legs before I go home. I think the path by the tidal pool will be relaxing."

Tessa put one arm around her friend. "You've done enough today. Take the day off. Unwind and I'll see you again soon." Tessa moved on to care for another garden site at the beach.

Roxanne placed her tools in the back of her truck as families with armloads of beach supplies passed her in the parking lot. Children with sand toys were rushing toward the beach, squealing with delight. She strolled toward the quiet area in the shade by the salt marsh.

A narrow path brought her behind the swimming pool and the children's splash pad. She waved to the lifeguard. He knew Roxanne since she and her NLBC team had gardened there for years. Playful sounds of laughter trickled through the trees until she arrived at the wild conservation area.

Along the walk were sweet-scented rugosa roses, beach plums, elderberry, and viburnum shrubs. A mockingbird sang out as she approached the lookout deck with a view of Long Island Sound. Again, Roxanne took a deep breath, relieved to have time and the beauty of her surroundings separate her from the dead man's eyes. A great blue heron caught her attention. He cocked his head, ready to dart onto some fishy prey.

Suddenly, Roxanne was pushed forward headlong into the reeds. She gasped and felt something give a quick tug on her waist. Stunned, she found herself stuck in a hummock of eight-foot-tall marsh grasses. Struggling, she had nothing to push against to raise herself up.

"Help!" she yelled hopefully. "Help! I need help!" Finally, she was able to turn around and clamber out of the tall reeds. The lifeguard from the swimming pool heard her cry and raced over to help.

"What happened, Roxanne? Are you okay?" He looked her over to see if she was hurt.

"No, I was pushed." She felt around her waist. "I've been mugged! My fanny pack is gone."

He looked around, then picked up her hat and water bottle. "I'll call the manager, Joe."

He pulled a walkie-talkie from his belt as she attempted to straighten herself out. "Joe, Roxanne has been mugged. Can you call the cops?"

Roxanne gasped, "Oh no! Not again! I just want to go home."

"We have to, Roxanne. It's our policy," he said calmly.

The young man looked so concerned, and she felt bad for him. He led her to a nearby bench. Joe and a couple of other men arrived.

"Roxanne! Are you alright?" Joe asked, exasperated as she was a friend.

"Joe, I am having one of those days where a beach chair and a stiff piña colada would do me good."

"I can provide both, but we have to talk to the police first," Joe cautioned gently.

chapter 4

"**Y**ou again?" the officer asked Roxanne.

"Yeah, I'm not happy to see you either," she said, feeling a bit dejected.

"It's Roxanne Samson, right?" He was writing on a small notepad.

"Yes."

"Do you want me to call the chief?" the officer asked.

"Goodness, no!" she said, alarmed. "My husband is busy enough. I don't want to bother him."

She reported the simple details of the mugging. "I didn't see him. I don't even know who pushed me, or if it was a guy."

The officer confirmed they were looking for a black fanny pack. Then he told her they would canvas the area and question people.

"We'll be back. Please wait with Joe, Mrs. Samson."

In the meantime, Joe led Roxanne to his office that had a wonderful view of the beach and Long Island Sound. The office was down the hall from the bar, lounge, and banquet hall.

"One piña colada coming up," Joe said.

"Oh, hold the alcohol, Joe. I feel the need to stay clearheaded right now." Joe strolled to the bar and gave the order to the bartender, deaf to Roxanne's request.

Roxanne smiled at him. "I really appreciate you taking time with me, Joe. It's been quite a day."

He handed her the drink. "Don't even think about it. We're like family. We all care for this old place like it's our home." He gave her a look of deep

21

concern. "I'm sorry this happened to you, Roxanne. It is so rare. Only the occasional missing bag or lost item is the usual around here. So tell me, what was that officer talking about when he said, 'you again?'"

"Oh!" She raised her hands for emphasis. "Just this morning."

"What?" he asked quizzically.

"I found a dead man in the Columbus Circle garden, Joe."

His mouth dropped open in horror. "Really?" he said aghast. "Who was it?"

"They don't know yet. He had no identification, and he wasn't a homeless guy." Her face was contorted by several emotions that made him start laughing. He tried to stop, but her expression was priceless.

"Yeah, you laugh," she chastised him, "but how would you like to be bending down in the garden and find a dead man staring up at you?" To show her displeasure at his callousness, Roxanne added, with some degree of sarcasm, "I nearly suffered whiplash and fell back on my bum."

"Oh geez, Roxanne, I'm so sorry." He imagined her recoil and slapped his knee as he started to laugh again.

Roxanne shook her head and, with a shadow of a smile, conceded to him. "I guess when you're removed from it, it sounds a little funny." Catching the moment, she taunted him. "What if you found him, Joe?"

He responded, "I would have jumped so high and run so fast that I would have been at the firehouse faster than making the call." She knew he would have. He continued describing the film reeling in his mind.

"I would have looked like one of the Three Stooges, flailing my arms while mouthing strange sounds as if a ghost were on my heels." Roxanne could picture Joe's soft, round figure suddenly moving at a speed it never does, running the two blocks. They both chuckled at the image.

They finally settled down, and Roxanne remarked, "Thanks, Joe. I needed a laugh, and you're a good friend. I've had a hell of a morning." She took a long sip of her drink.

Joe empathized, "I understand. Besides, a little laughter is good for your heart. You know tragedy and comedy are at opposite ends of the spectrum. When you have tragedy, sometimes you need a little of the other."

"Thanks, Joe," she murmured.

They both turned to the door after hearing knocking.

Police officers returned with Roxanne's fanny pack.

"Can you tell us what's missing?" an officer asked.

Roxanne opened it. "Here are my keys, my wallet with thirty dollars, my credit cards, but my license is gone."

"That's weird," Joe commented.

"Can we walk you to your car and escort you home, Mrs. Samson?" the officer asked.

"Normally I would say no, but today, I'll take all the help I can get," she answered appreciatively.

After she thanked Joe with a big hug, the officers accompanied her to her truck. She climbed into the cab. Everything looked fine but as she settled into the seat, she sensed something was wrong. Her thoughts raced. *That's impossible. The seat has been moved!* She adjusted the seat and started thinking. *Someone's been in my truck. What's going on here?*

She drove through the parking lot gates. The officers were behind her as she passed Neptune Beach and took a left on Ocean Avenue. Their home wasn't far, just down a few streets in a quiet historic part of New London.

As she was about to turn into her driveway, Roxanne was shocked to see someone leap off her front porch and dash toward the backyard. Startled, she stopped the truck in the road. The officers following her slammed on the brakes, nearly running into the rear of her truck. They watched her jump out and run toward her backyard. Both bounded out of the car and followed her to the back of the house, only to find her climbing an arborvitae tree and peering over the back fence.

"He got away!" she yelled.

The two men stood there in the middle of her Asian contemplation garden looking up at her.

"Who?" they asked in unison.

"The guy who just jumped off my porch," she answered, clinging to her branch.

"We didn't see him," they said simultaneously.

She looked at them queerly. And they looked at each other.

She quickly rattled off the details. "He's wearing a gray running suit, black sneakers, and has dark brown hair, sunglasses, and a baseball cap on."

"Come with us, Mrs. Samson," ordered one of the officers. "We're going to scope out the neighborhood."

"Ahh, okay," she said from her branch, "but first, can you help me get down from this tree?"

One officer cupped his hands while Roxanne held onto the shoulders of the other. Gracefully, they let her down and all quickly scrambled into the cruiser.

"Go to the right!" Roxanne ordered with confidence. The officers obeyed. "He could sneak through the yards to the next street," she explained. They drove up and down through the neighborhood for fifteen minutes, then cancelled their pursuit.

"Let's get you home, Mrs. Samson."

They entered her door and looked around the house. She went from room to room with them. It didn't seem he had been in the house. Roxanne made them iced tea. They went to the porch, gladly quenching their thirst. The officers kept a lookout, making sure the character was not coming back. The safety of the fire chief's wife was a priority.

"Okay, guys, that's enough excitement for today. I'm done."

"Yes, ma'am, we'll make a full report," the senior officer assured her.

"Ahh, can you leave out the part where you had to help me get out of the tree?" she quizzed with a smirk. "They don't really need to know that, do they?"

They chuckled. "No, ma'am, that won't be in the report."

"Thanks, guys, I appreciate it. I don't want stories of me up a tree circulating through the department."

The officers left, and their first order of business was to call Chief Samson to report what happened. After his morning meeting with Homeland Security, he left work immediately and headed home to Roxanne. But on his way, he made a call to Detective Morrison.

Chapter 5

Trying to settle down from the morning activities of murder and mugging, Roxanne made a sandwich and took it to their front porch with a book under her arm. She looked up and down the street. All was peaceful. She peered down each side of the house. One of the neighbor's cats came gingerly out of her herb garden. *Well, if the cat isn't bothered, the guy must be gone,* she reasoned. She sat down and heaved a sigh. Now alone, she wondered, *Am I safe? Should I be afraid? I'm exhausted.*

To clear her mind, she opened a botanical book on poisonous plants. Looking up the yew shrub *Taxus baccata,* she read, 'The yew was so deadly that often the first sign of toxicity was death. In ancient Roman times, a decanter made of yew wood was filled with wine to poison ones' enemies who drank from it.'

"Oh." She moaned and took a big bite of her sandwich when she saw the red and white fire chief SUV pulling up in front of the house. Sam came lumbering up the steps looking a bit concerned.

In a voice muffled with food, she asked, "What are you doing here?"

He smiled, sat down, and patted her hand. "I'm just checking on you."

She wrinkled her brow and said more clearly, "Oh, for Pete's sake, they told you."

"Of course, they did, dear," he replied. "They'd be in a heap of trouble if they didn't. You know that."

"Well then, I'm glad you're here," she conceded.

"Look," he said, "I think it's all connected."

"What is?" she asked.

"The murder, the mugging, and the guy here at the house."

"You do?"

"Yes." His face was pallid with concern.

"Well, in a way, I feel better," she said, surprising him. "At least I know I haven't turned into a bad luck charm. I was starting to take all this commotion personally, wondering if I needed to start doing more good in the world. Now, I can go back to being happy with myself knowing it's not me. It's the murderer." She paused and had a realization. "Wow, that doesn't make me feel better. What are we going to do? How concerned should we be?"

"I called Morrison. He's coming over." Sam squeezed her hand. "He thinks it's all related too. We don't want to let any details fall through a crack." Sam was silently brooding. *Who knows what this murdering, mugging idiot will do next. We must get a tight grip on this situation.*

"Oh geez, do you think I can change clothes before my next interrogation?" she pleaded. "I'm sweaty and overwhelmed."

Chuckling, Sam observed, "The one thing I can count on is your wisecracks."

"Well, life wouldn't be any fun if we forgot how to laugh," Roxanne answered back with a twinkle in her eye for him.

"That's our glue," he acknowledged, squeezing her hand. Sam was not surprised his wife was handling things so well, but he didn't want to take her strength of character for granted. Having seen people crack after too much stress was something he was trained to look out for. Besides, this was his love and he felt protective.

When Morrison drove up, they met him on the porch. Roxanne recounted the events at the beach and her concern about the man on their property. The detective took it all in before he updated her and Sam.

"Here is what we found out. I had our officers take the murder victim's picture around to all the Bank Street storefronts in case someone saw him recently. Georgi Algarve identified him, poor soul. He was beside himself. He was in despair. It was his boss that was murdered: Mitch Stockman, the owner of the Vinho Verde Wine Bar."

"Oh no, Georgi is so sweet!" Roxanne exclaimed. "I know him. We plant his containers and window boxes. I thought he was the owner of Vinho Verde!"

Morrison explained, "No, Mr. Algarve actually manages the business and is a partner. He says he owns a small percent. The man you found is from Long Island. He comes here to check on Mr. Algarve and the business. It's hard to say what warranted his murder, but I hope to find out soon enough."

Roxanne asked the obvious, "How do you think the mugging and the man here at the house tie into the murder?"

"It has to, Roxanne. It's too much of a damn coincidence. The murderer must think you saw something or found some evidence that could give us a clue. I can't say what because we combed the scene and didn't find anything apparent. When you first arrived at Columbus Circle, did you see anything unusual? A car, a person, anything you can remember?"

"Gee, Dan, everything seemed average to me, except my trampled flowers," she replied.

Roxanne reviewed the scene in her mind. "I parked my truck, grabbed my tools, hooked up the hose and then saw the dead man. It was quite an ordinary day until I found poor Mr. Stockman."

The detective theorized, "If that's the case, then the murderer must have been watching the scene. He followed you to Ocean Beach. If he inadvertently left something behind, he must have thought you found it."

She eyed her husband. "What are we to do now, Dan?" Roxanne felt insecure, and Morrison recognized his friend's needed assurance.

"Well, he saw the police with you here at your house. I think it's safe to say he won't be around again." Morrison glanced at the chief. "I'm waiting on forensics for more details. Right now, I'm on my way to interview Mr. Algarve. We've searched Stockman's condominium, and Mrs. Stockman will be arriving from Long Island tomorrow for questioning."

Roxanne sympathized, "Georgi is such a dear. I hope he's going to be okay."

"How well do you know him?" the detective probed.

The chief informed Morrison, "She knows everyone, Detective, and if you don't know that by now, you soon will. I think she is more popular than me because of her gardening committee. Since her group does all the local city garden sites, they end up meeting the neighbors, store owners, and even the politicians."

Roxanne added, "Georgi is one of the few who donate money to the Beautification Committee. He is on the City Center District planning committee, and he pays us to do the planters in front of his store. I've had coffee and scones with him on several occasions."

Morrison pushed his hand through his hair. "Is that right? Well…it's not protocol, but would you like to come with me to talk to him? Maybe we can find out why someone is following you."

"Sure thing," she quickly agreed.

"Wait a minute, wait a minute," Chief Samson protested. "Detective, do you really think that's a good idea involving Roxanne like this?"

Roxanne spoke before the detective could. "I'm already involved, dear, and Georgi is my friend. Maybe we can see this mystery done and over so we can all sleep tonight." He knew she was right, and he eyed Detective Morrison.

Morrison picked up the thread. "Chief, since she knows him, he might be more comfortable with her and probably reveal more or say something he wouldn't share with us. It could help us move this along. I'd like to see how Mr. Algarve responds around Roxanne and if she notices anything unusual about him." Morrison was asking for permission and the chief knew it.

"Alright, but I'm coming along," the chief asserted. "Let me change out of my uniform since I'm off duty."

"Okay, Chief," the detective razzed, knowing they were really never off duty, in or out of uniform.

***

Detective Morrison was about fifteen years younger than the chief's fifty-two years. Morrison was promoted to lead detective just three years earlier after being a skilled uniformed officer for thirteen years. When the position opened, Chief Samson gave him an excellent recommendation due to his work on a couple of arson cases they solved together.

Samson reported that Morrison had a razor-sharp mind for details and a bloodhound's instinct. He couldn't have solved the arson cases without him. Sam was now relying on the detective's shrewd abilities to protect his wife. Little did he know Georgi Algarve was about to introduce a whole new dynamic to the investigation.

Chapter 6

The door chimed as Detective Morrison, Roxanne, and Chief Samson walked into the Vinho Verde Wine Bar. Georgi, obviously frazzled, paced back and forth between the racks of wine bottles. He was talking to himself.

Interrupted by their presence, he looked up and recognized his friend. "Ohh! Roxanne!" he wailed with his arms in the air as he rushed toward her. His thin frame wore slim black slacks, a designer belt, and a starched, soft green shirt. "Oh, thank you for coming. You're such a doll," he crooned. She gave him a big hug, and he started to cry. Blubbering, he said, "What am I going to doo?"

"There now, Georgi," she assured him, patting his back, "we'll figure things out together." He hung on to her and didn't stop fretting until she said, "Georgi? You know my husband, Chief Samson." Georgi let go of her immediately, wiped his tears, and stiffly nodded to the two men.

"It's okay, Georgi, you can relax," Sam counseled. Georgi swiftly went into a femme fatale pose, hand against his forehead, hip swiveled, and he swooned, "What am I to doo?"

Detective Morrison raised his eyebrows, then cleared his throat. "Georgi, we have to review some details with you, as I have new information from Roxanne here."

Surprised and wide-eyed, Georgi inquired of Roxanne, "What is it, my dear?" Then he muttered, "Oh, oh, where are my manners? Come, sit down here at the tasting table."

The spacious room had a high ceiling with large rafter beams and floors of wide pine planks with a golden patina. Old brick walls were supported by

31

chiseled granite blocks. Tasting tables of polished oak stretched across the room. Multipaned industrial windows let in the eastern light and framed the view of the sailing and shipping activity on the Thames River. The chief and detective sat on one side of the table, and Roxanne sat opposite them next to Georgi.

"Georgi," Detective Morrison began, "I'm going to record this interview, and it will be part of our investigation." He placed his digital recorder on the table and added, "When you met with the police earlier today, they didn't tell you Roxanne found your boss, Mr. Stockman. I brought her here to help fill in more details so we can apprehend the perpetrator."

Georgi gasped as his hand went to his chest. "Oh, Roxanne, that's just horrible!" he squealed.

Roxanne told her story, including all that had happened at Ocean Beach Park and her home. Hearing she was mugged and someone was on her porch made Georgi start whimpering. "I don't understand," he groaned. "What if I'm next? What do they want? We're just running a simple business. Detective, what are we to do?" Georgi pleaded with him, his face and body contorted under the emotional distress.

The detective did not find this type of drama common, but he held his composure and explained, "Georgi, we have to follow basic procedure. We gather as much data and details as possible. That's what we are doing now. I put it all together like a puzzle. Tomorrow morning, Mrs. Stockman is coming in, and we'll interview her too."

With another melodramatic move, Georgi clasped his forehead and groaned, "Oh no! Uhh! She's not into this business, and that's another reason I am so upset. She'll close us down, and I so love the wine business, parties, tastings, vineyard tours, and catered events. Mitch loved this business too. He was here twice a month and was pleased with how I ran it."

Rambling on, he added, "But he loved her, I could tell, and she always wanted him home and not here, so I guess she loved him too. Detective, she hates New London. She is so over the top with 'Long Island this' and 'Long Island that.'"

"Okay, Georgi," Morrison commanded as he interrupted the emotional rant, "let's go over some facts, shall we?"

Georgi calmed down and tried to behave, but Roxanne knew that wouldn't last for long. She put her arm around his and hugged it to help him settle down. Chief Sam admired his wife's care and compassion.

"How's the business been doing?" the detective asked Georgi.

"It's been really growing each month by word-of-mouth. We have a wide range of patrons, all different ages, and many who travel quite a distance. We are open Wednesday to Sunday and thinking we need to expand our hours."

"Are you aware of any enemies of Mr. Stockman's, such as disgruntled vendors, employees, neighbors, anyone whom you can think of?" asked Morrison.

"I really can't say there are any enemies. I've been with him since he opened about two years ago. Mitch has been traveling to New London for several years, visiting and supporting local vineyards, buying wine, and creating relationships. He got along with everyone, really." Georgi's voice wandered off as he reflected.

Then he added, "We did have someone try to break into the basement through the back some months ago, but the place is built like a fortress out of granite and has barred windows. They only damaged the door and broke some glass." He paused a moment before continuing, "There is a scruffy delivery man we deal with who's always in a bad mood and a little rough around the edges, but for God's sake, no one's perfect!"

Suddenly, Georgi's body language drama returned. As his hand swiped the air, he laughed at himself. "We're all unique. Look at me!" His arms flung out wide, and he struck a pose. They all smiled knowingly.

Roxanne gave him a squeeze. "You're adorable," she said softly. He smiled at her and squeezed her back.

"Sooo," Morrison continued, "as I have here in the notes from this morning, Stockman came on the eight a.m. auto ferry from Long Island yesterday. He drove himself to Stonington to visit three vineyards, then he met you here at twelve thirty p.m. You unloaded the cases of wine from his vehicle and had lunch brought in. You had a two p.m. meeting here with Chamard Vineyards from Clinton, Connecticut."

"Yes," confirmed Georgi. He gazed toward the raftered ceiling and searched his thoughts. "Then we relaxed on the back deck. Mitch enjoyed a Havana Montecristo cigar while we shared a bottle of Paul Roget Champagne. Did you know this was a Winston Churchill tradition? Mitch loved imagining Churchill with the long torpedo cigar, pondering his place in the world with a glass of champagne." Georgi meekly smiled at the memory.

"And when did he leave?" the detective queried.

"At four o'clock, he left to drop off his luggage and rest at his condominium in Harlow Towers. He came back here for the six p.m. wine dinner event. It went wonderfully, and Mitch left at ten thirty for his condo. It's a short walk down the street. That's the last time I saw him."

Georgi became somber and stared at the floor. Tears trickled down his cheeks, and Roxanne handed him a tissue.

"What else did he do when he came to New London? And who did he know, Georgi?" asked Morrison.

"He's here twice a month, and our routine is always different. This time, he went to the vineyards in the morning directly from the ferry. Sometimes I go with him, but we had a wine tasting event last night, and I had to prepare."

Georgi paused, "He liked New London because no one knew him here, compared to the north fork of Long Island. He easily walked to restaurants on Bank or State Street to see what they were serving for wine. We often went to

Mystic, Stonington, and coastal restaurants to see what wines they were serving. He was a great boss."

Chief Samson spoke up. "Georgi, I'm concerned for Roxanne's safety. There is something missing in your story. No one seems to have a motive to kill Mitch Stockman."

Georgi reiterated, "I can just tell you what I know and who I like, and the only ones I don't like are that scruffy delivery man and Mitch's wife, who I don't really know. I don't think either one wanted him dead. Oh, I feel dreadful. How am I to go on?" He put his head on Roxanne's shoulder.

"Okay, Georgi," Morrison informed, "we'll do some more research. I'll be sending officers here tomorrow to go through the business books and look around a second time."

Georgi moaned, "Everything is going to change tomorrow when Cruella, I mean, Marissa gets here."

"Why is that?" asked Roxanne.

"Because," he replied, "she'll ask me to buy her out, which I can't do, or she'll close me down. I just hope she gives me some time."

Georgi looked out to the water, then mindfully put two fingers to his pursed lips and continued, "Come to think of it, Mitch didn't seem his jovial self. He told me I was doing a great job, and he was very pleased. I felt his sincerity. He said his wife wanted him home for the summer, and it would be two months before he would be back again. That was a surprise to me as he was here twice a month since the beginning. He kept an active hand in the business."

Then falling back into despair, he grieved, "I'm going to miss him. My whole world is falling apart." Emotions overcame him again; tears rolled down his face. Roxanne put her arm around him, and he leaned into her.

"It will take time, Georgi, but you'll be alright," Roxanne assured him. "Right now, we must find out who killed Mitch and that means helping the detective any way you can."

Morrison questioned, "Is the business incorporated, Georgi?"

"Well, yes. Mitch insisted upon it. He said it kept the paperwork easy. I just went along because it all looked fair to me."

"How does that play in, detective?" asked Chief Sam.

"It means the wife won't be able to touch the business right away. Also, as long as we are investigating a murder, she has to wait for us to finish our work. You have a little time, Georgi, but you might need a business lawyer to keep things straight."

"Thank you all," Georgi said. "And I feel a little better with you here, Roxanne."

Detective Morrison and Chief Samson stood up. Roxanne gave Georgi another hug and said as they all left the building, "Don't worry too much, and call me if you need me."

***

Out by the river docks, a man read a text message from a kid spying on the Vinho Verde Wine Bar. "The cops are leaving with the blonde."

"*Problemi*," the man said under his breath and then swore out loud, "*Mannaggia! Grande difficolta*!" (Problems. Damn! Great difficulty!)

Chapter 7

Vinho Verde – (Veen-yoh Vehr-day) - A popular table wine from Portugal that has a fresh lemony-crisp flavor. It is light green in color, ideal with fish, and low in alcohol content.

Day 1 – 6:30 p.m. - The Vinho Verde Wine Bar

Georgi's wine dinner, scheduled for sixteen patrons, could not be abandoned due to Mitch Stockman's demise. The reputation of the Vinho Verde rested on their exclusive clientele. Georgi also felt pressed since he had purchased the food and received prepayment for the event. With the help of his supportive waitstaff, he was determined to carry on, yet he felt the burden of sorrow and worry that now weighed upon his twenty-nine years.

At six thirty p.m., the Vinho Verde was primed. Soft jazz music floated through the rafters, creating a relaxed atmospheric mood for the diners. Elegant vases of white Phalaenopsis orchids graced the long oak table. Each place setting had distinctive wine glasses aligned for the tasting and were accompanied by polished silver and cloth napkins.

Georgi stood by and waited for the guests to settle. He appeared as usual, his hair razor-trimmed on the sides with a full tuft top, a starched lavender dress shirt with sleeves rolled neatly below the elbow, and gray silk blend slacks. He tried with difficulty to not focus on his friend and boss, Mitch Stockman. Albeit the standard sparkle usually visible in his eyes had dimmed.

Georgi did his best to gather up the enthusiasm required to entertain the sizable group. The waiters served the appetizers and poured the first wine. The young sommelier held the stem of the wine glass with two fingers and rang a small bell.

"Good evening, everyone. Before you is a lovely chilled, bubbly red Shiraz. It is great for a hot summer's day. It is a party starter with its fruity musk, cleansing fizz, and medium body. The hint of sweetness is delightful."

Georgi found his rhythm and turned up the charm. "The Shiraz grape is a fruity Australian, and this offering is from Penfolds Wines." Georgi gave his fruity representation with a twist of his hip and shoulder, a turn of his head, and a smile. "Sounds nice, doesn't it?" Everyone chuckled.

"Compared to the well-known Syrah grape of France, the Australian Shiraz is made from riper grapes, more fruit-driven, higher in alcohol, less obviously tannic, and peppery rather than smoky. Usually, the wine is more approachable within the first two years. Believe it or not, it is also sensational at another time of year: with Christmas turkey! It is well-known to complement the fixings and flavors of a festive holiday meal."

Georgi gave them time to ask questions, sip their wine, and enjoy the appetizers. When the guests were ready, his servers presented the next course, and Georgi announced the wine.

"Our next wine is an enchanting Sauvignon Blanc, and it is crisp, dry, and refreshing. Saltwater Farm Vineyards, here in Connecticut, age the wine in stainless steel tanks. This elegant libation brings to you the full flavor of the Sauvignon Blanc grape, which originates from the Bordeaux region in France." Everyone followed Georgi's lead, swirling the glass, noticing the wine's color, and sniffing its perfume before taking a sip.

"Please notice the notes of lime zest balanced by clean minerality and the exotic fruit finish with a hint of white pepper. This lovely wine will deliciously complement our locally harvested oysters in our shiitake mushroom soup. Please enjoy!"

The patrons murmured their enjoyment of aromas and flavors while cooing over the pairing and delectable soup.

Upon readiness of the next course, Georgi rang his small bell to announce it. "My dear guests, here we have a beautiful Pinot Blanc wine from Shinn Estate Vineyards on the north fork of Long Island, New York. The grapes are grown sustainably on their enchanting biodynamic vineyard. We are serving the wine with luscious warm lobster and fresh spring greens."

Everyone took a sip and a taste, then melted into a dreamy utopian place, floating on a flavor wave that rippled across, then out, evidenced by their verbal 'oohs and aahs.'

Georgi highlighted, "This lovely Shinn Vineyards Pinot Blanc wine is vibrant and fruit-driven. It can balance on your tongue the rich creaminess of lobster tossed in lemony aioli wonderfully. I find that enjoying wine with a complementing food is a synergetic education of both, like a fine dance in your mouth."

In the traditional way, Georgi kissed his fingertips and loudly made the sound. "Mwah! Isn't this delightfully fun?" His patrons happily nodded, savoring the wine and food.

The last course was dessert. By now, the conversations were louder and filled with laughter. To get their attention, Georgi rang the little bell.

"Attention, everyone, we have two desserts for you to choose from: chocolate cherry torte or rhubarb and custard pie — a recipe passed through my family." The diners made their dessert choices and were served as Georgi prepared to announce the wine selection.

"I would like to present our next wine: a Napa Cabernet Sauvignon from Jonathan Edwards Winery here in North Stonington, Connecticut. Mr. Edwards travels every year to California to utilize their grapes and make fine wines there," Georgi emphasized, "that he brings here for us to enjoy. It is a lushly flavored, bold, dry red wine aged in oak for eighteen months. This wine is the perfect accompaniment to either of these fine desserts you have before you. The intense flavors are rich in cassis, dark chocolate, and fresh earth.

"Our second virtuous wine from the vine is Inniskillin's Sparkling Vidal Icewine, originating from Niagara-on-the-Lake, Ontario, Canada." Georgi looked over his guests, raised his eyebrows, and accentuated, "Yes, my friends, I said icewine. They harvest the grapes only after they have frozen on the vine. This allows for a sweet, more concentrated wine. Served cold, this delightful libation will shimmer over your tongue. The natural acidity balances well with the luscious sweet nectars of mango, lychee, citrus, and pineapple. Both of these wines offered will meld lovingly with either of these delectable desserts."

The guests made their wine choice and were served. Georgi rang for attention and intoned, "As we are about to sip in celebration of the new growing season, please raise your glasses high. I would like to offer you a toast from my great-grandfather. 'Thank you all for joining me on a journey into wine civility, and when you recall our time together, I hope it is with jovial sincerity.'"

One guest added, "Hear! Hear!" They sipped and clapped cheerfully, admiring his flair for making their evening memorable.

Georgi added his final announcement. "If you desire, I have a marvelous organic coffee from Native Coffee Traders of New York; also, our outdoor deck is available so you may swoon over the starlit night reflected in the Thames River. Thank you ever so much for traveling with me among the grapevines and our momentary escape from the outside world." The patrons clapped, then mingled, appreciating Georgi's knowledge and generous personality.

***

By the time the patrons and waitstaff left, it was nearly eleven o'clock p.m. Georgi was exhausted and emotional. He locked the front door of the Vinho Verde after hanging a sign: 'Closed due to a death in the family. We will reopen soon.' His heart sank while wondering what his future would hold. He stepped onto the sidewalk.

The golden glow from the streetlamps cast Georgi's shadow on the 1780s granite structure of the Vinho Verde. He listened to the clip-clop of his Italian leather shoes on the uneven cobblestones. Georgi's slim form of five feet ten inches was suddenly elongated as his shadow stretched down the small side alley where his car was parked. He heard a distant foghorn and looked up to see the mist moving down the Thames River. A shiver ran through him, not from cold but from grief. He unlocked his burgundy PT Cruiser and slipped behind the wheel, feeling the tiredness wash over him. Suddenly, his door was yanked open, and someone shoved his head into the steering wheel violently. Georgi squealed.

"Now listen here, twinkle toes," a man's hot breath exhaled into Georgi's ear and gripped tightly onto his tufted hair. "What did the woman with the police tell you?"

Georgi whimpered, "She told me she found Mitch dead, she was mugged at the beach, and she saw someone at her house. That's all."

"Did she find anything?"

"No, no, she didn't!" Georgi yelped.

"Where is Stockman's laptop?" the attacker demanded.

"I don't know!" Georgi pleaded. "He kept it with him all the time."

"That's what I want to know, good boy," the gruff voice snarled. The thug slammed Georgi's temple into the steering wheel, and he passed out.

Georgi finally woke with a massive headache and started to cry. Discombobulated, he held his head and moaned, "Ohh, ohhh, I have to call Roxanne." He looked at the time, almost midnight, so he called Detective Morrison instead.

chapter 8

Day 2

Fire Chief Samson left early this morning for work. This was the big day; the Secret Service was to establish their presence in New London and Groton. The president was to deliver the Coast Guard Academy commencement speech in five days. It was a special affair for the state of Connecticut, and the meeting required the state police, local fire and police chiefs, the naval admiral of the Groton Nuclear Submarine Base, the local FBI contact, the coast guard admiral, and the emergency medical services to be present.

Up to one month prior, the Secret Service had met with the state and local precincts. Extreme vetting and background checks had been made on all crews involved, including their spouses and children. This was protocol for any presidential visit.

This morning's official proceedings, managed solely by the Secret Service, were to review security installments. This included the arranging of all law enforcement on highways, bridges, and waterways and preparing for their closure on the morning of the visit.

In addition to all this, the commander in chief's blast-proof limousine and a convoy of SUVs were being flown in on cargo planes along with multitudes of radio, surveillance, and security equipment. The whole ordeal was a multimillion-dollar necessity.

***

At nine o'clock a.m., Roxanne answered a call from Detective Morrison, who explained Georgi's circumstance of being attacked. He asked if she could meet him at Georgi's Hempstead Street apartment at eleven a.m.

42

Roxanne was dismayed and alarmed to see Georgi with a bandage on his forehead and looking pretty haggard. She rushed to his bedside. "Oh, Georgi! This is terrible. I'm so sorry this happened to you! Detective, what's going on?" she asked frantically.

"Georgi, tell Roxanne what the guy said to you."

"He wanted to know if you found something, Roxanne. Did you? Did you find something?"

"Like what? He beat you up for that?"

"He wanted to know what you told the cops and what you found," repeated Georgi.

"What I found? What I found was a dead man!" Her hands went to her head, "I can't believe this! Oh, Georgi, I feel so badly. He beat you up because of me." Moving her hands over her heart, she felt panicked.

"No," Detective Morrison inserted. "The thug beat him because some evidence was left behind, and he thinks you found it. And it must be linked to Stockman's murder. Possibly, now that he thinks you did not find anything, he will leave you alone." Pausing, he took a deep breath and continued. "Look, Roxanne, I'd like you to check the crime scene with me again, in case we missed something. I have to interview Stockman's wife today, so let's see if I can tell her anything other than more bad news."

"Ohhh," Georgi moaned, "I can't deal with her today."

Roxanne decided for him. "Georgi, you won't have to meet with her today." She narrowed her eyes at Morrison. "Right, Detective?"

"Right," he agreed. "It's unnecessary in your condition, Georgi."

Roxanne compassionately held his hand. "You rest up, Georgi, and take care of yourself. Okay?"

He smiled. "Thanks, that makes me feel better. But I'm worried about you! He was a very mean man!"

"Did you see his face?" she asked.

"No, I didn't. I felt his hot breath in my ear…," he gulped, "and heard his horrible voice." Georgi whimpered and held his head.

"There, there," she soothed. "We don't need to talk about it anymore. Take a couple more pain pills, and I'll bring you some food. What would you like?"

Georgi brightened up. "Can you bring me a large decaf latte with extra brown sugar and a heated apple tart from Muddy Waters Café?"

Roxanne smiled, holding his hand. "Sure thing! An apple tart it is," she said and winked.

He squeezed her hand and cooed, "You're a good friend."

Detective Morrison and Roxanne walked down the grand wooden staircase of the Victorian duplex. Once out the door on Hempstead Street, Morrison turned to her and said smiling, "You're very sweet to him."

"Thank you," she smiled. "Georgi is a dear heart, and he's taken a beating for me. It's the least I can do to treat him to a coffee and a tart. He is honest, true, and sweet." Then she laughed to herself, "I've told him he eats so many tarts he'll become one, and he giggles saying he adores the idea."

Morrison laughed, "It could be he has already turned into one…but I won't say another word about that. You two are quite a pair, aren't you?"

She mused, "We have beauty and good taste in common, and he's a nicer friend than some."

Morrison opened the door to his SUV for her. "Well, I have people from our forensic team meeting us at Columbus Circle. The man who beat Georgi asked him about Stockman's laptop, so we now know there is some connection to the business." After Roxanne climbed into the SUV, Morrison respectfully shut her door.

He entered the driver's side. "This case is heating up quicker than a summer on greenhouse gases, Roxanne. You know, the mayor has contacted me saying he can't have this ruining our tourist season. Rumors fly around here too easily. Of course, I told him we are doing all we can. So we need to-find the perpetrator and close this case ASAP, as usual.

"Besides, the president is arriving in five days, and I don't want this to interfere with secret service procedures. I suspect they'll leave us to handle our local problems. No need to divert their attention away from presidential protocol."

Roxanne nervously clenched her hands. "Detective, I have to admit I'm fearful for our safety. It's hard for me to stop thinking about these incidents, and Sam will be very concerned that Georgi was beaten up. I hope we find the evidence you need. I'm feeling helpless. Georgi and I need peace of mind. You know I like to be positive, but this is really scaring me."

Morrison assured her, "Roxanne, I'll work on this day and night for you and the chief until we get this solved. Look, I have officers canvassing the area, and the Long Island police department is working with us. Believe me, I'm pulling out all the stops."

"Thank you, Dan. I know you are. It's just unsettling."

Chapter 9

Roxanne spotted the yellow crime scene tape wrapped around her garden charge as they drove down Bank Street. It was a morbid addition. Even though the garden boasted a colorful array of annual flowers (the white and blue scaevola, yellow lantana, pink petunias, blue salvia, and a host of perennials), they all looked like prisoners behind the 'Do Not Enter – Crime Scene' tape.

The finely crafted statue of Christopher Columbus stood in the center at sixteen feet tall. The white marble shone as it did when dedicated by the Italian community in October 1928. He stared silently toward the sea, ignoring all the fuss below his feet.

Upon walking toward the garden, Roxanne assessed the scene. The tape entwined the sentinel pair of rose of Sharon trees that flanked the majestic Columbus. The spectacle felt surreal. Suddenly, a flash of Mitch Stockman's haunting face reappeared in Roxanne's mind. She held her chest, feeling dizzy, and took a deep breath to settle down.

Morrison's voice gratefully interrupted the image. "I never really looked at this statue much," he mulled. "I guess his attire must be authentic to 1492." Columbus's clothing style was layered and looked feminine compared to today's standards. His hair was split in the middle and shoulder length.

Roxanne was relieved by his comment and snickered, "I drove by here with my niece when she was quite young, and she thought it was a statue of a New London bag lady holding her lunch. She'd heard us talk about homeless people in the area, so she thought the statue was for them."

"Well, from the mouth of babes, the truth is innocent," he noted. "Now, I'll look at this statue in a different way." An idea crossed his mind. "There could be an alternate plaque here," he said with a smile. "'Let us eliminate homelessness.'"

"Ahh, they'll never go for it," Roxanne shook her head. "Although, think of it this way, Dan. Everyone was homeless when they first came to America until they made a home of their own."

"I believe you're right." He reflected on her point. "Maybe we need to consider history before judging. I do say one of my heroes is Ms. Z., the director of New London's shelter. She's been a constant help to folks who need a home here in town."

Dan was interrupted by a dark-haired woman officer approaching them. "Roxanne, this is forensic officer Carolena Sanchez, our crime scene specialist. Her keen sense and vast knowledge have helped us out a few times. She's found key evidence in the past that others have missed."

"Glad to meet you. We need all the help we can get," Roxanne admitted. "My friend Georgi was beat up last night, Officer Sanchez. The beast asked him if I had found something here in the garden."

Smiling broadly, Sanchez's warm personality overflowed. "Oh, Mrs. Samson, you can call me Carolena. We are in a garden on a beautiful sunny day. Now, let's see how I can help."

Carefully, Carolena scanned the garden. She had already reviewed the case file, photos of the murder scene, and the plaster casts of footprints. Various litter and cigarette butts had been gathered, cataloged, and held for analysis. The first accounts of Stockman's body and the site made it clear a mighty struggle had ensued. But Carolena wanted more.

"I understand he had Taxus baccata in his mouth. That was a good catch, Mrs. Samson." And with a bit of whimsy in her eyes, she whispered, "The potential for absolute death in a garden is nature's best kept secret." Morrison raised his eyebrows at the thought. Carolena continued more empathetically,

"It's too bad a nice man was a victim here, and several of your plants have been trampled too."

"I know, I'm looking forward to watering the garden as soon as it is allowed." Roxanne was hopeful it wouldn't be long.

Piquing her interest, Carolena asked, "Please show me how you water the garden."

"I do it from that ground-box spigot over there." Roxanne pointed at a green square on the surface of the lawn.

"Let's have another look at it," Carolena directed. She quickly lifted the green lid with gloved hands and asked, "Boss, they did brush this and inspect it yesterday, right?"

"They did and only found Roxanne's prints," Morrison replied. They all peered down into the box below the ground. A simple garden spigot was inside with a cavity below it.

"That's it. You just attach the hose here," Roxanne pointed.

Carolena's gloved hand swept through the hose attachment. "Well, if the murderer is looking for something and he went to all the trouble of involving you and your friend Georgi Algarve, I have to look deeper. I'll check everything again, boss. It could be in the soil or maybe it's still on the victim."

"I'll call the medical examiner myself to find out if there is more the body has to tell us." Morrison offered, "Check in with the canine unit that was here yesterday. Take a fresh look at this whole scene, Carolena, and expand it. This perp is acting desperate. And we have no witnesses yet."

"Okay, boss, I'll get right on it, and I'll bring in a metal detector to see what more I can find." Carolena Sanchez radioed the station and asked one of the guys to bring several key pieces of equipment.

Roxanne confided to Morrison again. "Dan, I'm not used to being involved in anything that I would read about in the papers. This incident with Georgi is just too much. You really need a lead!"

Morrison understood. "With the police all over this, I expect he'll leave you alone." A sudden, odd feeling caught his attention. He looked over his shoulder nonchalantly. He scanned the streets, wondering if the perpetrator was watching them right then. "Look, Roxanne, let me drop you back at Georgi's apartment." Passively, Morrison climbed into his vehicle while keeping an eye out through his rearview mirror.

He stopped at the Muddy Waters Café. Roxanne stepped out of the SUV to pick up the coffee and tarts. Morrison radioed his men, ordering them to check cars, stop people on the street, and broaden their search into the neighborhoods surrounding Bank Street. He dropped Roxanne at Georgi's and proceeded to call his assistant detective, Jack Peabody. He told him to question the delivery men and distributors who commonly had access through the Vinho Verde basement.

***

Not far from Columbus Circle, a young man was pretending to hang out in his car, yet through his rearview mirrors, he watched the scene. He texted his employer, "Cops searching site with blonde...she just left...cops still there." The return text instructed, "Stay and see if they find anything."

chapter 10

Mitch's wife, Marissa Stockman, took a taxi from the Long Island ferry directly to Harlow Towers to check on their condominium. Her deceased husband's leather traveling bag was on the king-size bed, opened and disturbed. She looked through it for anything important. Moving swiftly into the office to survey his desk, she noted some of his papers were out of alignment. Since he was a meticulous neat freak, she wondered why he'd leave behind even slight disarray.

She searched the desk for business paperwork, a flash drive, or his laptop, which he always carried with him. Finding none of these, Mrs. Stockman looked across the room to the vineyard wall photo and raced toward it. Removing it, she revealed the keypad and tapped out the code word, WINE, and pulled open the safe. The only content was a small stash of cash. *I thought there'd be more.*

A loud buzzer suddenly jolted her. She closed the safe, rehung the picture, and answered the intercom call from the doorman. "Mrs. Stockman, Detective Morrison is here to see you."

"Oh! Well, send him up, Maurice."

"Yes, Mrs. Stockman."

The elevator door opened, and the detective stepped into the spacious penthouse. Multiple windows captured the expansive view out to the Thames River and the sound. He quickly observed the condition of the condo, neat and refined. Then his eyes took in Mrs. Stockman.

She was a natural beauty. Her soft, auburn, shoulder-length hair was swept to one side of her oval face. Her slim figure was hugged by a soft, camel-colored dress. He noticed a scent of expensive perfume.

"You surprised me, Detective. I was planning to meet you at the police station in a half hour." Mrs. Stockman stepped forward to shake his hand.

"My deep condolences, Mrs. Stockman. I'm sorry to be meeting you under these circumstances," Morrison said kindly. He had followed her from the ferry docks and wondered why she sidelined to the condominium.

"You will have to excuse me," she said. "I'm still in shock and feeling quite out of sorts. I've had no sleep."

"I completely understand, and I apologize, but I need to ask you some questions so I can find your husband's perpetrator," Morrison assured her.

"Of course, let's step into the living room, shall we?"

Instinctively, he went to the window as he asked, "Have you noticed anything out of place?" His gaze traveled to the yellow-taped garden far below. *How strange, a view of the murder scene.*

"I'm not sure," she hesitated, "but I rarely come here. This is Mitch's place mostly. I thought he might have left his laptop or a flash drive on his desk. His papers were askew, and that's odd because he liked everything in order."

"The forensic team was here yesterday checking for prints or anything that might be helpful." Morrison reminded her of their conversation and observed her reaction.

"Yes, of course. You mentioned Georgi gave you a key," she said without wavering. "Did you find his laptop or anything helpful? I want to know why this happened," she said, crossing her arms and folding them against her waist in a protective pose.

Morrison answered gently, "We did not find his laptop, and we are still investigating. Did you need the laptop?

"Mitch always had it with him, and I wanted to take it home with me." Marissa Stockman moved toward the window and looked out. Slowly, she backed away with horror. "Was that where he was found?" Gripping the back of an upholstered chair, she held on while her fingernails bore into the fabric.

"Yes, I'm sorry to say." Morrison empathized, "I know this is very difficult." Mrs. Stockman composed herself, and the detective continued. "Could you tell me how your husband came to New London from Long Island?"

She answered in a daze, "He bought this condominium as an investment and a place to stay while he checked in on his business." Her voice now quivered, "Who could have done this, Detective? It's just so horrible, so absolutely horrible." She choked back tears and searched for a tissue in her purse.

Morrison gave her a moment. "I'm trying to figure that out, ma'am. How many people do you know in New London?"

"Oh, I only know Georgi and hardly at all. I've only been here twice over two years. He manages the Vinho Verde. They're business partners in love with wine. I don't relate because I don't drink wine. I've teased Mitch and told him wine and Georgi are the other women in his life," Marissa admitted with a sad smile crossing her face.

Gesturing with the tissue in her hand, she continued, "Honestly, I've never been around Georgi long enough to get to know him. That's just the way it is, what can I say?" She looked at him hoping he understood. And he did, in a way.

"I see. Can you think of anyone who disliked your husband or any reason someone would want him gone?" Morrison tried to be delicate, but the job was to ask tough questions.

"No, no," she said emphatically shaking her head, "he was well-liked by everyone, as far as I know." Then, as she thought a moment, she suddenly became angry. "I told him to leave the wine business behind so we could travel. I told him not to come to this godforsaken place, New London. But he wouldn't listen. He thought if he bought this nice condo, I would change my mind and spend time here with him.

"I'm a realtor in North Fork, and this town, I must tell you, is just not me. Now, look what happened to him. He's dead!" She started to cry. Her cool demeanor was gone. Unfolding the tissue, she turned away to dab her eyes and nose. Then regaining her composure, she became angry again. "He must have come across some riffraff here in New London," she speculated.

"Sorry, ma'am, but don't you have riffraff on Long Island? In my line of work, they are everywhere," countered Morrison.

"Certainly not," she said with a huff. Her composure kept cracking. "Look, Mitch was hoping I would like it here." Tears welled up in her eyes. "I can't believe this has happened. We talked about spending more time together this year. I convinced him to stay in North Fork for the summer. We have close friends and business acquaintances coming to visit, and I wanted him around to entertain with me." She carefully dabbed her eyes.

Morrison diverted. "Mrs. Stockman, it is procedure that while we are investigating, we have to ask you to put a hold on any changes with your finances. And we'll be looking into credit card activities, contracts, and so on. We will also review your husband's wine business and investigate the financial activity until we discover motives. What other businesses does he have? Any in Long Island?"

"Mitch invested in small vineyards there and here in Connecticut. He has his own money, and that is where he wanted to spend it. He wanted to be invested so he could have cases of their first successful vintage."

"Are you involved in any aspect of his wine business?"

"Good God, no! I am not interested at all! I want nothing to do with it or New London. This business took my husband away from me," she retorted angrily as teardrops again trickled down her cheeks.

Morrison noted that her tears and anger were normal grieving.

"I'm sorry," she said realizing she was ranting. "New London is just not my style." She wrinkled her nose as if she smelled something foul. "Do you think Georgi is involved?" she asked fearfully.

"He is not a suspect at this time," answered Morrison.

"Mitch spoke so highly of him." Then she pondered a thought. "Like I said, I don't really know Georgi well enough, but…he will inherit the business."

"Really, now," the detective's curiosity was piqued.

"Mitch knew I wasn't interested in the business. But wine was his absolute passion, and he loved anyone who shared that passion. I'm not sure Georgi even knows, but that was the agreement we had. He wrote it up in his will. My lawyer has that information."

"Did you know Georgi was beaten up last night?"

"My goodness, no!" She raised her voice, "What happened?"

"The thug was looking for your husband's laptop and something left behind at the scene. Was Mr. Stockman carrying anything else of importance on him?"

"No! Well, I don't know," she blurted as she looked around the room. "I can't think of anything. Is Georgi okay?"

"He will be," Morrison assured. "Now, if anything comes to mind, anything at all, please let me know right away. How long will you be staying?"

"I must get back to my daughter tonight. How long do you think this investigation will take?"

Morrison repeated his often-used line, "We are waiting for the autopsy to be completed and the medical examiner's report to be finalized. It usually takes a few weeks. But I do have one unusual question complicating things. Do you specialize in plants and horticulture or know anyone who does?"

"Do you mean a gardener? I have a brown thumb."

Morrison added, "Or a landscaper, pharmacist, or herbalist?"

"For goodness sake! I know of gardeners and landscapers on Long Island, and I have a pharmacist. Whatever do you mean?" she asked, feeling deeply perplexed.

"It's an ongoing investigation, and we have to ask all kinds of questions, Mrs. Stockman. Again, I am very sorry about your husband. We're hoping the autopsy will tell us more. In the meantime, please call me if you think of anyone with plant knowledge or anything else that comes to mind. Here is my card. Good-day, ma'am." Morrison nodded in respect and entered the elevator.

Once the doors to the elevator closed, Morrison slipped his hand inside his left pocket and pulled out his digital recorder. He spoke into it, "This ends my questioning with Mrs. Stockman at one p.m. on June ninth. Check her acquaintances, bank accounts, life insurance policies, and real estate dealings."

Morrison preferred to tape preliminary questions with family or possible suspects in their personal environments. Over the years, he found it worked out well especially when comparing it to a statement, if it was required at the station.

The elevator descended. Morrison rubbed his chin with deep thoughts. A possibility dawned on him. *Georgi may have wanted the wine business for himself, all along. A motive!* The elevator door opened to deliver him from the heady heights of the posh Harlow condos to the now infamous Bank Street.

Chapter 11

Roxanne nibbled on an apricot scone as Georgi sipped his latte and crunched on his warm apple tart. "It makes me feel better already," he said, "cinnamon apples in a puff pastry. It's as if all is right in my world. As if Mom is here, and apple tarts just came out of the oven."

He had a warm glowing smile below the bandages wrapped around his head. Roxanne was glad to see him settled, enjoying a moment of pleasure. She didn't want to spoil the peace with questions about the mugging or Mitch's death. She decided to just be a friend and sit with him, engage in small talk, and wait. Wait for him to be ready to talk. "The poor guy has been through enough," she thought.

After he finished eating, Roxanne carried the plates and cups to the sink and cleaned up.

"Georgi, I'm going to let you rest now. Do you have anyone who can check in on you later?" she asked from the kitchen.

"Oh yes, I lined up a whole crew," he explained as Roxanne came back to listen. "At two o'clock, Bruno is coming by until he starts his night shift as a waiter. Then at five p.m., Sketcher and Brian are bringing dinner, and at eight p.m., my friends Marco and Gigi are bringing a movie. We'll watch that until I fall asleep, and they'll let themselves out."

"Well," Roxanne said with hands on her hips, "you have a better group of friends than I do!"

"Oh no, Roxanne, that's not true. If you were mugged and told all your friends, you would have food and movies for a month!" He gently reached out to hold her hand. Looking at her sincerely, he said, "You're a good friend. Remember the time you found me locked out of Vinho Verde one morning when I went to water the window boxes? You called your locksmith friend. And remember when I had to travel to Europe for over a week for wine business with Mitch, and you watered my plants, and you let a delivery man in with cases of California wine we were desperate to receive? So now I can add this to the logbook list of all you've done for me. Thank you."

"I remember," she said and gave him a hug. "Okay, Georgi, you rest up now before your next visitor arrives, and I'll call you tomorrow to see how you're feeling." She kissed him on the cheek and let herself out.

As Roxanne approached her truck, she looked across Hempstead Street to the original 1652 town cemetery. The sign read, 'Ye Antientist Burial Ground.' Its ancient tombstones were sunken and tilted with age. Small, eerie angelic faces were almost hidden under pale green lichens. An enormous beech tree stood like a guardian. Its long, leafy tendrils draped over the hallowed ground as if protecting the tombstones beneath its wide canopy. Roxanne suddenly felt extremely vulnerable. The whole situation washed over her as she remembered a tombstone epitaph.

Stop traveler as you pass by,
As you are now so once was I,
As I am now so you shall be,
So prepare for death and follow me.

Saddened by the thought, she drove toward New London's City Center District. She traveled past the tall brownstone steeple of St. James Episcopal Church and said her own silent prayer for help. When she came upon the Soldiers and Sailors Monument on the Parade Plaza, her eyes roved up the tall monument to the heroine at its highpoint. The female figure, holding a palm frond, represented peace and liberty for all who fought on the shores of America.

The two days of tense events, and now the tombstones, triggered Roxanne's emotions. Her mind raced with thoughts of the dilemma they were in. Squeezing the steering wheel hard, she said aloud, "How dare they harm Georgi and kill that poor man!"

A horrible, helpless feeling overtook her as tears streamed down her face. She exhaled a loud sigh and continued to drive. She turned onto one street after another until she passed through granite pillars and parked her truck beside Fort Trumbull, which loomed to her left.

The current stoic fortress was built after 1839. It is grand in size but plain by design. Historically in 1777, its location was the artillery center for the young colony. Infamously, it was overtaken in 1781 when the English, led by the traitor Benedict Arnold, landed ashore and burned down New London's city center. It was a great devastation to the town, which took thirty years to recover. Many widows and their children were left homeless and in despair.

Roxanne looked at the tranquil panoramic view of the Thames River out to Long Island Sound. It was one of her 'good places' to think things through. She heaved another sigh, trying to calm herself. Her eyes lowered to a grassy knoll and followed a stone wall. Massive black cannons aimed seaward caught her attention. Stacked beside them were cannonballs of war, ready to be loaded.

A new feeling surged inside Roxanne. A ripple of energy crossed over her arms as she shuddered. Suddenly, she was overcome with a new energy, warrior energy.

Angrily, she pounded her fists on the steering wheel and demanded out loud, "How dare they harass us. They have invaded my life, my peaceful happy life."

The images of her contented life faded, as if a fog had descended, and a strange invasion came with the mist, replacing peace with death, insecurity, and threats. Her days of gardening, reading, volunteering, and family gatherings had been brutally overrun.

She stared at the cannons and pounded the steering wheel. From the safety of her truck, she shouted, "I don't accept this! They have to catch this killer!" Her anger fell into sobbing.

Chapter 12

Detective Morrison drove his official traveling office, the SUV, through the crowded corridor of Bank Street. He waited to follow Mrs. Stockman. *Will she connect with someone else?*

Her taxi passed art galleries, a fair-trade store, a salon and spa, bistros and then flew past the Vinho Verde Wine Bar. Morrison positioned his SUV into a quiet corner of the ferry terminal parking lot. He sat with arms crossed, and his dark blue eyes watched Mrs. Stockman with suspicion.

She exited the taxi with movie-star grace. Her silk scarf billowed aloft as she strode across the tarmac like a model in a photo shoot, boarding the high-speed ferry. Morrison scanned the area for any dubious onlookers.

While the attendant helped her ascend the gangplank, Morrison gave a discontented grumble. *I have no evidence to hold her. It's just a hunch, but I don't like this one bit. What if she choreographed her husband's demise? She has the money and a holier-than-thou attitude.* Struggling, he argued with himself. *I don't care how good she looks or smells. Murderers don't have a look. They just need a motive.*

By morning, Morrison expected to have his hands-on banking business, insurance documents, and possibly Mitch Stockman's will. *Maybe a lead will surface tomorrow.*

***

Roxanne drove away from Fort Trumbull and the cannons of war and stayed on the shoreline road. Her mind whittled away at ideas. *I need a fresh perspective…there must be something I've missed in these events.*

On this stretch of Pequot Avenue, large homes and private beaches were dotted along the sound. The expansive view included several lighthouse landmarks: New London Harbor Light on the shore, Ledge Light at the mouth of the Thames River, Avery Point Light on Groton's shore, and Race Rock Light bordering the sound and the Atlantic Ocean.

Roxanne found a place to park. Spying a pair of graceful white swans feeding, she rolled down her window. Calm water gently lapped and swished small stones on the beach, quieting her nerves. She inhaled the salty air deeply and leaned back in her seat, closed her eyes, and lost herself in the sounds....

Several minutes went by when a small idea floated toward the surface of her mind. She followed it. *Hmm, how to lure a witness...and catch a killer?* Emerging from the drifting thoughts, she called her husband at work.

"Sam, I have an idea. Can I stop by?"

"Yes, I'll be free in ten minutes," he agreed.

"Okay, I'll be right there," she said eagerly.

Driving quickly away from the sound along the Thames River, Roxanne passed Mitchell College's buildings and beachfront and Fred's Shanty, a popular clam shack overlooking the docks of a large marina. Once near the center of town, she paused at the imprisoned Columbus Circle garden, then took a right on Bank Street and landed at the engine house. The tall garage doors of the 1880s brick building were open, and one of the men saw her coming.

"Hi, Cliff," she called, "where's Sam?"

"Upstairs in his office," he answered.

"Good, I have a fire of my own today!"

"Well," Cliff chuckled, "I hope he can put it out for you."

She shrugged as she strode past the fire trucks and headed up the stairs. Peeking around the edge of the door to Sam's office, she whispered, "Are you free now?"

"For you? Of course!" he said looking over his glasses at her. "Close the door, will you?" He pushed aside the papers on his desk. She pulled her chair close to him. "So what's this idea you have?" he asked."

"I want to ask Detective Morrison to tell a lie."

Sam let out a long, rolling laugh. His chair tilted back, and he slapped his stomach with the idea of lying to Dan Morrison. "Whatever are you talking about?"

"Look, if he tells the press that we found an object in the garden at Columbus Circle, possibly that creepy killer will stop bothering us. And I'm thinking if we offer a reward for information on Stockman's murder, maybe someone will come forward. Then we will have this thing resolved once and for all." She looked at him in suspense, hoping he would agree.

"Well, who is going to post a reward?" he asked.

"We will," she answered.

"You mean you and me? How much money do you have in mind?"

"Enough to get someone's attention," she replied. "Besides, whatever was lost likely incriminates the killer. Doesn't it make sense?" Roxanne asked, feeling desperate. "Look, I just want my life back, Sam, and poor Georgi, you should've seen him. He has a big bandage on his head, and he's black and blue."

She took a deep breath. With empathy, Sam exhaled heavily and took her hand. Roxanne was used to his long thoughtful pauses, a trait that made him a great chief over the years.

"Let me call Dan," he said, looking deeply into her eyes. "I will ask him to come down here."

"Thank you, dear." She heaved a sigh of relief. "Do you think he'll go for it?"

"It's doubtful," Sam speculated, "but it doesn't hurt to review the idea with him."

Detective Morrison was able to meet them in short order. His dark khaki pants and blue, pressed shirt with tie and badge around his neck were part of the official package. His discerning dark blue eyes and black Irish hair rendered him naturally handsome.

"What's going on? Do you have something new?" Morrison asked.

The chief spoke. "Listen, Dan, Roxanne has an idea that I frankly agree with, and it might help advance the investigation."

"Anything sounds good at this point," Morrison said uncharacteristically and added, "I'm being harassed by my department heads. The ferry office has called saying we must solve this murder because the residents of Long Island are alarmed over Stockman's death, and the ferry office doesn't want to lose sales, especially from that side of the sound. The New London storefronts and restaurants are concerned about decreased business. I'm being pressured from all sides. What do you have?"

Chief Sam fixed his gaze on Morrison and continued, "We all believe the murderer is looking for something from the site. If you claim to have found new evidence, it will achieve several things. It might get him off Roxanne and Georgi's backs, and he might take some action that would expose him. On top of that, Roxanne suggests we post a reward for information. This could encourage a passerby from that evening to come forward. Is it possible there is more than one person involved?"

"It's possible," Morrison conceded, rubbing his chin and feeling the five o'clock shadow emerging.

Not waiting for a further reply, Chief Sam continued, "There are too many moving parts, Dan — four incidents: Columbus Circle, the beach mugging, the house, and now Georgi. Maybe there is more than one guy. The reward may flush someone out."

Looking sideways at Roxanne, Dan Morrison responded, "Well, it's not my nature to mislead anyone...but that's in my personal life. This involves catching a killer; public safety is at stake, and we need to get the job done. I could announce that we found evidence. I could say people were intoxicated, and there was a fight that resulted in an accidental death. A reward might provoke someone to come forward, but I want you to realize we don't know how this will play out, and you should be prepared for unknown consequences."

Roxanne interjected, "Look, Detective, this is affecting our lives. I've had enough!" To stress the point, she made the motion of 'cut it' across her neck. "At least putting out this false information may throw the killer off me and Georgi and place him in your hands!"

Detective Morrison looked at Chief Sam and back to Roxanne, a rare smile crossing his face. "I think you're onto something here. You could be my new secret agent, Roxanne," he said with a genuine smile that made him even more handsome. "However, I do want to have Marissa Stockman aware of the reward idea and see if she will support it and fund it. I'll contact her and tell her I'm announcing uncovered new evidence. I want to assess her reaction.

"I also have the press to meet with before the evening deadline. So we'll see how this works out. I'll be in touch soon. Thank you both."

After he left, Sam said, "Roxanne, dear, don't you get any ideas about what he just said about being a secret agent. I know once your mind connects with your intuition, you're like a little piranha, eating away at ideas from every angle."

"Well, isn't that why he offered me the job?" she queried.

"Wow, that was a job offer?" he countered.

"Well, it all depends on your point of view, doesn't it? It sure sounded like one to me." She smiled mischievously.

Sam put his head in his hands and ran them through his thick white hair. He shook his head. "Oh no, Roxanne, this is serious. I don't want you poking around these folks. Their business is death with a capital D. Your job is done and over. Besides, we have the president coming to town, and that is enough right now."

She knew he was concerned for her, so she pulled back from her rash talk. "You're right, dear. Let's see what happens after the announcement and reward notice. I'll back off." She gave him a big smile, slyly enjoying her new secret agent status.

He reached for her hand and implored, "Promise me, Roxanne, you will give this a few days before you do anything." Roxanne and Sam were sweethearts in high school and married for twenty-five years. He admired her calm exterior, knowing the force of the fire within. So far, their mutual respect kept the balance in their relationship.

"I promise, honey, and I really mean it. I'm just giving you a hard time. I'll sink my energies into the gardens, and I'll be just fine."

He sighed with relief. "Okay, then, let me get back to work."

"Happily," she chirped, jumping up and giving him a peck on the cheek. "Thanks, honey, I'll see you later." She stepped out of the office and took a quick left.

"Oh, there she goes!" he muttered.

In a flash, she glided down the fire pole, giggling.

Chief Sam winced. *How many times have I told her? She can't do that! It's a liability!*

chapter 13

From his helm on the Sea Jet, Captain Matthew Griswold gave the order to release the high-speed ferry from the dock. He blew the deep-toned horn, letting passengers know they were about to cast off. Simultaneously, a working cargo train slowly passed Union Station, which was close to the shipping docks. A long shrill train whistle responded to the high-speed Sea Jet's horn. Whoooo-whoooo! The conductor waved out his window. Captain Griswold sounded back another deep-toned response and waved.

Griswold loved the great outdoors and loved his job. Before landing this position eight years ago, he retired after twenty-two years in the coast guard. Seafaring history was long in his family. He carried within a wistful boyhood memory of when he and his dad climbed the 166 steps of the Groton Monument, an obelisk near his family's namesake, Fort Griswold, on the riverside in Groton.

From atop the 135-foot viewing windows, his young boy's eyes peered out and sighted his first love: sailing ships. It was then he also felt the call of the sea and learned of his maritime lineage. His grandfather teased him and said the mermaids wooed the Griswold men. But his family's nautical disposition was more like sea kelp with deepwater roots that grew naturally in salt water.

Since 1639, the Griswold family were some of the first settlers, seamen, and whalers in southern Connecticut. Matthew Griswold IV was voted governor in 1785 and promoted Thanksgiving as an official holiday to carry on the Pilgrim tradition of giving thanks. The Griswold's colonial pursuits were liberty in the young America and financial prosperity as landowners, mariners, and boatbuilders. Their heritage stood as strong as the masts on their famous merchant ships, the Black X Line.

Captain Griswold had sailing in his blood. His passion was to live near the water, dock on the land, and set sail as often as possible, leaving and returning like a tide. He loved both the departure and the return equally. He felt sailing made him a better person, appreciating his family and the land more because of leaving, yet always returning. In turn, his wife and children appreciated him more too.

Ferrying the Sea Jet high-speed passenger catamaran and the *Mary Ellen* vehicle carrier required the captain to be away from home overnight because of his route to Long Island. Not long at all compared to serving in the Coast Guard. Besides, time away made his wife's kisses sweeter when he returned.

From Captain Griswold's vantage point at the helm, he could see Mrs. Stockman. She had come into New London on his morning run from Long Island. He knew her through her husband, the jovial, easygoing Mitch. Word traveled quickly across Long Island Sound that his regular passenger, Mitch Stockman, was murdered.

He watched her on the open deck as her light auburn hair and yellow scarf lifted and floated in the breeze. He felt for her loss, not able to imagine the shock of this young widow who appeared to be in her early forties.

Once underway, Griswold put the second officer in charge of the wheelhouse so he could greet the passengers. He noticed Mrs. Stockman as she stepped up to the bar, ordered a drink, and strolled to the open-air deck. Her eyes were hiding behind large designer sunglasses. He pondered how the eyes reveal so much about someone, if they are engaged in a conversation or withdrawn, if there is emotion or indifference. 'Windows to the Soul,' his mother called them.

Griswold considered approaching her to say he was sorry, say how he knew Mitch and enjoyed their conversations, say how Mitch chatted with him often and told him about his wine business and his home on Long Island with his new wife of four years. He could say how he felt Mitch and he were similar, traveling to and away from home and appreciating all of it. After much thought, he decided it was best to leave her with her grief, and he climbed the small iron staircase to the helm to maneuver the ferry through the currents that churned at the mouth of the Thames River.

Beyond Ledge Lighthouse, he was in the open waters of the sound. Griswold had his second officer take charge again. Straightening his uniform, he descended the narrow steps to the deck below and the bar. He was about to step out of the shadows of the stairwell when he saw one of his deckhands approach Mrs. Stockman. He whispered to her and handed her an envelope. She briefly said thank-you, then just as quickly turned away and clenched her hand.

Griswold stopped and stayed in the shadows, wondering what this young man passed on to her and what he had whispered. He considered his next move when he saw her take off her sunglasses. He watched her svelte form approach the bar for another drink. She then sat at a small table by a window and opened her hand.

Cautiously, she opened it and inside was a note that contained a memory stick. Griswold watched quietly. A flash of anger crossed her face. She folded the note around the memory stick, slipped it in her purse, and eyed her surroundings warily.

It was then the captain moved out of the shadows and toward her table.

"Mrs. Stockman, I'm Captain Griswold," he introduced himself as he stood with his hands behind his back and gently nodded to her in respect. Griswold had handsome dark hair with gray flecks, a short well-trimmed beard, and looked ten years younger than his early fifties.

Slightly surprised, she said "Oh hello, Captain," looking apparently taken aback by his sudden appearance.

"I want to extend my condolences for the loss of your husband, Mitch."

"Oh, thank you," she said, shifting uncomfortably in her seat. "It's been very difficult as you may imagine." Her eyes fluttered downward as her voice trickled over him like a gentle stream on a hot summer day. Griswold was caught off guard by her demure femininity. Composing himself, he volunteered some sociable information.

"Mitch and I came to know each other quite well on these trips when he checked in on his business here in New London. He had shown me your photo, as he was very proud of you. He was a friendly soul, and I will miss him." Griswold searched her eyes as he spoke. There was something lacking, and he thought maybe she was still in shock.

"Yes, that is very considerate of you to tell me," she said softly. "I didn't realize he had many friends here. I was busy with my own work and didn't manage to travel with him. He did love his wine business and meeting people who loved wine. It's terribly difficult to believe this has happened; it's all such a shock." She pursed her lips and looked down at the table.

Griswold gently replied, "If there is anything I can do to make your travels more comfortable, please do not hesitate to let me know. I imagine you will be back and forth a few times until things are settled?" he inquired.

She looked up at him, startled to think that it might be true. "Oh, I don't know. It's up to the police, really." Then catching herself, she switched her tone and added in a smooth, silky voice, "Thank you, Captain, for your kindness." She extended her hand to shake his. As he reached for her hand, he looked into her eyes. They were an unusual blue-green and with her fair complexion and auburn hair, he found her quite-stunning.

Then purposely to catch her off guard, he asked, "Was my deckhand Johnny able to assist you in some way?"

Ever so smoothly, she pulled her hand back and said, "Yes, he helped me with my bags, and I gave him a tip." She shifted again in her seat. He watched her lying eyes turn cool as she controlled her emotions. "Thank you, Captain, for your concern." She nodded with respect.

The bartender leaned in, "Here is your drink, ma'am."

The captain backed away and tipped his cap, "Good-day, Mrs. Stockman."

He returned to the bridge and observed his second officer piloting the Sea Jet flawlessly while approaching Little Gull Island. Griswold announced over the loudspeaker, "Ladies and gentlemen, you will see the seals are out today and have gathered on the Little Gull's rocky shore, sunning themselves." He proceeded to inform, "The first Little Gull Lighthouse was installed in 1806 and in 1869, it was replaced by the current eighty-one-foot stone tower with a brighter second order Fresnel lens."

It was four-ten p.m. when Captain Griswold smoothly steered the Sea Jet into the Orient Point Terminal on the tip of the north fork of Long Island, New York.

Griswold said to his crew in the wheelhouse, "Right on time, mates. A good forty-minute run. Be ready for the return in an hour."

"Yes, sir," the crew chimed. They afforded him more respect than the other captains because of his coast guard career, but he was fairly relaxed about it. He liked order and discipline but didn't require overt bootlicking to maintain his command.

Griswold stood at the end of the boat ramp to say, 'Good-day,' to the passengers as they disembarked the ferry. He looked for Johnny, the young deckhand. His thoughts raced as he considered Mrs. Stockman. *Why did she lie about giving him a tip? What did he give her? He's not in her league. He's a guppy in her sea of influence.*

Griswold waited for his crew to clean up the ferry, grab their bags, and head off the ship to the local snack bar to relax for a short time. Since Johnny lived in Greenport, he was off until the morning shift.

Johnny stepped off the ramp. Griswold asked, "Johnny, can you spare a minute?"

"Sure thing, Cap. What can I do for you?" He was a clean-cut kid. His navy polo shirt and khaki pants uniform were clean and crisp, his belt and boat shoes matched. He had been working for the ferry service just two months.

"Take a short walk with me, will you?"

"Yes, sir."

"I just want to tell you that you've been doing a fine job this spring." He walked Johnny back to the locker room.

"Thank you, sir, I like the work, and it pays for my online school."

"Johnny, I have to ask you something about one of our passengers."

Unfazed, Johnny asked, "What's that, Cap?"

"I saw you hand something to Mrs. Stockman. What was it? I'm concerned for your safety because her husband was found murdered yesterday."

"What? I didn't know that!' he said, sincerely astonished.

"So tell me, what is going on? What did you give to her?"

"I, er, gave her an envelope from Charlie Brass, the dockworker. He pointed her out and asked me to pass it on to her. He said she left it behind and wanted to be sure it was returned to her. That's all. I didn't know her husband was just murdered!"

The captain lifted his cap and scratched his head, "That's it?"

"Really, Cap, that's all I know. I don't want to get mixed up in anything."

Griswold looked the boy over, then analyzed his behavior and his eyes. He believed him.

"Has Charlie asked you to do anything else?" the captain asked.

"No, sir, I promise you."

"Johnny, stay alert for anything unusual. Someone murdered Mitch Stockman, and he was my friend. We need to pay attention until they catch the killer. Anything at all, you report to me only."

"Of course, sir. I just need to keep my job." Visibly nervous, he swiped his dark blonde hair to the side.

"If Charlie asks you to do anything, just go along with it and get back to me, okay?"

"Yes, sir, I will do that. I don't want any trouble."

In a fatherly way, the captain put his hand on Johnny's shoulder and quietly said, "There are all types of characters in the world, Johnny, and most will do anything for money. I know Charlie. He's a good guy, and he's been here for a long time. But Mrs. Stockman's husband is dead. I'm just saying to be careful."

"Yes, Captain. Thanks for the tip. I'll be more alert now."

"Okay, I'll see you tomorrow on the morning run." Griswold watched Johnny swing his backpack over his shoulder. *He's a good kid*, he reflected.

Griswold walked out to the observation deck for some fresh air and to eat his sandwich. His gut felt an atmospheric shift, like when the barometric pressure drops before a storm, not visible but sensed. Yet in this case, it was a storm made by man, not by weather. Little did he know, there was no measurable length and breadth to this man-made tempest. Its environs were far-reaching, much like a hurricane with incalculable troubling disturbances.

chapter 14

Marissa Stockman hugged her daughter Vanessa while looking out to the sound in the small town of Orient Point on Long Island. Her view from the second story of their home was hard-earned. Her years as a real estate broker had paid off. The business practically ran itself now with the agents she employed. Her summer plans had taken a terrible turn. Mitch's death felt insurmountable, and the fear of the unknown overwhelmed her.

"I'll watch over you, Mom." Vanessa hugged her tightly. Her long dark hair draped over her mother's shoulder. She just finished her third year of university in New York City and was home for the summer. Marissa was relieved. Her friends, her business, and now her daughter would keep her busy while she would try not to be consumed by the loss of Mitch.

"I can't believe this happened," Marissa said, squeezing her daughter. "We were to spend the summer off together, enjoying ourselves. A second honeymoon he called it." Tears streamed down her face. She allowed her daughter's sleek hair to soak them up. Vanessa held her tighter and silently her tears continued.

"I'm so sorry, Mom. Mitch was so good to you."

Her mother heaved a massive sigh and replied, "I have to get ready to meet the florist, darling, for the funeral. Do you want to come?"

"Is anyone else going with you?" Vanessa asked, concerned.

"Yes, I asked Jenny from the office. She said she would be available."

"Mom," Vanessa gently wiped a tear from her mother's cheek, "I'll run some other errands for you, if you don't mind. Maybe I'll pick up your dry cleaning and order food at Gabriela's Catering so we have something when people stop by."

"Oh, yes. That would be lovely, dear." She stroked her daughter's hair while looking into her dark brown eyes. "What would I do without you? Thank you, honey." Marissa kissed Vanessa's cheek.

Immediately after Vanessa left the room, Marissa pulled the memory stick out of her purse. She locked the door and went to her laptop in the adjoining sitting room of her master suite. She stood, looking at the screen. A boldly stated message popped up:

> **Do as I say or your daughter will suffer!**
>
> **Mitch didn't want to play but I know you will.**
>
> **Put $10,000 cash in one of your red Realty envelopes.**
>
> **Address it to Johnson Jones for pick up only.**
>
> **Put it in the mailbag the day after tomorrow on the 7am**
>
> **Long Island Sound Ferry.**
>
> **P.S. No Cops or there will be No Vanessa!**

Marissa's knees buckled under the horror. She fell into a chair, succumbed by the thought of harm to her daughter. Her thoughts raced. *Oh my God! Oh my God! What am I to do?* Hugging a pillow, she rocked back and forth. She thought of Mitch. *How did this happen to us? Who are these people?*

For a moment, her mind took over and urged her to check the memory stick for more information. Another file was on it. She clicked it open. Suddenly in a flash, Vanessa's face popped up, smiling on the screen. Marissa burst into tears and clutching the pillow, she buried her face to muffle her sounds. She moved to her bed and curled into a ball, weeping.

Vanessa walked by her mother's door and heard the sobbing, thinking they were tears for Mitch. *Mom finally met the right man, and now he's gone. This is devastating.*

Chapter 15

Early the next morning, Roxanne decided her garden needed a good cutting back. Spring flowering shrubs had bloomed, and new growth was bolting forth. Judiciously, she lined up several tools: a crossover hand pruner and loppers, a polesaw for trees, and an electric hedge trimmer for shaping the shrubs. All ready to go, she started snipping and clipping.

First, she pruned the lilac Sensation, the only one that has a smooth fragrance and dark purple petals outlined with a white edge. Next was the lightly perfumed early blooming viburnum x burkwoodii. Then she climbed a ladder and trimmed the pink thornless rose, Zephirine Drouhin. Tolerating part shade and poor soil, its best trait was imbuing its surroundings with a sweet fragrance. It was interwoven on the arbor with a kiwi vine, the variegated one with pink and white leaves. It offered delicious, tiny fruit that the squirrels and birds devoured, leaving her and Sam a few handfuls for dessert.

Roxanne moved on to her David Austin rose bushes, rich yellow of Graham Thomas and the warm pink rosettes of Gertrude Jeykll. Gingerly, she snipped off the dead wood and spent buds. She whizzed through the privet hedge with her long hedge trimmer. It was one of the main privacy walls to the backyard.

The physical activity of cutting and clipping was a rewarding way of cleansing her of her frustrations. The garden labor, fresh air, and sunshine finally released her mind from worrying thoughts.

Standing by the small pool in her Asian contemplation garden, she took a moment to admire the multiple tints and tones of green in her hostas and the graceful sweeping bend of the Hakone grass under the Hinoki cypress. She had separated her yard into three distinct garden rooms.

She moved on to review the annuals in the front yard that were-beginning to fill in well among the mixed border of perennials and shrubs. The multicolored zinnias, pink and yellow lantanas, and brilliant blue scaevola would all bloom well in the sun.

Taking a moment, she swallowed some water and observed her small kitchen garden. A rectangular-raised herb and vegetable bed satisfied her cooking needs, producing chives, thyme, parsley, rosemary, tarragon, and sage. She even had a spot of catnip for kitty. Later on, there would be fresh tomatoes of various heirlooms, yellow string beans, peppers, and cucumbers.

After several hours passed, her cell phone rang, interrupting her contentment. "Hello?"

"Roxanne, we know who has the motive!" Detective Morrison declared.

"Oh good! Who?"

"It's Georgi Algarve!" Morrison replied quickly.

She threw her loppers on the ground. "That's impossible!"

Morrison tried to explain, "We've read the will and business contracts and Georgi inherits the Vinho Verde, Roxanne, the whole business, including investments in several wineries. It seems he has the most to gain financially since Mitch's wife is already wealthy and doesn't want the business."

"I don't believe it. It can't be, Dan. No, I don't think he did it!"

"Well, he may have hired someone," the detective suggested. "His neck was snapped, and a preliminary toxicology report has confirmed that poisonous plant in his mouth is Taxus baccata! I'm still waiting for further results, but this was a hit, not an accident."

Emphatically protesting, Roxanne said, "No, no, no! It's not possible. Maybe someone slipped Mitch a Mickey. Georgi doesn't have a bone in his body that could do that, and besides, he wouldn't beat himself up! Have you talked to him?"

"Not yet, but I'm planning on going down there soon. I'd like you to be there when I question him. I don't think he will lie to you," Morrison said persuasively.

Unimpressed, Roxanne retorted, "You mean when you accuse him? Oh, I don't know, Dan. I don't think I'm ready to do anything like this. What am I, the good cop while you're the bad cop?"

Thoughts flashed through her mind. *Oh, what should I do? He's innocent. I really should be there for him. He's been such a dear to me this year. He let me use Vinho Verde for an impromptu birthday party.... Maybe I can help him.* She spoke up before Dan's thoughts had come together.

"Okay, I'll do it," she conceded. "You must know I don't believe he did it."

Gratefully, Morrison acknowledged, "I know, I know, but you will be honest with me if you see or hear anything unusual. You know I have to do this and follow the leads."

Roxanne paused, feeling a level of stress on her shoulders she was not accustomed to until recently. Her life was usually uncomplicated as a wife, gardener, and community volunteer.

"Can you meet me at the Vinho Verde?" the detective asked.

"Sure, when?"

"As soon as possible," he said hopefully.

"Ahh, okay, I can be there in forty-five minutes. See you about eleven thirty."

Roxanne sat in thought on the rock wall with lavender on either side of her. She ran her hand over the silver-gray leaves and flowers, then breathed in the scent. "Hmm, patience and focus," she said aloud and sighed. She had learned the aromatherapy of lavender, waited a minute, then mumbled, "Humph. This is not working!"

She pondered her dilemma. *This feels wrong.* She picked up her cell phone and called her husband. "Sam? Dan just asked me to meet him at the Vinho Verde. He found paperwork that makes him think Georgi has a strong motive for Mitch Stockman's murder, and of course, I don't agree."

"What? Don't you get involved, Roxanne," counseled Sam.

"I have to," she said softly. "I have to help him, protect him. I don't think he did this. Besides, he is banged up, the poor fellow. This doesn't make sense. Dan says he inherits the Vinho Verde, plus investments in wineries on Long Island. He says Georgi has the biggest motive because Mitch's wife is already wealthy."

"I know what Morrison is trying to do, but I think you have done enough," Sam urged her. "I'll call him right now and tell him I don't want you involved."

"Don't you dare. I called you for support," Roxanne countered, finally grasping her mettle. "I have to help Georgi! Look, Sam, it doesn't harm me to be there for him. I'm going to do this. I'll call you as soon as I can. Bye." She hung up, not waiting for his response.

Sam heard the dial tone. "For Pete's sake," he muttered.

chapter 16

Roxanne cleaned herself up and met Detective Morrison outside the Vinho Verde. She took a deep breath as she followed him inside. "Hello, Georgi," Morrison said.

"Oh, Detective," Georgi acknowledged him as he continued arranging one of the tables with fresh flowers. The light from the tall multipaned windows beautifully lit the lofty space of dark wooden rafters. His heels clopped against the heavily worn floors. Roxanne admired the pumpkin pine floors and caught sight of the cast-iron nails deeply set in the aged, wide planks that were part of the historic whaling commerce from the years of longshoremen. Georgi and Mitch had brought in sophisticated lighting, flowing drapes, and a bar of stainless steel to complement the old-world charm of the granite and brick building.

Georgi's designer slacks swished as he crossed the room to shake the detective's hand. He gave Roxanne a gentle hug.

"You're looking much better, Georgi," Roxanne observed as she glanced at his head.

"It's the pain pills, a good night's sleep, and some stage makeup from Bruno," Georgi replied. "Come in, I'm just keeping busy. I don't know what else to do until I hear from Mrs. Stockman." His face became downcast.

Morrison stood at the tasting table. Roxanne and Georgi joined him. "Well, that's why I'm here," he said with an official tone.

"Oh?" Georgi's voice rose, his eyes widened, and he seemed to be holding his breath. He stared at the detective, waiting for the words that may determine his future and that of the Vinho Verde.

Trying to settle on where to begin, Morrison hesitated slightly. "Ahh, did Mitch discuss his Last Will and Testament with you, Georgi?"

"Why, no! Why would he?" Georgi asked nervously.

"Because you are in it," Morrison revealed.

"What! That's not possible. I've only known him two years," Georgi said in an incredulous tone.

"It's been confirmed, which means you have a lot to gain from his death," Morrison probed.

"That sounds just horrible!" Georgi exclaimed. His hands went to his face. "Whatever do you mean?"

Roxanne piped in, "Georgi, you didn't know about Mitch putting you in his will?"

"Why would he leave it to me?" Georgi pointed to himself as his voice rose to a higher pitch.

Roxanne looked at the detective, as if saying, 'I told you so.' But Morrison was just starting.

"Georgi, you are the sole inheritor of this business. Mitch left it all to you. You have the most to gain. His wife is filthy rich. She doesn't like this business nor coming to New London."

Georgi sat on a barstool, put his face in his hands, and sobbed uncontrollably. Roxanne forcefully whispered to Dan, "That's quite enough, Detective! He didn't know about Stockman's will, so he didn't do it." She put her arm around Georgi. He leaned on her and sobbed on her shoulder. Roxanne looked up at Morrison as Georgi's full weight was upon her small frame. She could barely hold him up. Her legs buckled as she shook her head at Morrison and mouthed, 'Help.'

"Georgi!" the detective snapped loudly. Georgi straightened up and wiped the tears of confusion and grief from his face. Roxanne handed him some cocktail napkins. He patted his face with them and blew his nose with dainty puffs. Morrison's hand went to his brow, and he rolled his eyes at the display. Roxanne noticed his impatience.

Forcefully, Morrison announced, "I must take you to headquarters, Georgi, due to this new information. I will need an official statement from you, and I'd like you to come now."

"Am I under arrest?" Georgi wailed. "I can't take this. I think…I think…I'm having a heart attack!" He started gasping for breath. "Uhhh, uhhhh, I can't breathe," he wheezed, waving his hands in front of his face, which was turning beet red. Roxanne dashed behind the counter for a bag and pulled Georgi down to the floor.

"Breathe into the bag, Georgi, and put your head between your knees," she ordered as she shot a 'look to kill' at the detective. Then calmly, she asked, "Can you fetch him a glass of water, Detective?"

"Yes, yes." Morrison handed it to him. "Here you go, Georgi. Now don't get so upset. This is for routine questioning. You're not under arrest. Just calm down."

"That's ridiculous," Georgi muttered. "How can I calm down? You just told me terribly good and terribly bad news. I inherit the business, and I have the most to gain from the death of my boss and friend. I'm so confused."

Roxanne sat on the wooden floor with Georgi. She attempted to calm him. "It is okay, I'm right here with you, and I'm not going to let anything happen to you if I can. I don't believe you had anything to do with Mitch's death." She opened her small purse and pulled out some lavender oil. "Here, Georgi, smell this. It will help calm your nerves and focus the mind. It's an old-time remedy for stress."

Georgi inhaled the lavender and cooed, "Ohh, that's lovely." Simultaneously, he heaved a big sigh. Taking a few more inhalations, he exhaled. "Thank you, Roxanne, I feel better already." He squeezed her hand and put his head to hers. She sighed too.

Morrison shook his head, looking down at the duo on the floor. "Look, Georgi, I need a statement from you, and I asked Roxanne to come with me since she knows you. I thought it would help. Will you please come to the station?" Morrison tried being more cordial.

"Only if Roxanne comes with me," Georgi pleaded like a little child.

"Fine with me. Let's go then," coaxed Morrison.

Roxanne looked up at the detective and asked, "Ahh, Detective, how about I drive him down, maybe in a couple hours? We'll have some lunch and then see you."

Dan Morrison had his hands on his waist while he thought about it. *Maybe a little time will calm this character down. I don't need this kind of meltdown at the station.* Resolved, his hands went into the air to make a statement. "Fine, but make sure he shows up, or we'll have a warrant issued. As far as the department is concerned, he is a major suspect."

Catching a glimpse of himself in a mirror, Morrison quickly put his hands in his pockets, wondering if Georgi's drama was rubbing off on him. Agitated, he announced, "Okay! I'll see you after lunch." He turned and left the building.

Roxanne had other plans and was buying time.

Chapter 17

Roxanne helped Georgi off the floor and led him to a chair. Noticing an old phonebook under the service counter, she grabbed it and splashed her hand across the pages looking for a phone listing. "Found it!" she declared. Pulling out her cell phone, she punched in the numbers.

"Yelloh, Attorney Cornelius Pendergast's office," sang the voice. "May I help you?"

"This is Roxanne Samson. Corn, is that you?"

"Roxy, honey, how are ya?"

"Don't call me that, Corn!" she protested.

"But you call me Corn, and it's fun!" he jested.

"No, it isn't! I can't stand that nickname."

"Okay, alright, what kind of trouble are you in?"

"I'm not in trouble!" she asserted.

"But you're calling me, and you never call me. Sam is the only one who calls me in your household. Are you up to something with this murder?"

"Oh, for gosh sakes, did Sam call you?" she replied, somewhat peeved.

"Of course, he did. He said he didn't trust you. You have a mind of your own and for some odd reason, he didn't know what you would do next. He asked me to be on the ready. So I'm on the ready. What do you have for me?" asked the lawyer.

She groaned. "Aargh, everybody always knows what's going on. Geez, how come I can't surprise anyone anymore?" she huffed. "Well, it doesn't matter. I want you to come with Georgi Algarve and me to the police headquarters to talk to Detective Morrison. I want you to be Georgi's lawyer and advise him so he doesn't get in any trouble."

Silence answered. "Did you hear me?" she asked.

"Is this a favor to you, Sam, or Georgi?" asked the lawyer.

"All of us, gosh darn it, Corn. I can't take any more stress, and I want your help. Yes or no?" she demanded.

"Yes, yes, I'll help. Let's meet first. Come to my office."

"Good! I'm coming now. And Corn, since it's lunchtime, why don't you have that nice office assistant order some food for us, and we can talk and eat."

"Yes, ma'am! I'll get right on it. See you soon."

"Marsha!" He yelled, "Order some food for our new clients," then hung up the phone.

Roxanne smiled. Cornelius Pendergast was the best lawyer in New London. From across the room, Roxanne assured, "Don't worry Georgi, we've got Corn now."

Blinking his red puffy eyes, Georgi asked, "Corn?"

"You'll see. Come on, let's go have lunch. I'll drive."

"We're having corn?" he queried.

Driving from Bank Street toward Huntington Street, she passed Union Train Station, took a left up Federal Street, and drove by the police headquarters.

Georgi noticed, "Isn't that headquarters building dreadful? All square, cold, and mean like Detective Dan Morrison. It figures that's where we're going to meet him."

Roxanne stayed positive. "Don't worry. We'll work it out, Georgi." She made a quick turn onto Huntington Street, and for Georgi's sake, made a dramatic presentational wave toward the adjacent buildings. "Behold the Pillar Houses! Cornelius Pendergast's office is in one of these four prestigious Greek Revival buildings, built in 1835. It is still called Whale Oil Row due to the whale oil industry that funded all their construction." The pristine white successive buildings had a quadrupled effect of structure, design, and bold columns.

"Ooh," Georgi cooed, "I just adore grand architecture. I'm feeling better already. He must be wonderful if he works here."

***

Pendergast's secretary Marsha escorted them to the boardroom. On the table, she had laid out a small spread, buffet style, including bottled water, iced tea, a fresh spring salad, and small triangular sandwiches. A rotund balding man with suspenders stepped into the room.

"Yelloh, Roxanne!" he said enthusiastically.

"Corn, I want you to meet Georgi Algarve, the new owner of the Vinho Verde Wine Bar."

"Roxanne!" Georgi scolded, "it's a little too soon to say that, don't you think?"

"No, I don't. It's true, and you need to get used to it. Plus, I think it's wonderful that Mitch thought so highly of you to honor you in this way. It means you deserve it," she added for good measure.

Georgi lowered his head to his chest. "I just didn't think of it in that way, being an honor and all...." his voice trailed off, and Roxanne wondered.

"What is it?" she asked.

"I think I'm going to cry again," he whispered.

"Now you stop that," she said in his ear. "Corn is here to get to know you, and you can't be carrying on like that, now can you? So pull yourself together."

Georgi breathed in deeply and nodded to her, straightened himself up, and put his hand out to shake Corns'. "It's nice to meet you, sir. Thank you for seeing us on such short notice."

Cornelius laughed. "Not to worry, my boy," he assured as he slapped Georgi's shoulder, startling him. "I cannot resist when my friend Chief Sam calls. You need help, and I'm available."

"What?" Georgi looked at Roxanne.

"It's okay Georgi," she patted his arm. "Let's sit down and eat, shall we?"

"Certainly," said Corn in his notoriously loud voice. "Please sit and tell me all you know while we eat."

Roxanne and Georgi related the whole ordeal. She began with how she found Mitch in the shrubbery with a poisonous plant stuffed in his mouth. Then how she was mugged at Ocean Beach, after which she saw a gym-suited prowler on her porch. She accompanied Detective Morrison to tell Georgi about Mitch and that very evening, Georgi was beaten in the back parking lot. Today, the detective told Georgi he is the sole inheritor of the Vinho Verde. This made Georgi the prime suspect in the murder since Mrs. Stockman was already wealthy and not at all interested in the business.

Corn pitched forward in his conference chair. "Well, that's quite a sequence of events, isn't it?" He took a long sip of his iced tea and narrowed his eyes.

"Why were you mugged, Roxanne?" he asked just as she was about to bite into her triangle sandwich.

"I don't know." She shrugged and explained, becoming animated, "It doesn't make sense, Corn. Whoever did it grabbed my fanny pack, and my license was gone when the police retrieved it. Then when I sat in my truck to go home, I could tell someone had been inside it because the seat was moved. And when I drove up to the house with the police behind me, a man was on my porch. He jumped off and ran away." Roxanne gestured through the whole description. Corn could tell she was wound up.

"So they must think you found evidence at the murder site that would incriminate the killer," he offered. "Maybe you know something you don't know, you know?"

"I suppose, but I didn't, and I don't. Why did they go to my house?" Her voice crackled with exasperation. "I didn't find anything, see anything, and I don't know anything!" she proclaimed as her arm went into the air, holding the triangle sandwich in hand.

Distracted, Corn's eyes moved up her arm to the sandwich. He wondered if she would eat it or throw it. "Okay, okay," he said, reassembling his thoughts, "but why did they beat you up, Georgi?"

"Well, that's just it," Georgi replied, riding on Roxanne's exasperation. "The guy asked if the blonde found anything. After I said no, he knocked me out by smashing my head into the steering wheel." He put his hand to his head, pointing out the recent injury and bandage.

"Oh," Corn said, taking another long sip of tea. In deep thought, he furrowed his brow and pursed his lips. "A businessman like Stockman has plenty of people who would have a motive for his murder. There is more going on here than Georgi inheriting the business," he surmised.

Roxanne blurted out, "We have to find out what it is, Corn. When we see the detective, we don't want Georgi to be accused, now do we?" Anxiously, Roxanne reached out her hand across the table to Georgi who grasped it tightly. Suddenly, Corn saw the movie image of *Thelma and Louise* cross his mind. He shook his head to delete it.

"This is a mystery much bigger than the two of you." Corn waved his sandwich at them. "We need to help Morrison with a list of who else could be involved in Mitch Stockman's death. I think he is jumping the gun by saying you're his prime suspect. He just needs to talk to a few more people close to the family and the business, and he'll unearth more leads. I also wonder what the forensic team has discovered and what the medical examiner has to say." Cornelius now stared ahead, considering possible motives of a killer.

"Georgi, just because you're in Stockman's will isn't reason enough. Who else was in the room at the wine tasting that evening?" Corn asked.

"It was a group celebrating a birthday."

"Not a likely group of people to want Stockman dead," Corn responded. "And how about your staff?"

"They are part-time and thrilled to have a job." Georgi added, "They're not very likely either."

Cornelius Pendergast yelled, "Marsha!" startling Georgi and Roxanne. Marsha stepped in. "Find out who drew up Mitch Stockman's will, would you? Call around. We want to know when he made it out." She nodded and left the room.

He eyed Georgi and asked, "Where were you the night Mitch was murdered?"

"I was at work until eleven p.m., drove home, and arrived around eleven fifteen," Georgi replied.

"Did you go out after?" shot Cornelius.

"No, I stayed in the rest of the night," volleyed Georgi.

"Can anyone vouch for you?"

"No, I was alone."

"Well, that's not good," he muttered.

"No kidding. Do you think I want to be alone?" Georgi commented glibly.

Roxanne patted his hand and added, "We don't know the time of death, Corn. Maybe that would help."

"We do have an idea of Mitch's evening," offered Georgi. "He was at the wine tasting event at six p.m. He left about ten thirty and said he was going to visit with Tony at the bistro for an espresso before heading to his condo at Harlow Towers."

Corn deduced, "So that could bring it to sometime after eleven that he was attacked at Columbus Circle?"

Georgi imagined poor Mitch leaving the bistro and ending up in the shrubs. "It's possible," he murmured.

Cornelius asked, "Where was he found?"

"He was found in the garden just outside the bistro, right behind Christopher Columbus's statue," Roxanne answered. Georgi's emotions overcame him. His head slowly sank to his chest.

"Georgi," Corn snapped, jerking him out of it. "You need an alibi. Is there anyone who saw you on your way home? The timing is too close to you leaving work, especially if Tony was the last person to see Stockman alive."

Georgi visualized leaving work that evening, taking the short drive in his PT Cruiser to his Hempstead Street apartment, and grabbing the mail. "Ohh! Ohh! Mrs. Wolcott! She was home! She heard me come in," Georgi said excitedly.

"How do you know?" asked Corn.

"Because she was playing the song "I Will Survive" by Gloria Gaynor. I started singing it in the hallway, and she started singing behind her door and then she came out into the hall in her bathrobe and pink slippers. We belted out the whole tune together. Gloria would have been proud of us," he smiled, cherishing the happy memory. "Then Mrs. Wolcott invited me in for some cookies, and we sat on her Victorian chaise together, dipping them in milk. I went to bed at midnight."

"Oh," said Corn, "well, that alibi will do."

Roxanne patted Georgi's hand and giggled. So did Georgi. Corn looked down at his notes and smirked while shaking his head, imagining the whole scene.

Cornelius let out a satisfied sigh, leaned forward, and looked over his reading glasses at Georgi, then Roxanne. A slight smile emerged while he rubbed his hands together. "Not to worry, my friends. All is well in the hands of Cornelius Pendergast. I know how to manage the detective. Let's go to our meeting, shall we?"

Chapter 18

Across the street from Attorney Pendergast's office, J.J. zipped along on his skateboard, weaving around cars and daredeviling over the curbs and sidewalks. Elevated high above him, pigeons perched and cooed in the brownstone steeple of St. James Episcopal Church. This Gothic Revival giant was erected in 1847 and was designed by the famous Richard Upjohn, who had just completed Trinity Church in Manhattan.

J.J. stopped and sat on a knee wall in the shade, waiting. Finally, he observed Georgi, Roxanne, and a portly man in a suit step from the law offices of Whale Oil Row. The threesome walked to Governor Winthrop Boulevard, passed the Holiday Inn, and continued to the police headquarters. Directly across from headquarters was the ferry terminal entrance located on the Thames River.

J.J. took a hard right and swooped down Eugene O'Neil Drive past the newspaper headquarters for *The Day*, then took a left onto State Street, to the city center Parade Plaza. He swerved around the Whale Tail fountain and landed to the left of Union Station. Hiding in the shadows, J.J. took out his phone and texted a message, "Blondie, boy-George, and Lawly going to cops."

***

Inside police headquarters, Detective Morrison welcomed them all into the meeting room. "I see we have company." He nodded to Attorney Pendergast. "Pendergast," the detective warmly extended his hand.

"I'll be representing Georgi," Pendergast stated.

"Yes, I assumed. Please have a seat." Detective Morrison took out his pen and tapped it on his pad of paper, looking curiously at the three of them.

Pendergast took the opportunity. "Are you planning to place Georgi under arrest?"

"No, no," Morrison said with certainty, "we just need an official statement from him as to his whereabouts the evening his boss, Mitch Stockman, died."

"Well, that'll be easy enough," the attorney said, looking toward Georgi. "You tell him what you just told me, Georgi." Pendergast looked back at the detective and raised his eyebrows high enough to signify, 'wait to hear this one.'

Georgi described his disco song duet with Mrs. Wolcott. Detective Morrison officially recorded the statement while trying to keep his sober composure. Pendergast reminded him that Georgi's alibi was solid. The wary detective promised he would be confirming the story with Mrs. Wolcott.

Georgi piped in, "Ask Mrs. Wolcott the name of the song. It was the Grammy-winning hit 'I Will Survive' by Gloria Gaynor." Suddenly, Georgi became squeamish and mumbled, "It seems ironic, doesn't it? I survived and Mitch didn't."

Morrison said, "Right, Georgi, so that was the song you were singing. Let's see if Mrs. Wolcott remembers all these details."

"Oh, she will," sang Georgi.

Attorney Pendergast interrupted, "That's enough commenting, Georgi."

Georgi hung his head and with only his eyes, he looked up at the attorney. "Okay," he said humbly.

"Wait," demanded Morrison, "Georgi, tell me what you know about poisons."

"I don't know anything about poison!" he cried.

Pendergast returned sternly, "Georgi! Don't say another word." Then quietly, "Detective, you're barking up the wrong tree!"

Roxanne spoke up, "Detective, there must be someone else out there who knows poisons."

Pendergast quickly ordered Georgi and Roxanne, "You two are dismissed! I'll meet you outside."

Quietly, they left the room. In the hallway, Georgi whispered to Roxanne, "That Detective Dan Morrison is bitter like a harsh wine with overt tannins. He is so acidic he reminds me of raw rhubarb — tart and puckering. He makes me cringe. I don't like him anymore."

Georgi was on a roll, "And for that matter, your Attorney Corn was vastly different in there, all gruff and serious. He's a bit of a rumpot, isn't he?"

"Whatever do you mean?" asked Roxanne, confused.

"He's stout, well-rounded, and colorful, but he comes with a kick!" He paused and explained in a quiet undertone, "It's a fruity German alcoholic punch, and he reminds me of it, that's all."

In her most solemn voice, Roxanne said, "That's the way it goes, Georgi. It's business, all business, once you enter a police station. It's formal, no niceties, no joking around. It's as serious as death should be."

Georgi's mood changed again. Trying to keep his voice down, yet still in a melodramatic tone, he added, "This is horrible! How do you go on with life when someone close to you has died? There is a part of me that doesn't think it happened. It's as if I had a bad dream, and now I'm awake and it's over. I'm normally happy and then suddenly I realize I'm living a nightmare!" His arms thrust skyward. "Mitch is gone, and I'm by myself to run his business!" His heralding arms collapsed weakly to his sides, and he slumped. "He was the best boss ever. I'm so torn up. I feel horribly sad. I don't know what is up or down anymore." A silence fell between them as he became tearful.

Roxanne locked her arm onto Georgi's and gave it a squeeze. She knew just how he felt, after having lost a close cousin when she was young, a few dear pets, and her father. She had seen loss but also knew of it through her husband's work as a firemen and rescue worker. He had seen families distraught by fire and accidents. She too wondered, *what is the answer?*

"Look," she said, "there is no way to deal with this properly. Everyone has their own way to grieve. I think it is best to be yourself, and I think that if Mitch were right here with us, he would say, 'Georgi, I had a good life while I was here. I want you to have a good life too. Now carry on.' He doesn't want you moping around. There is no honor in a head hung low. Keep your chin up and be your cheerful self. Yes, this has changed things, but that is the journey of life. It's an adventure, and we're in the thick of it together."

Georgi squeezed her arm back and said, "I don't know how I could do this without you. What an odd set of circumstances that brought us together. Thank you, Roxanne. You're a dear friend."

Pendergast emerged from the meeting, releasing them of the police station. They walked back to the office together.

***

Pushing off on his skateboard, J.J. weaved onto Water Street toward the police station. He perched himself so he could watch the windowed reflection of Lawly, Blondie, and boy-George pass right behind him. J.J. pretended to be listening to his iTunes. He picked up his board and walked behind them, hoping to overhear something that would earn his keep.

Chapter 19

The quick walk up Governor Winthrop Boulevard to his office gave Attorney Pendergast time to discuss his outcome with Georgi and Roxanne. "Well, I've got you covered, Georgi," he declared. "Don't you worry, the detective will be calling me now. If he shows up at your storefront, you just tell him to see me.

"You might be a likely suspect on paper, but I don't believe you did it. There must be someone out there who wanted Stockman dead. There has to be another motive the detective isn't aware of yet. Can you think of anyone?"

Georgi shook his head. "Everyone around Mitch that I've known was friendly. I just don't understand. I thought it was a random mugging at first but not now! We have to figure this out!"

Pendergast conjectured, "If it weren't for the plant in his mouth, you being beaten up, and Roxanne getting mugged, we might have thought this guy murdered him out of random anger. But he has a bigger mission. Georgi, you need to look into your business records; try to find some connection that set up these circumstances. The detective will do his part, but you may have the key, and you just don't know it yet."

With vigor, Georgi answered the call to duty. "I will make it my homework, sir,"

"I have a bit of an idea," Roxanne inserted. "Since the detective is going to ask Marissa about funding the reward for information, he'll be putting it in the paper. Georgi, you and I could hang the reward posters all around town and spread the word in the neighborhood. Maybe someone will bite. The sooner we are free from this, the better."

"Definitely," Georgi agreed. "Let's do it. There must be someone out there with some clue. I wonder if there is anything else we could do." Georgi's fingers went to his lips, tapping them as he thought.

"Oh! I've got it!" he declared excitedly. He stopped short, then twirled on one foot to face Roxanne, finishing his move with wavering jazz hands. "Maybe in a few weeks, I'll then host a memorial event for Mitch at Vinho Verde. It will honor him and celebrate his life. Mitch has lots of friends here. It could be a fabulous way to celebrate my dear friend in the fashion he loved: with wine, food, and socializing."

Georgi's imagination roamed. "We could set it up and ask Detective Morrison to check out the people who attend for more leads. Who knows, maybe the killer would come if he is posh." Georgi jumped and grabbed Roxanne. "We could get a lead and clear my name and when he is caught, our lives will be safe and calm again!"

As they were congratulating each other, Pendergast croaked, "Wait a minute here! You two must be out of your minds! You're both ridiculous! You've lost your common sense. You don't put yourselves on the street and start setting traps! First, you need to see what happens with the reward announcement. Morrison may receive false leads from the riffraff around here, you know, the dock rats and slippery eels that slink around doing deals on the streets. Then add in young treasure-seekers with nothing else to do. Come on! You're risking your lives with those ideas!"

He huffed and puffed, then continued. "I've seen this happen. Morrison will get more leads than he'll know what to do with, and you may be stirring a large pot of trouble. Who knows what kind of characters are following you? Who knows what you'll be dredging up from the depths of that trouble pot?"

Georgi perked up and argued, "But this is the way to get results! Just like wine, we are setting a trap, like when a vintner collects the sediment with a vintrap or fermentation trap. We are merely creating a situation where the killer or anyone involved with him becomes trapped naturally. But we," Georgi grabbed Roxanne, "provide the filter to catch them."

Pendergast stopped, cocked his head, and looked at Georgi from a new angle. "I'm not sure, young man, if wine wit is a proper metaphor, but I do respect your point."

"That's exactly why this is going to work," urged Roxanne. "I can feel it. Gardeners have good intuition. When we know, we know. We feel it in our bones. Come on, Corn! Besides, Detective Dan has already agreed to post a reward and is calling Mrs. Stockman. It will be at least $1,000. And if the killer isn't caught, a memorial event is going to happen anyway."

Pendergast growled, "Aargh, you never know what you'll attract, Roxy, you never know." She scowled at him in response.

Dutifully, Cornelius Pendergast thought hard before objecting anymore. "I'm just saying, I don't like you and Georgi doing anything overt. You are my clients. I'm here to give you advice. I don't like it one bit, you being on the streets."

Another frustrated grunt escaped his throat. "But I also know I can't stop you two schemers." He reflected on the idea a little more and warned, "Look, think it through, will you? I don't want you to be targets." His eyes narrowed to tiny slits.

Still displeased, he pontificated, "If Morrison and your husband Sam approve of what you're doing, then fine. But be sure to tell them I did not advise you to put up reward posters. And worst of all, hosting a memorial service to catch a killer. Okay?" Then he muttered, "Let's hope it's all over with before that day comes."

"Sure, Corn, we'll do as you ask and be in touch." Roxanne winked at him.

Corn admonished her, "You're a terrible liar, Roxy. You've got me very concerned. I will call Morrison and Sam myself if you don't." He sighed loudly. "Be careful, watch your back, and call me with updates. Okay?"

"We will. Thank you, Corn." Roxanne gave him a friendly pat on the arm.

"It's a good thing I've known you forever," he mumbled at her.

Then Georgi put out his hand. "Thank you, sir," because he didn't know what to call him anymore. Attorney Pendergast or Corn? Roxanne and Georgi walked to her truck as Pendergast strolled toward his office.

***

J.J. dropped his skateboard to the ground and took off. He weaved his way down the incline of State Street and stopped and sat on the stairs of the impressive First Congregational Church. The magnificent gray stone steeple loomed over the novice spy as the well-intentioned saints who resided there whispered divine guidance in vain.

He texted the message, "need 2 CU 911," and sent it. Lifting off his perch, J.J. swerved down the street, passed the train tracks toward Fishers Island's ferry dock, and zoomed to the boardwalk by the pier. Sighting a vacant bench, he did a sidewinding trick on it, then caught the board on the way down.

"C U on State St @ Sarges," the return text ordered.

Chapter 20

Roxanne dropped off Georgi at the Vinho Verde Wine Bar and went home to garden. While removing the deadheads from the flowers, she looked up to see Sam arriving home from work.

"Hi, dear," she sang.

"You're in a cheerful mood." Sam grabbed his jacket from the vehicle and followed her into the house.

"What's going on?" he asked, half wondering if his wife was up to any shenanigans. He knew her all too well: once she was involved, she was fully committed to the very end.

"Georgi and I saw Corn, and we went to Dan's office at police headquarters. It all went well," she answered.

"It did?" he queried, wondering if she wasn't leaving out a few details.

"Well, fine enough." She paused a moment. "After our meeting, Georgi and I came up with a great idea to flush out some leads!"

"What are you talking about?" Sam asked, standing still and suddenly concerned.

She described their idea of putting reward posters around town and Georgi hosting the memorial event for Mitch at the Vinho Verde, and this would hopefully flush out some leads for the detective.

"What?! Are you nuts? This is not a Sherlock Holmes story. This is not the game of Masterpiece Mystery. This is not how killers are caught!" Unconventionally upset, he took a deep breath, then slowly said, "I did call…and involve Attorney Pendergast…so he could calm you both down and knock some sense into the two of you! How? How is it that you take a murder, with Georgi being a major suspect, and turn it into hanging posters in town looking for a parade of suspects and a memorial service to expose a killer?"

Sam shook his head while staring at her in disbelief. "How can you do this? How about you do nothing and let Detective Morrison do his job?" He put his palm to his forehead and let out a big sigh. "Ughhh."

"Listen," he said thoughtfully, "I married you because you are fun and interesting, never a dull moment. You love to socialize, cook, and entertain. You've been the perfect wife. And now you want to use all those lovely qualities to trap a killer. I can't believe it. Never...never would I have imagined this. I think you're insane!"

Roxanne rattled something in the kitchen. "What are you doing?" he asked rather roughly.

"I'm making us some chamomile tea to help you relax." She gave him a cheeky smile.

Sam laughed sarcastically and lowered himself into his big leather chair. "I'm going to need something stronger," he asserted. "How about a chamomile hot toddy for the special occasion of dealing with my eccentric wife?" He stretched out his body, then reclined further into his favorite spot.

"I think that's something my grandmother drank," Roxanne noted, "but all I have is honey right now."

She carried two cups over to a small side table and then knelt by his chair, putting her hand in his. "Listen, dear," she said softly, "there is a method to my badness, I mean madness." She giggled slightly. He watched her eyes twinkling. "I do believe someone may come forward with something. But we have to get the word out about the reward. Do you think people on the street read the paper? Of course not," she answered herself.

Watching her beloved listening attentively, she continued. "This could shift Georgi off the detective's radar! And help catch whoever mugged me! Then if the murderer happens to be someone possibly with money, who isn't a low-life, and who knew Mitch, they might go to this memorial event. And here is where we'll have the detective and his guys watching, listening, and questioning people discreetly."

Sam did not respond. "Come on, it's not that bad an idea, is it?" she cajoled, looking up at him dramatically.

He paused and then laughed, and she did too. He patted her head and said lovingly, "Not bad, Miss Marple, not bad. Go over the idea with Morrison, as he is in charge of this investigation. And you do know he will be checking in with me. So don't get any more crazy ideas."

"Yes, dear, I'm never crazy. I'm just enthusiastic! Once you understand my method, everything makes sense," Roxanne asserted, now emboldened.

"Yes, the method of your badness!" he teased as he gently took her chin and kissed her sweetly.

She replied, "My grandfather always said, 'If you can't be good, be careful.'"

"Ha!" Sam sounded. "I don't think your grandfather was talking about muggings and murder! No wonder your grandmother drank hot toddies with a husband like that."

She smiled and gave him a hug and a kiss. "Thanks for being understanding," she whispered.

"My sweet," he said, holding her close, "I don't understand you. But that's all right with me."

Chapter 21

Roxanne called Detective Morrison to discuss the memorial event and the reward ideas. "Did Mrs. Stockman approve funding the reward, Dan? Georgi and I would like to put up posters around town."

"Well, I did talk to Mrs. Stockman," Morrison answered. "I explained to her that since you and Georgi were both mugged, you asked if a reward could be offered. I told her you were willing to fund it but only if she agreed. And I was glad to hear that not only does she agree but is offering a $5,000 reward!"

"Oh, that's wonderful!" declared Roxanne.

"But," Morrison emphasized, "and this is a big but, I will let you hang posters only with one of my officers escorting you and Georgi. And let's keep it down to ten, please. I can't spare a man all day."

"I'll make the posters up on my computer right now!" Roxanne said, enthused.

"The memorial event should wait, in my opinion," Morrison added.

"But Dan, you might unearth more leads," Roxanne protested.

"Yes, Miss Secret Agent," he said in a teasing voice, "but I'd really like to do some more investigating. Just hold your horses, please. I heard from the coroner that Mitch died between eleven fifteen p.m. and twelve thirty a.m. Mrs. Wolcott confirmed Georgi's alibi and arrival time at home. But he could have gone back out that night, so Georgi is not off the suspect list yet."

"Detective, you are just doing your job," conceded Roxanne. "I'll make the reward poster and pass it by you first. Georgi and I will put off planning the memorial event. Thank you for all you're doing, and I know you will catch the guy sooner or later."

"We will and hopefully sooner. Good-bye, Roxanne."

Putting her artistic scrapbooking computer skills together with a poster program, Roxanne added a nice photo of Mitch that Georgi gave her. She stared at the handsome face of a man around fifty and wondered. *Why did this happen? He looks so vibrant and full of life…. Did he have an argument? I wonder how much money he loaned the different vineyards. Did they reason getting rid of him, they would be rid of their debt too? Hmm, anything is possible.*

***

In front of Sarge's Comics on State Street, J.J. slid into his boss's car. He held his skateboard between his knees. His boss admonished him sharply with perfect English, highlighted by an Italian accent.

"What's the matter with you? I don't like meeting. No one should see us together. I told you the first time we met that it would be the last and all our business would be on the phone. What is so nine-one-one urgent?"

"Hey man, this is important. You're gonna thank me when you hear what I know, and you'll never see me again." J.J.'s bold declaration included his own type of body language and slang common to a sixteen-year-old skateboarding dude on the streets of New London.

In an adverse tone, the boss asked, "What do you have for me?" The suave hair, cologne, Bulgari sunglasses, and expensive Italian suit were lost on J.J., who only noticed the boss's ride, a luxury car.

"Man, I got something that helps me and helps you. They're planning to put up a reward for at least 1000 bucks on information leading to that murder. You know, the one that happened there at that statue of Columbus." J.J. was quite pleased with himself at figuring things out and his undercover work.

The boss turned in his seat to face J.J. "Are you sure? *Cosa faro adesso?"* (What am I going to do now?)

"Yeah, and Blondie came up with the idea to start putting reward posters up everywhere. So I figured you're not having me watch Columbus Circle for nothing, so I put two and two together, and what I'm thinking is you're gonna want to pay me a 1000 bucks for all this information, you see. Cuz I'm gonna go collect it from them if you don't pay me. I see it as a win-win either way, man."

"*Stupido imbecile*," the boss spat in his native Italian and motioned with his hands. "Where do you get off telling me what I'm going to do? *Chi vuole troppo non ottiene niente"* (He who wants too much gets nothing). The boss threw the car in gear, sped off, and murmured in disgust, "*Che Cazzo*" (What the hell).

"Hey, man, don't get all mad on me, dude. I just need to help my momma with the rent. I appreciate you paying me a hundred bucks and all, but this is business we're doing, right? That's why you hired me. It's business."

In silence, the boss headed past the ferry docks, took a right under the Gold Star Memorial Bridge past the Old Mill, and drove to the entrance of an abandoned park. It was a hilly haven of overgrown green, situated by the Thames River. "Where are you going, dude?" J.J. asked. "I don't live near here."

The angry boss man pulled over and grunted, "You do now." He punched J.J. in the head so hard, the kid was knocked out in an instant. He then snapped his neck with a swift twist. The iTunes cord was still hanging below J.J.'s ears.

The well-dressed killer drove to the river's edge where thickets grew high by the old train tracks. He opened the door and dragged J.J.'s limp body into the gully toward the shore. Grabbing a thick bittersweet vine, he finalized his wrath by wrapping it around J.J.'s neck. With ceremonial indifference, he gave

J.J. a swift kick and watched his body roll beneath overgrown brambles. The tune "Take Me to Church" by Hozier played out of J.J.'s earbuds.

"*Lontano dagli occhi, lontano dal cuore*" (Out of sight, out of mind), grumbled the conspirator as he sped out of the park.

chapter 22

Later in the day, Diego took his German shepherd, Max, on their ritual drive to Riverside Park. He placed the car at the base of the hill by the water of the Thames River. Max broke into a gallop, making his rounds sniffing out any new scents and making a few of his own.

Diego smoked a cigarette and stared out at the fast-moving tidal current that traveled under the expansive Gold Star Bridge. He leaned against his blue vintage Mustang, handed down to him from his dad. The heartfelt music of Luis Fonsi echoed from his sound box. The instrumental guitar and island beat of the song "Despacito" honored his home country of Puerto Rico and had him dreaming of dancing with his girl.

Max was sniffing by a tree, then trotted the degraded asphalt road toward the fence of the Coast Guard Academy. He disappeared into the overgrowth of plants by the shore. Diego let him be for a while. Eventually, he called out, "Max, what are you up to? Max, come here." There was no response. "Max!" he yelled.

Diego knew his dog; he always returned unless he found a dead fish. He certainly didn't want him rolling in the stink and carrying it into his 1969 classic.

Diego whistled and called, "Max, where are you?" Finally, he spotted the dog's hindquarters and tail wagging furiously. "Come, come here, you," he commanded.

Diego edged closer as Max ignored him. "What have you got there?" Diego inched down the steep incline, carefully grabbing onto the weeds. "*Mierda!*"

he swore, stunned by the vision of a boy staring up at him with vines wrapped around his neck.

"Get out of there, Max! NOW!" he yelled. Max listened to the panic rising in Diego's voice. "Come on, Max, we're out of here! *Ahora! Mierda!*"

Diego loaded Max into the car and sped off. Banging his fist on the dashboard, he cursed again. "*Mierda!*" He raced to the top of the hill past the gates of the Park and stopped. "*Mierda!*" he swore again and called 911.

"Nine-one-one, what's your emergency?" asked the dispatcher.

"There is a guy that looks dead here at Riverside Park."

"Your name, sir?"

"Diego. My dog found him."

"Stay right there. I'm sending over an officer."

The emergency response services arrived, and Detective Morrison followed them in with the police and his team of investigators. They questioned Diego and had the forensic officer analyze his shoes and tire treads and check his dog. Upon having all his contact information, they released him.

Observing the body, Morrison noted: male teenager, recently dead, still warm, no defensive wounds, iTunes still playing. The bruising to the face is recent with blood pooling and color near the surface of the skin. He was most likely rolled out of a car based on the bent vegetation, and it wrapped around him.

Next to Morrison was a uniformed policeman. "What do you think, Officer McNamara? Do you know him?"

"It's J.J., sir. We all know him. He's usually downtown skateboarding, like many of them, by the State Street skate shop. This is not his neighborhood. It's unlikely he skated over here." The officer collected his thoughts and considered the scene. "He was harmless, Detective. Someone dropped him here." McNamara looked around, "Where's his board? He's never without it."

Morrison scanned the overgrown site and spouted to his team, "Put a dog on this scene, see if there's any evidence we can work with, and tape off the park entrances." The team went to work.

Morrison questioned, "What's going on, McNamara? We have two bizarre murders in three days."

McNamara remained quiet, knowing he didn't expect an answer. Together they walked along the edge of the chain link fence placing colored markers upon any possible clues.

The detective pulled a stick of cinnamon gum from his pocket and offered it to McNamara, who rejected it. Morrison removed the wrapper and folded the gum into his mouth. "Listen, Mac, ask the guys at the HIVE Skate Shop on State Street about J.J. and if he was involved in something. And check in with the owner at Whaling City Boxing. You know him, Mac? He trains a lot of the youth, and he might have overheard their talk. The kids may be aware of these activities happening on the streets. See if you can find me a lead. And bring Peabody in on it with you."

"Sure thing, Detective, I'm on it." McNamara made arrangements with the assistant detective, Jack Peabody, and left.

Morrison pulled a contact card from his inside pocket and proceeded to call the number. "Agent Koster, this is Detective Morrison. I just want to notify you that there has been a murder at Riverside Park, next door to the Coast Guard Academy. I don't think there is anything you need to be concerned about here, but I'm just following protocol and letting you know."

"So you don't feel it has anything to do with the president's upcoming presence at the Academy?" Koster asked.

"No, sir. At this time, there is no indication that it connects with the president's visit. As you said last month at the briefing, no surprises and no snafus."

"That's right, Morrison. Keep me posted if anything comes up."

Pacing the crumbling pavement, Morrison considered the abandoned area and the old bathhouse. It was a derelict and forsaken building covered in graffiti and vines. He recalled the 'once upon a time stories' of when families gathered here, picnicking and swimming in the Thames River.

Crowds from as far away as New York would off-load from the trains that ran along the shoreline. Now the tracks were unused and blocked from the rusted-out ramps, and a six-foot chain link fence barred today's visitors from accessing the water.

Morrison was hard-pressed to imagine how this location was one of the yearly outlooks for the famous Yale-Harvard Regattas. They began in 1878. The popular attraction was the competition and the buff athletic men racing their crew boats.

A huge grandstand was erected to seat 3,000 fans on the Thames, and an overwhelming crowd of 25,000 showed up. Over the years, the crowds grew so large that notably in 1925, an estimated 100,000 attended the race, including two packed observation trains of thirty cars. On that day, they witnessed Yale roaring from behind, upstream on the Thames, breaking a record of twenty minutes, twenty-six seconds.

While Morrison waited for the coroner, he noted the only thing lurching forward at Riverside Park were the overgrown weeds and the time on his clock, counting two murders in three days.

Chapter 23

Marissa Stockman sent the signature red realty envelope with $10,000 in cash in assurance of her daughter's safety. It was now in the large canvas mail sack on the ferry. She left the house early to guarantee it would be on the seven a.m. Sea Jet departing Orient Point for New London. Today, the red envelope was for the transaction of life; it held the promise of a safe future for her daughter. Just as instructed, she addressed it to 'Johnson Jones, for Pickup Only, Ferry Office, New London.'

The Sea Jet made the quick trip across the sound and arrived on schedule at seven forty-five a.m. The large bin on wheels holding the mail was taken off the boat. A man in a gray suit watched the activity from across the parking lot and waited for an opportunity. After the passengers disembarked, he attempted to coax a deckhand to pull the envelope for him, but the guy wouldn't take the bribe. "Goody Two-Shoes," the thug snarled under his breath.

The mail bin was wheeled inside to Sandy, the office clerk. She lifted out the presorted mail and put it in a cubbyhole below the service window.

New London's newspaper, *The Day*, was on the counter. While taking a sip of coffee, Sandy saw the front-page headline about another murder. *Oh dear! First Mr. Mitch and now someone else! What is this town coming to?* She glanced at the details. "Johnson Jones, known to family and friends as J.J., sixteen years old, was found deceased at Riverside Park. Please contact the police with any information." Wow, the poor parents, she thought. She imagined her nephew who was the same age. *I wonder if he knew him.*

109

Sandy was going through her paperwork and record keeping when a man came to the counter. "I have a package to pick up from Long Island." She looked him over, noticing his expensive suit and tie.

"Sure. Your name, please?"

"Johnson Jones," he said, tapping his fingers on the counter.

Sandy peered at him over her eyeglasses. A four-foot-tall counter was between him and her. Her muscles tensed. She had been working there for twenty-three years, and suddenly this very moment was the test of her people skills. Stay calm, she said to herself. Time to put on an act, Sandy. You can do it. Just pretend you're on a bad date and be nice until it's over.

"Just a minute," she said calmly. Below his view behind the counter, she sorted through the box of mail. "Let's see," she murmured out loud. "Julie Morgan, Connie Chance, Robbie Sturgeon, Rosemary Moore, Deonn Dyermejian, Paula Masterson," and then she saw his name. The red envelope blared at her senses. Her hands shook as she put it under the pile. "Nope, nothing. It's probably coming in on the three thirty ferry. Come back at four o'clock," she announced with a very matter-of-fact tone.

"Are you sure?" the man asked, clearly surprised. "They told me it would be here."

"Of course, I'm sure," she said. "Four o'clock." The man turned around, obviously very disappointed. As soon as he left, Sandy called the police.

"I have an emergency at the Cross Sound Ferry office. It has to do with the murder of Johnson Jones. Come quickly before he gets away!"

"Who?" asked the 911 operator.

"The murderer! Goodness me! Hurry, hurry! I'm going to watch him until you get here."

She saw the man approach a silver sedan and speak to someone through the passenger window. Sandy attempted to read the license number, but it was out of sight, and the car sped off quickly, leaving the man standing there. He walked toward the train station, passing the long car lines to board the ferry. Crossing an expanse of tarmac, he then darted through the Coast Guard Museum construction site.

"Oh no!" Sandy made quick moves from window to window, peeking through the blinds. "He's going to get away! What do I do?"

"Whatever are you talking about?" her boss yelled from his back office.

"I'll be right back," she returned. Sandy ran out the door and leapt down the back stairs just as the police pulled up.

"There he is," she whispered into the car. "That's him in the gray suit and black glasses."

"What about him?" the officers asked.

"He came to claim mail addressed to Johnson Jones. You know, the kid who is dead! He could be the murderer!" She stopped whispering and sternly belted out, "Go get him, for Pete's sake!"

The police raced their vehicle to the end of the tarmac just as the guy skipped over the train tracks and headed inside the station. One officer radioed for backup as his partner took off on foot. He jumped one set of tracks and simultaneously, "Whoo! Whoo!" The high-speed train pulled in for a stop. He leapt out of the way, just in time, to the track beyond.

Rather than race around the train, the second officer swiftly decided to go through the middle of the stopped train. In one door and out to the other side. Train schedule announcements echoed off the high, beamed ceilings of the historic 1848 building. A third and fourth officer arrived from the street side.

The one in charge rattled off a description. "Medium build, male, six feet, gray business suit, mid-forties, dark glasses, dark hair." Systematically, the officers combed the inside of Union Station. People were coming and going among the long wooden benches. Finally, they located him in the men's room, washing his hands.

"You're coming with us. We're taking you in regarding the death of

Johnson Jones."

"I was just doing an errand! I'm clean!" he gestured by holding up his hands.

"Oh, a wise guy! Your hands may be clean, but what about the rest of you?" the officer scoffed. "Cuff him!"

***

At eight thirty a.m., Morrison made a call. "Mrs. Stockman, I need you to come into New London. I have some information regarding your husband's murder."

"Can't you tell me over the phone?" she asked nervously.

"No, ma'am, I'm sorry I can't."

Mrs. Stockman squirmed. "Listen, Detective, I can't come. I'm overwhelmed by everything as it is. I'm having a service for Mitch next week, and I have my daughter here for the summer. It's all too much right now." She never wanted to see New London again.

"I understand. But if you don't come, I'll have to have you served by your local marshal," persisted Morrison.

"What? Why?" Pangs of fear gripped her heart. She worried about the ransom money and her daughter.

"I need to talk to you in person, Mrs. Stockman. That's how important this is."

"Detective, I would greatly appreciate it if you would come here and not involve the local authorities. To be honest with you, I'm afraid for my life and my daughter's."

"Can you enlighten me a little?" he asked dryly.

Mrs. Stockman whispered, "Someone is blackmailing me." Vocalizing those words made her feel ill, and she shivered with fear.

"Why are you being blackmailed, Mrs. Stockman?" he queried, now very curious to her state of affairs.

"Why? They've threatened to kill my daughter," she whimpered.

"Look, that sounds like a good reason to be afraid, but we caught the guy who went to pick up your package. I need you to come in. I will send you an escort."

"You know about the package?" she gasped humiliated, then held her breath. The next thing Morrison heard was a whisper. "I need to stay with my daughter, Detective." He could hear sobbing.

Morrison paused, knowing he had to remain neutral. "Mrs. Stockman, I will send you an escort on the eleven a.m. Sea Jet leaving Orient Point." She was silent.

Another moment passed and a trance-like voice answered, "I'll be there."

She slowly hung up the phone and held onto her stomach. Suddenly, she was relieved. *They caught the guy. My daughter is safe.* Rocking back and forth, she cried.

Chapter 24

Marissa Stockman waited at the Orient Point Ferry terminal for the arrival of the Sea Jet. Detective Morrison surprised her by stepping off the ferry to greet her.

"You are my personal escort, Detective? I'm surprised." She showed small relief.

"It made sense for me to see that you are safe," he offered.

Morrison gestured her onto the boat as he explained, "This has turned into a complicated case. I'm very interested in hearing what you have to say for yourself." His sport jacket and tie, neatly combed hair, and polished shoes let her know he was on official business. Badge and gun could not be far from sight.

She quickly made an introduction as a smartly suited man in his fifties stepped forward. "I'd like you to meet my attorney, Jonathan Blum." They shook hands.

"I shouldn't be surprised your counsel is with you," Morrison replied, undaunted.

Her attorney made a suggestion. "It's a bit awkward, but I'd like to ask that we keep conversation off the topic until we are in New London at police headquarters."

Detective Morrison sighed. "How about I meet you before we disembark?" They both nodded. "I'll be in the wheelhouse visiting with the captain if you need me," he informed. Marissa and her lawyer gladly granted him leave, and they now could discuss her situation privately.

114

***

Captain Griswold was at the helm and knew Morrison well. "Hey, Detective. Are you here to meet up with Mrs. Stockman?"

"Yes, but she brought her own escort today, her lawyer, so I have some time on my hands. I'll visit with you for a while, if you don't mind?"

"Of course not," Griswold answered graciously. "She may well need her lawyer. I haven't had the chance to tell you what I saw when she last traveled with us two days ago."

"What's that? I'm all ears and stuck with you until we cross the sound," Morrison jested. He leaned against the wheelhouse wall and watched as the Sea Jet picked up speed, passing the simple black and white striped Orient Point Lighthouse. Once they were past the rough waters near Plum Gut, Griswold appointed his second-in-command to take the helm.

"Let's sit in the galley, Detective," invited the skipper.

In a private area with a television on the wall, the duo sat at a small table. Captain Griswold began his story.

"She was having a drink when I saw Johnny, one of the ship stewards, whisper to her and hand her a small folded envelope. So, I decided, when given the opportunity, I would speak with her to get a sense of what transpired. Since I knew her husband, I gave her my condolences. I then asked her about Johnny. She told me she gave him a tip. She tried to act nonchalant about it." Griswold wiped his brow.

"Since she was dealing with her husband's death, I left her alone. Later, I asked Johnny what it was he gave her. He said it was a small envelope that one of the dockworkers asked him to pass on. Evidently, she lied, but why?"

Morrison rubbed his chin, pondering her actions. "Thanks for the information. She's in hot water with me already. You know, poison is a woman's game."

Eyebrows raised, Griswold probed, "Why do you say that?"

Morrison explained, "Mitch Stockman was found with a poisonous plant in his mouth, and sixty percent of women choose poison to kill. It's easier for them to keep their veneer of innocence.

"Do you remember the movie *Arsenic and Old Lace*? It was based on a woman in Windsor, Connecticut. The *Hartford Courant* newspaper article, in 1916, was titled "Murder Factory." She used arsenic and conspired to have wills and life insurance policies made out to line her own pockets. They say she may have done in up to sixty people."

Captain Griswold's surprise was not lost on the detective. "That's a true story?" A hint of anguish was on his face.

"How well did you know Mr. Stockman, Griswold?"

"He traveled with us often, about twice a month. We enjoyed many conversations about the history of wine in Connecticut, Long Island, and around the world. He was one of the very few I would visit regularly on the ferry."

Griswold became more thoughtful and confided, "It's a shame. I sure will miss Mitch's positive attitude about life. It was as if wine pumped through his veins. I remember him telling me about helping prune the dormant grapes at the vineyards in March. Following that, he said he loved celebrating spring and would look for the first breaking buds sprouting a green promise from the old gnarled vines.

"His next milestone was spying the tiny beaded clusters that formed in June. 'Small enough for a fairy necklace,' he'd say. Later in the season, he called them 'jeweled spheres full of potential,' then he would ceremoniously glorify each event with an excellent bottle of wine from some distinctive region. He was quite the poet.

"In the fall, he was jumping with excitement for the harvest. I remember when he would bring me a fine vintage and tell me, 'Captain, make sure you have lamb with this one. Season the lamb with rosemary and fennel, and you and your wife will fall into a heaven of flavors.' I told him he was a grape artiste; his paint palette was food and wine, and his taste buds were the canvas of ambrosial flavors. Then we would laugh at ourselves."

Griswold awoke from his happy recollection. His tone became serious. "For God's sake, you think this was intentional?"

"It was intentional, Griswold. And Mrs. Stockman is looking very suspicious. Who is this dockworker that passed her the note? He may be the key to prove her innocence, blackmail or worse."

"It was Charlie Brass. Charlie's been here forever. He's sixty-five and about to retire. He's loyal and reliable," replied the captain.

"Well, let's talk to him. Is he working today?"

"He'll be at the dock when we arrive," confirmed Griswold.

The two men went back into the wheelhouse, and Griswold took control of the helm. He passed Harbor Light, a white octagon monolith on New London's shore and banked toward the mouth of the Thames River. The Sea Jet zoomed along, and the next lighthouse came into view.

"Did you know, Detective, they made a postal stamp of Ledge Light?" The square, red brick Colonial Revival lighthouse with white trim and multipaned windows grew in size as they approached. It was a proper four-story house and appeared to be floating on the water. It was perched and fastened to an underwater rock ledge, hence the name Ledge Light.

Always ready to share some history, Griswold added, "In 1909, two wealthy men, Harkness and Plant, helped fund the building. They wanted to be sure that no average lighthouse would be within view of their waterfront estates. Back then, lighthouses were usually made of metal piping. Lucky for us, these men had good taste. When you pass it several times a day like I do, you recognize it's a work of inspiration."

Appreciating Griswold's attention to detail, Morrison stared out to the lighthouse, and his thoughts wandered onto his case. *Maybe the fates are smiling on me today. I understand Stockman better from Griswold's friendship, and I have a new lead to follow with Charlie Brass. Mrs. Stockman has a great deal of explaining to do.*

Yet, little did he know, the fates, the directors of destiny, might have been smiling for their own maniacal amusement.

As the Sea Jet turned into the Thames River, Griswold reminisced, "Sometimes I think of my family's history. They maneuvered tall ships through these waters going way back to the 1700s. Nowadays, the huge cruise ships, the Coast Guard's boats, and the Navy's nuclear submarines navigate here."

Morrison reminded him, "The annual Sailfest will be here soon, the reunion for tall ships from around the world."

"Yes, that's true. The Morgan whaling ship from the 1800s and the US Coast Guard's *Barque Eagle* from 1936: they'll both be on tour. As usual, we'll be crowded with tourists for the big firework show too." Griswold glanced over at the detective, "It's only a few weeks away."

Morrison was imagining the throngs of people on City Pier and in the streets of New London. He confided, "I'm in the hot seat with the city. I need to solve these two murders ASAP, especially now that I know they're connected." The detective eyed Griswold. "It's looking like Mrs. Stockman is in deep. I certainly hope she didn't hire a wild man who's turned into a serial killer on us." He sighed excessively. "People from Long Island are asking the ferry office if it's safe to come to New London. You see what I'm leading to, Captain?"

Griswold looked at him askew.

With a wry smile, Morrison answered, "It's the Long Island blue bloods blaming the New London blue collars for the inconvenience of a murder. And blue is the only thing they seem to have in common."

Griswold laughed, knowing full well the distinct differences the detective was pointing out. He saw it every day on his trips back and forth over the sound.

"Everyone wants to be safe and sound, and it's easy to blame the other guy. Life is more complicated than that, right, Detective? It's not so black and white; there's every shade of gray." Morrison nodded in agreement.

Griswold approached the New London dock and the panoramic view of the historic City of Steeples. Multiple church spires pierced the sky. In the 1800s, ship captains flush with money from whale oil funded church construction of their religion. Hence, many steeples rose to meet the higher realms.

With ease and grace, Griswold turned the ferry around and backed her between two piers. As the passengers disembarked, the detective caught up to Mrs. Stockman and her lawyer. He asked them to wait on board in the enclosed dining area.

Detective Morrison and Captain Griswold met up with Charlie Brass on the docks.

"Charlie, can I talk to you a minute?" asked the skipper.

"Sure, Captain, what can I do for you?" Charlie was a rugged fellow in good shape for mid-sixties and sported a shock of white hair that made his dark eyes stand out. His skin was tanned and weathered from years of working outdoors.

"Charlie, this is Detective Morrison of the New London Police Department. He has some questions for you," Griswold explained.

Morrison took his cue. "Mr. Brass, a few days ago, you gave something to Johnny, the deckhand, to pass on to Mrs. Stockman. What was that?"

"Oh, that," replied Brass. "Some guy came up to me and said he had coffee with Mrs. Stockman, and she left something important behind on the table. It was a small envelope. She was walking onto the Sea Jet when he pointed her out, the slim woman in a dress. He asked me to give her the envelope, so I said I'd pass it on. He thanked me and tried to give me a twenty-dollar bill. I said, 'No, thanks, I'll make sure she gets it.'

"Well, I got busy and at the last second, I gave it to Johnny, told him her name, and described her to him. That's all there is."

"What did the guy look like?" Morrison asked.

"He was nothing special, average looking in a gray suit and tie, dark hair, dark glasses, about six feet tall, maybe in his forties," Charlie replied, scratching his head.

Charlie's easygoing attitude didn't set off the detective's alarms. Morrison pulled out his phone and showed him a picture of the man they apprehended at the train station. "Is this the guy?"

Charlie took a quick look and said, "He's similar but no, that's not him. He has the same look but a different face, and this one is older than the guy who approached me."

"Thanks, Charlie. If you think of anything else or see the guy, give me a call." The detective handed him his card and shook Charlie's hand.

"Keep your eyes peeled for me, Griswold," requested Morrison. "There's plenty going on between here and Long Island to keep us both busy, and I need all the help I can get."

"You bet," Griswold responded and shook his hand, "and I'll bring your cargo down for you." They both smiled, knowing Marissa Stockman was some kind of cargo.

chapter 25

The man responsible for J.J.'s death was in his silver sedan, pondering his next move. Having left the ferry terminal without $10,000 in the red envelope, he drove away until he found a private location in Cedar Grove Cemetery. Reflecting upon his situation and miffed his hired hand did not retrieve the money, he now had to wait for the next mail drop at four p.m.

Did Stockman's wife fail to mail the envelope? I doubt it. It's just the mail schedule, he told himself. *Ho la sua attenzione* (I have her attention).

His bigger complication was the victim's name, Johnson Jones, aka J.J., was on the front page of the local newspaper. Annoyed with the events, he loudly expressed, "A snafu! *Non posso crederci* (I can't believe it)!" He continued the rant, grumbling at his misfortune. "It usually takes weeks or months before they discover a body! I should have eliminated the *moccolo* (snot) later. *Mannaggia* (Damn)! This has jeopardized the plan!"

Brooding, the Italian devil reconsidered his circumstances and measured his wits against the small town of New London. Arousing his bravado, the professional bolstered his own ego. *I'll use their ignorance against them. No different than anywhere else. These people are stupido! I always win, ad infinitum.*

The brute reviewed his options. Manipulating Marissa Stockman and Georgi were not a problem, and the police were easy too. They operated in predictable patterns. All he had to do was to keep them guessing.

Redirecting his energy for killing J.J. too soon, he determined how he would influence the situation. He drove the rental car out of the quiet heart of the 1850s cemetery. Winged angels and forlorn statues looked down on him from the somber glade of tombstones and beckoned him for benevolence. He ignored them.

Driving to the local soup kitchen, he persisted toward achieving his first goal: find another man in need of work. He fancied a fresh gamble. *It's time to give the roulette wheel another spin.*

High on adrenaline, the schemer slowly approached the food bank on Montauk Avenue, a local hangout for those in need of assistance. At ten a.m., several men were lollygagging, as usual, outside the building. He sized them up quickly. A scruffy dark-haired fellow with a strong build was his anointed target. He looked to be Italian and was the right size. With diabolic poise, the gentleman pulled his fancy silver sedan in close and lowered the window. "Buongiorno, excuse me."

The tan-skinned man perked right up and went to the car to address its smooth operator, who smelled like money. "Buongiorno, sir, how can I help you?" he asked, disclosing he had Italian heritage.

"I need a driver for the day. Do you know the streets of New London?" the rogue asked, looking him over, trying to decide if he'd bet money on this man.

"Of course," said the out-of-work drifter who quickly looked over his shoulder at the guys behind him, making sure they would not crowd in on his new opportunity.

"I'm available," he acknowledged, gesturing his hands outwardly, showing he had nothing else to do.

"Okay, no questions, good pay, and clothes are provided. Capisce?" asked the gentleman.

"Yes, sir, very good. Capisce." He surveyed the luxury ride and salivated.

"Get in, and I'll drive you to the location," the new employer offered.

The man eagerly jumped in, leaving behind his buddies of desperate circumstances. The gentleman employer drove him to the Holiday Inn located in downtown New London. They rode the elevator to the top floor and walked to the end of the hall with a windowed view of the Thames River waterway.

The new hire whistled long and low. "Wow, it's sure a pretty picture from up here."

Then they entered the finely appointed room with a picture window and direct skyline view of several church steeples. Yet, this day, the only worship was to the god of money.

The assassin asked, "Are you a size forty? I think one of my suits will fit you."

"Yes, I am. Good guess," the man said, dazzled by the attire.

"Look, I have to step out and arrange for the car. Why don't you clean up, take a shower, and I'll pick you up in forty-five minutes. Can you be ready?" he questioned.

"Yes, sir, I will, and thank you," replied the drifter, as he pressed the fine silver-gray suit between his fingers and smiled. *It's like winning the lottery*, he mused.

The gambling contractor felt the same as he drove toward 'Auto Row' on Route 1 and Broad Street. It was once a small family-owned car business but over the years, its progeny spread like spores off a wild mushroom, encompassing all four corners and down the streets.

As one dealer's lot adjoined another, glinting vehicles of every make and model were represented. The man quickly turned into the lot where he could rent a car for the day. He arranged to pick it up in an hour. He then drove down Broad Street, eyed a barbershop, and decided to drive his new hire there for a trim and a shave.

Once his man was freshened up and looking like new, the instigating gangster asked, "Are you hungry?" It was nearing noon, and he figured the guy would eat. He didn't want him to work while hungry.

"Yes, I could eat," the freshly polished pawn replied.

"Good. Let's go to Tony D's and have a decent lunch. But first, we'll pick up the car."

The two men in their light gray Italian suits, dark Bulgari shades, sleek haircuts, and fine leather shoes could have been brothers.

"Those shoes fit you fine?" the boss asked.

"Yes, a little big but no problem." The tool smiled. "What do I call you? My name is Victor."

"You can call me Mr. Silver, and how about if I call you Mr. V instead of Victor?"

"You can call me whatever you like. You're the boss," the new hire answered, quite pleased.

Mr. Silver gave further directives. "You can keep the suit and bring the car back tomorrow by noon to the dealer. How does that sound?" he asked.

"Wonderful, Mr. Silver. Thank you for the job and the clothes."

"Oh, we Italiani must look out for each other. That is our way, capisce?"

Mr. V showed his teeth. "Capisce, boss."

At Tony D's Italian Restaurant on Huntington Street, the two men ate three courses, drank wine, and had conversation about their Italian heritage and families as if they were old friends. They finished with a fine grappa, a grape based brandy, and salted pistachio nuts. Then Mr. Silver gave Mr. V explicit instructions.

"I want you to drive today on this route for the next two and a half hours." He unfolded a city map on which he had highlighted in yellow the streets Mr. V was to travel. It formed a large circle around New London, then through the center of town onto Broad and State Street, and around again. "Just take this route and repeat it until three forty-five p.m."

Emphasizing his words, Mr. Silver added, "Follow these instructions explicitly. At four p.m., I'll have a package for you to pick up at the ferry office. It's addressed to Johnson Jones and is in a red envelope. They will give it to you with no questions.

"When no one is looking, I want you to put the red envelope in this manila envelope, fold it in half, and put it in your inside jacket pocket. Take this leather satchel. I want you to open and close it as if you put the envelope in it. Make

124

sure you have your back to anyone who may be there. Then put the satchel over your shoulder. This is just for appearances."

Mr. V listened intently as his new boss finished his instructions.

"Leave the building by the door that is near the water. As you go down the ramp, you will see a man with a black cap standing by the tugboats. He will ask you for a light for his cigarette. Give him a light with this lighter." He handed him a small gold lighter with an eagle crest and continued. "Discreetly hand him the envelope. Then proceed to your car and take this route. Go directly home. You can take your friends and family out for a meal on me. Here is your pay."

Mr. Silver handed him a white bank envelope. Mr. V looked inside and counted five one hundred dollar bills. He smiled broadly.

"Yes, sir," said Mr. V.

"Take your pay home first, and put it away in a safe place. I don't want you carrying this much cash on you for this job. Just keep a single hundred-dollar bill on you in case you need it. Capisce?"

"Capisce, boss, no problem. I got this. Is there anything else I need to know?"

"As long as you follow these instructions to the letter, I will have more work for you. Now, repeat them back to me so I know you have understood. Then all will go well."

His new hire recounted each step with precision, and Mr. Silver reviewed his body double with pride.

Chapter 26

Roxanne completed her garden maintenance at Green Harbor Park and traveled home. It was lunch time; she made a sandwich, grabbed a book to read, and relaxed on her back deck. With her current interest in poisonous plants, she found a helpful book, Dangerous & Deadly Botanicals. It revealed many of the historic accidental ways flora had inflicted hallucinations on people, often with vile symptoms and horrible deaths.

Just as she was finishing her lunch and perusing her book, Georgi called. "I know I have to wait, but I'm still preparing for Mitch's memorial at Vinho Verde. Do you think you could help me with ideas to decorate the inside? I was dreaming of lots of fresh flowers and plants that I will extend onto the patio. What do you think?" he asked.

"I think it sounds expensive, Georgi. Are you sure?" Roxanne queried.

"I can write it off as an interior design expense. Besides, Mitch deserves the tribute," he attempted to justify the expense.

Roxanne imagined the effort of him caring for the plants. "Georgi, if you keep it simple and elegant, I think it will be a lovely affair. Look, I just finished with work, and I'm free for an hour. Shall I come by?" she offered, knowing he was in need of guidance.

"Oh, that would be fabulous!" he answered with a bounce in his voice. Then unable to contain his enthusiasm, Georgi started dancing in place. "I'll call Marco," he added. Roxanne could hear his foot clogging over the phone as Georgi went on.

"Marco always has great ideas, and he might have a nice bobble or two from his antique and restoration shop that we can use as decoration." Georgi hung up and kept dancing his way across the floorboards, feeling better than he had in days and grateful he could keep busy.

Soon enough, Marco and Roxanne met at Vinho Verde to review Georgi's ideas. They decided to install Italianesque columns from Marco's shop and added large urns with ferns and orchids. Another thought was to soften the brick and stone walls with cascading drapes by mounting them in key areas.

Satisfied with their choices, they were preparing to leave for Marco's to check for additional items when Georgi saw an envelope on the floor by the door. He retrieved it, opened it, and gasped in horror.

In clear, bold, black marker, it read:

Are you next? Not if you pay up – Put $10,000 in a green Vinho Verde envelope. Bring it to the library stacks and place it next to section 641.2. Do it by 4 p.m. No cops or you're DEAD TOO!

A jolt ran up Georgi's arms and through his body. "Ohhhhh!" he squealed, fanning himself from the shock. "What am I to do? He's going to kill me!"

Roxanne and Marco stood stunned and read the note over again.

"That's only two hours away," she gulped. "We have to tell the detective, Georgi!"

Gesturing wildly, he yelped, "No! No! We have to do what the note says, or he'll kill me! I'll be dead in a shrub just like Mitch! Oh my God, it's awful! I can't take this!" he loudly whined, looking as though he might hyperventilate.

Roxanne took control. "No, Georgi, don't buy into this. He's trying to scare you," she explained.

"Yeah, it worked. Can't you tell? Look. I'm shaking I'm so frightened." He held out his tremoring hands.

Roxanne urged him, "Look, the detective will know exactly what to do. He will help us. What if this guy demands $10,000 every week?" she posed. "Why would he stop? Once you pay, you're hooked into him."

Georgi looked at her, realizing she knew better, and he was overwhelmed. Roxanne picked up her phone and dialed the detective. Marco tried to settle Georgi down. "She's right, and you know it. Let them help, Georgi. There is no way we know what to do. Roxanne knows best. Her husband is dealing with emergencies all the time. Listen to her."

chapter 27

Detective Morrison was in the process of interrogating the man in custody from the train station. He was the one who at 8 a.m. tried to retrieve the red envelope with Johnson Jones' name on it from Sandy. Morrison wasn't getting anywhere with him. Mrs. Stockman was in another room with her attorney. She said she had never met the man in the gray suit and dark glasses. The guy in the other room confirmed he did not know her, but Morrison suspected them both of lying.

The detective listened to the man's story about why he went to pick up the envelope addressed to J.J. "I jumped at the job. It was six thirty this morning, and I was standing outside in the line for temporary work next to Fiddleheads grocer when this guy drove up in a silver sedan. He asked me to run an errand and wear a suit. He went by the name Mr. Silver. He drove me to the train station where I changed my clothes. I was paid one hundred dollars to fetch and pass on a red envelope addressed to Johnson Jones. When the envelope wasn't there, I met him outside of the ferry office and told him. He was upset but he told me to keep the suit, and I was on my way. He said he'd pick it up himself at four p.m."

A knock at the door interrupted the interrogation. "Detective, I have a very urgent call," announced the clerk. Morrison left the room.

Curious it was from Roxanne, he asked, "What's happening, Roxanne?"

"Georgi is being blackmailed!" She explained and read him the note.

"When did this happen?"

"Just now!" she pleaded.

"I'll be right there." Morrison felt her distress.

"No! No, Dan," Roxanne whispered urgently, "the note said no police or Georgi's dead."

"Then I'll meet you at the back of Muddy Waters. Be sure to place the blackmail note into a baggie without touching it. I want to dust it for prints. There is not much time." Morrison was surprised by the brazen perpetrator. *That just means he's a fool and easy to capture.*

Roxanne continued to whisper, "Okay, it will just be me. I'll tell Georgi and his friend Marco to wait while I meet you. Then we'll try to act normal until we hear from you."

Morrison's mind rolled with the idea. He said aloud, "Roxanne, there isn't anything normal about this case or any of you, but you go ahead and try."

Roxanne scoffed, "Pff, I know. This is flipping crazy, Dan."

"I'll meet you there in ten minutes," he responded.

He was juggling Marissa, her lawyer, and the gray-suited man. He put all of their questioning on hold and took off for Muddy Waters Café with his assistant detective, Jack Peabody.

Roxanne discreetly passed off the threatening message and envelope. She returned to the Vinho Verde and announced to Georgi, "I know it might feel like a time to drink wine, but I purchased scones and apple turnovers. How about we brew a pot of tea while we wait for our instructions from the detective?"

"Oh, you're glorious, Roxanne," Georgi sang. "I'm always ready for a nosh when I'm nervous."

"I'll put the kettle on," offered Marco.

"Don't you two worry." She added with confidence, "The detective is having the envelope dusted for fingerprints and will call us soon."

"Should I run out and withdraw $10,000?" Georgi's voice rose almost to a squeak.

Stunned, Marco gasped, "You have $10,000?"

"Not me, silly, the business. Mitch left me the bank account, and I'm a signatory."

"Ohh! Well, haven't you risen above us all?" Marco waved his face with a cocktail napkin. Then with an afterthought added, "Or wait...since we're friends...that would make me somebody too." Marco exposed a broad, smug smile as if he had suddenly become rich.

Swatting at him, Georgi mocked, "You're ridiculous. It's just business, that's all. Get your head out of the clouds." Then he swatted him again. Marco's expansive smile remained, like the Cheshire cat.

Eventually, a call came in from Morrison, and they all listened together on speakerphone.

"Do you have ten grand, Georgi?" he asked.

"Yes, in the business account."

"How do you feel about setting a trap for this guy? We'll get him when he picks up the envelope." Morrison was hoping Georgi had the wherewithal to go through with his plan.

"Uh," Georgi thought it over, "is there any way we can use fake money instead, Detective?"

"Hmm, Georgi," the detective hummed, "I don't have any on me, and neither does the bank. We will catch him, and you will recover your money. Besides, he needs to see you go to the bank and follow his cues. Can you do it for Mitch's sake?" Morrison asked, leaning on Georgi to help him close the case.

"Okay, but you big shots should really have props in your line of work," he admonished.

Morrison continued his instructions. "I want you to be seen and obvious when you go to the bank and to the library. Have your friend Marco go with you. And Roxanne, I'd like you to go to Chief Sam's office and wait there."

131

"Okay, Dan, thank you! I'm relieved you're going to catch him," Roxanne said.

"We plan on it," the detective assured.

"You better," pleaded Georgi. "It's my life and my money you're playing with."

Chapter 28

Frustrated by her circumstances, Marissa Stockman felt completely justified for having a Beretta Bobcat revolver in her purse. She leaned in toward Detective Morrison, defending her actions vehemently. Her attorney, Jonathan Blum, sat beside her.

"Of course, I brought a gun. I need to protect myself. I can't count on you!" the widow spewed with intensity. Her eyes glared at the detective. "Consider my husband!"

The gun was found when she passed through security, setting off alarms and creating a scene. Attorney Blum was red in the face with exasperation. "You don't bring a gun to a police interrogation for your husband's murder! Especially since you put $10,000 in the ferry mailbag for a dead boy to pick up! You can't justify it!"

"Look, you two," she demanded, "if this man, who you have in custody, isn't the killer, then the killer is still out there. What are you going to do?" Her voice reverberated in the small room and on hearing her own desperation, she suddenly wilted with exhaustion, "This is my daughter's life, my life!"

"Mrs. Stockman," Morrison said sternly, "I want you to know something you may not realize." He bent forward for his delivery and pointed his pen at her. "Right now, you are my prime suspect. You have the money. And your motives are multiple. You could have a boyfriend or a jealous lover. I don't know you. Your actions have been suspicious. If you hired this monster to kill your husband, why should I be surprised he blackmailed you for more money and threatened your daughter's life? How else would he know you have a daughter, unless you told him or you know him?

"Can't you see you look guilty?" Morrison brushed the sweat from his brow. "You wrote the name of a murdered sixteen-year-old on your red realty envelope." Marissa bent her head and sobbed, exhausted by the whole ordeal.

Attorney Blum loudly persisted, "Now wait a minute, Detective, she's the victim here. I believe her. Unless you have proof of her guilt, there are no grounds for your accusations. This is all circumstantial evidence."

Impatient, Morrison announced, "Well, Attorney Blum, we may just have proof in the next few hours. I'm keeping this man we have in custody and you two in my office until four p.m. We will see who picks up that red envelope with $10,000 at the ferry office. Once we have him, we will have the rest of the story. One way or another, I will know today whether Mrs. Stockman is involved in these murders."

The detective surveyed Marissa Stockman neutrally. Her tearstained cheeks did not deter him from his goal. His conviction was to trust no one. Even though she was elegant, beautiful, and classy, she still looked suspicious. The detective's personal mantra stuck in his head: 'Just the facts. Trust your instincts.'

Morrison left the small room to give them a break. He sat at his desk to review his plan. Almost the whole police force was tied up in tracking down this game-playing killer. At four o'clock, they would be in two locations: the New London Library and the ferry office, about a half mile apart. There were five plainclothes officers covering Georgi's money drop at the library. An unmarked cruiser was stationed by the secure entrance to the ferry terminal. Both traps would be ready and set.

The detective was concerned that all they had to go on was a silver sedan and a description given by the scapegoat in custody from the train station.

Morrison recalled the verbal portrayal: middle-aged man, six feet tall, short dark hair, a sharp nose, and slightly tan skin. There was a hint of an accent, yet excellent English. He was clean-shaven and wore sunglasses, a fine gray suit, white shirt, tie, and black leather shoes. Ironically, he looked just like the man describing him.

chapter 29

Georgi drove his PT Cruiser to the bank to withdraw the money with Marco by his side. Stuffing the cash into the green Vinho Verde envelope, he continued to the library.

The granite library, built in 1890, was an architectural gem, a handsome Richardsonian Romanesque style. It was on the corner of Huntington and State Street. Georgi parked in the rear to enter the 1970s addition, as ordered by Detective Morrison.

Squeezing Marco's arm, Georgi requested, "Wish me luck." Marco assured him, "Don't worry, the police are watching, and they'll protect you. I'll wait here with the car running."

Georgi trotted up the interior staircase. Navigating through the original grand entry, he arrived at the information desk and asked where the 600 stacks were located. The librarian pointed him in the direction of another level of stairs. Once in position, Georgi scanned through the books and realized they were all about winemaking and vineyards. *Who is this guy? He picked the wine section?*

Checking his watch, Georgi selected a location among the books numbered 641.2. He kissed his green Vinho Verde envelope and placed it carefully. Taking one step away, he stepped back to fuss with it. *Obvious but not too obvious,* he thought.

Keeping his eyes downcast, Georgi, the new smooth operator, looked to the sides as he approached the staircase. He saw no one suspicious, so he cautiously descended. Suddenly, he spied a library worker pushing a cart of books. In his mind, he panicked. *She's heading to my stack! Oh no! She's going to find the green envelope!* Peering at her through the stair balusters, he watched her as she stacked and sorted a few books. She then moved on to the next row.

Phew, Georgi sighed. He pranced down the stairs and out the door to Marco, waiting in the car.

"That's done," Georgi pronounced proudly. "Let's meet Roxanne at the Washington Street Coffee House."

"What? I thought the detective told her to go to the fire station and wait."

"Well, she has a mind of her own," Georgi asserted, smiling like an imp.

"And so do you," laughed Marco, shaking Georgi's shoulder.

They drove down Huntington Street, passing a silver sedan parked in front of the four-cornered granite steeple of St. Mary's Star of the Sea. The driver watched Georgi as altar boys streamed out of the church in their black and white robes. They held the doors open as pallbearers walked a casket out, and the mournful congregation followed.

Taking two quick left turns around the block, Georgi and Marco met Roxanne inside the coffeehouse. She sat at a table with a lemon scone, cupping a mug of Earl Grey tea. Above and around her hung local artwork; the owners had created a makeshift gallery in their high-ceilinged lofty space. A small stage for bands was set up in a corner for evening gigs and nearby was a large window-wall along the street. The well-worn hangout had a comfortable vibe for young and old.

Glad to see them, Roxanne remarked, "Well, you made it!"

Georgi recounted every nervous detail of placing the money in the library while he drank lemonade and split a sandwich with Marco.

"It's the policemen's job to catch the guy now," Roxanne posed. "We'll just wait for a call." She picked up and waved her cell phone. "Isn't it funny how I've hardly used it, and now I can't live without it?"

Georgi smiled, "Welcome to the twenty-first century, Roxanne. You're about ten years late." Marco and Georgi chuckled, actually giddy with relief, hoping the whole ordeal would be over with soon.

As they chatted lightly, Georgi thought he recognized a girl outside the building. He wasn't sure due to the hooded shirt she was wearing. He knew so many people downtown, and she looked familiar. She was chatting with someone on the street in a silver sedan. The car sped off quickly. She walked toward the coffeehouse. The tall glass window-wall gave Georgi a full view of her. Entering, she placed her order at the counter and pulled down her hood. Georgi gasped.

The sound made Marco and Roxanne look at him. He grabbed both their arms. He hunched over the table and whispered, "That's the girl! She's the one who was pushing the book cart in the library. What is she doing in here?" Imagining the worst, he yelped, "Oh my God, my money!"

Suddenly, a group of people from outside raced toward the coffeehouse. The glass wall allowed a clear view of these random, yet odd-looking people.

"What's going on?" Roxanne asked. "Did a show just let out at the Garde Theater?" Several people pushed through the doors forcefully. They huddled around the young woman before escorting her into the hallway that led to the bathrooms.

"Let's go," said Georgi, pulling Roxanne and Marco. They leapt out of their seats, knocking a coffee table as they ran toward the hallway.

"That's her!" screeched Georgi, flailing his arms. "That's her. Where's my money?" he demanded, fighting his way, trying to pierce the human barrier of the now obvious plain-clothed police.

"Georgi, back off," yelled one officer. "Miss, where is the envelope?" he asked her.

"I handed it to that man who just left in the silver sedan," she protested.

"You what?" screamed Georgi.

138

"Be quiet!" yelled the undercover officer. Georgi fell back onto Marco who caught him.

"Which way did he go?" the officer asked the girl.

"Towards Starr Street," she replied. Immediately, three of the five officers ran out. The officer in charge radioed the news to Detective Morrison.

Speaking to the young woman, the officer ordered, "Miss, you're coming with us. You have the right to remain silent...." He read her the Miranda warning while handcuffing her and taking her to the awaiting unmarked car.

One of the remaining officers barked an order at Roxanne, Georgi, and Marco. "You three go to the station and report to Detective Morrison, now!"

"Well," Georgi said in a huff while straightening himself and brushing his clothes smooth. "Nothing like trying to cover your butt by ordering people around," he retorted. "That was my money you lost!"

"Shh! Georgi, behave!" Roxanne scolded, "They are on our side, remember that."

Georgi turned into a sullen marshmallow, hunched his shoulders, and shuffled to the door. Then he expelled a dramatic sigh.

chapter 30

The well-groomed Mr. V followed Mr. Silver's details to the letter. He arrived at the Long Island Ferry office at four p.m. and asked for the mail addressed to Johnson Jones.

Sandy did as Detective Morrison had instructed. She handed the red envelope to the gray-suited deceiver, noticing he was practically identical to the man whom she had encountered in the morning. Sandy watched as he moved to the other side of the room near the tourist brochures. From her vantage point behind the ticket counter, it seemed he inserted the envelope into his leather satchel.

Carefully, the body double, positioned the satchel, folded the red envelope into a manila one, and discreetly stuffed it inside his jacket. Then he pretended to place the envelope in the satchel. He positioned it over his shoulder and casually walked out the door to his awaiting liaison near the tugboats.

Sandy alerted the undercover police by hopping up and down in the window. The officers saw her signal and waited for the culprit to approach his car. With great annoyance, Sandy observed Charlie Brass asking the man for a light to his cigarette. The man obliged, presenting the gold, eagle-crested lighter.

Sandy complained loudly enough for her boss to hear. "Oh, Charlie, I told you to quit smoking. Get out of there. The guy's a murderer, for Pete's sake."

Sandy's boss yelled from his office, "You did your part. Let the cops do theirs, for God's sake. This is not a TV show you can choreograph. Haven't you watched any of the police reality shows?"

Sandy rolled her eyes, wondering if her soulless boss had even a small bone of compassion in his body. Shaking her head, she remembered he didn't. Sandy continued to watch as the scoundrel outside walked to his silver sedan. Before he entered the car, the undercover police were all over him with guns drawn. They took him down and handcuffed him.

Relief swept through Sandy as she jumped with arms raised in the air. "Yes!" she yelled as if a goal were scored by her favorite football team. She raced into her boss's office. "They've got him, boss. My second capture today!"

He looked up at her with a deadpan expression. "Good. Could you put the newspaper's classifieds desk on the phone? I want to report a job opening for your position because now you work for the police." He took a chomp out of his afternoon candy bar and loudly slurped from his fourth coffee of the day.

Sandy punched her hand with her fist, pretending it was his face. "One of these days, boss…it's going to be to the moon." He laughed at the Jackie Gleason *The Honeymooners* reference. Then she added, "You could thank me for cleaning up this mess of murder and mayhem affecting the ferry's business. Or maybe the owners should."

"I don't care; I'm retiring soon," he said with a fake grin. "It's a lot more fun irritating you."

Sandy grumbled and turned away, knowing after twenty-three years, he was a hopeless ignoramus.

Chapter 31

Detective Morrison now had three accomplices in individual interrogation rooms at police headquarters. Two were men — one apprehended at the train station and Mr. V who was captured at the ferry terminal — and the library girl who had passed Georgi's Vinho Verde envelope to another man in a silver sedan.

Assistant Detective Jack Peabody was shaking his head in disbelief. Morrison had his hands on his hips and asserted, "Look at these two guys, Jack. They have the same build. They have dark hair, tan skin, and are in matching gray Italian suits with the same expensive leather shoes and sunglasses. They're practically identical!" Pacing in front of his desk, Morrison stopped, scowled and then grumbled, "This is ridiculous!"

"Each of them have a hundred-dollar bill in their pocket," he ranted. "And where are the envelopes with the $10,000? I cannot believe the officers were thrown off by a seventeen-year-old girl. How did she slip out the back of the library, past the pizza restaurant, down that exterior staircase to the coffeehouse parking lot? Obviously, she was far in advance of the officers! Did she have dumb luck?

"Aargh, do I have to be everywhere? Those officers were in the wrong place at the wrong time." Morrison loosened his tie and glared at Jack. "The girl actually had time to pass off the envelope with Georgi's money. What a fumble!" He motioned, holding out his hands. "We had five, Jack, count them, five officers on this frickin' envelope. Did no one see her?" Morrison slicked his hair with his hands, then clenched the ends as if he wanted to strangle someone.

Jack Peabody had not seen his boss lose his cool like this before, yet he understood the pressure. The local homicides in New London were typically uncomplicated. Typically, they were related to turf wars, drug crimes, or domestic violence.

Yet, Jack was well aware of the tale of his boss's exceptional work on the infamous arson case in town. Morrison had solved it with Fire Chief Samson. Jack recalled the *Day*'s newspaper write-up:

> Neighbors called in a sign of smoke coming out of a broken window in the old shoe factory. When the firefighters arrived, the rafters of the building were strung with gasoline-filled balloons. Hunting down the source of smoke, Samson's crew found smoldering rags in the nick of time. Had the rags fully ignited and reached the balloons, they would have burst and blown the place sky-high, effectively destroying everything. After three weeks of concerted effort, Officer Morrison homed in on a network of hired criminals from New York. It's the age-old story of a defunct factory owner trying to make money off their fire insurance.

Since the story was in the papers for weeks, it put Morrison in the limelight and led to his promotion to detective in the department.

Watching this case evolve with now three men dressed like look-alikes had Jack wondering. *There are so many moving parts and players, it feels like a 3-D video game with a replicator punching out clones of this perpetrator.* Jack watched his boss pace back and forth and figured common sense would prevail. Morrison would return to his calm and collected self. But suddenly, Jack was jolted by Morrison shouting.

"Neither of these two lackeys have much to say, except that the guy who hired them looks like them. The last guy already wants to lawyer up and won't talk or tell us where that red envelope from the ferry terminal ended up."

Throwing his hands in the air, Morrison strutted down the hall. Like a bloodhound on a trail, he stomped toward the command center with Jack following behind.

Several officers were reviewing digital data illuminated on large screen displays. Video runs were being scanned; ViCAP, Violent Crime Apprehension Program, data files of the FBI were searched. A wall-size whiteboard had lists of locations and the common threads of events and murders. Morrison delivered instructions to each group, and walkie-talkies squawked orders to help the teams keep abreast of the situation.

Detective Morrison expelled, "Find Charlie Brass! I want him here ASAP. He was the last one in contact with the guy at the ferry terminal."

chapter 32

Meanwhile, Georgi, Roxanne, and Marco were escorted into the boardroom at police headquarters. Marissa Stockman and her lawyer were sitting there.

Marissa asked Georgi, "What are you doing here?"

"Me! What are you doing here?" Georgi countered.

"I'm trying to save my daughter's life," she implored.

"What are you talking about?" Georgi asked, dumbfounded.

"The man who murdered Mitch threatened to kill Vanessa. He blackmailed me into sending him $10,000. He had me put a name on the envelope that happened to be the kid who was murdered yesterday, Johnson Jones."

"Oh my God!" Georgi, Roxanne, and Marco exclaimed in unison.

"The guy blackmailed me too," Georgi asserted. "He threatened to kill me and told me to put $10,000 in an envelope." Biting his nails, he then wailed emphatically, "This is insane!"

"Why is he involving you?" Marissa asked, perplexed.

"I don't know! He had me place the envelope of money in the library at four o'clock."

Marissa offered, "But the detective set him up to get my envelope at four o'clock from the ferry office."

Since both looked confused, Roxanne took the opportunity to interrupt and jump into the conversation. "I'm Georgi's friend, Roxanne. I'm sorry to say I found your husband, God rest his soul. Please let me help you figure this out," she offered, truly hoping she could help.

Marissa became anguished, moving her hands to her face and then to her heart. "Oh my God, I can't take much more of this." Attorney Blum broke professional protocol and put his hand on her shoulder to console her.

Roxanne softly resumed. "So, if this guy blackmailed you both, how can he be in two places at once, unless he has people working for him?" Mumbling out loud, she added, "This is far more complex than I would have guessed."

"He must have people working for him," murmured Marco who was now sitting next to Georgi, trying to keep him from biting his nails down to the quick.

Attorney Blum strained to comfort Marissa by stating the obvious. "I believe that's why we are here. The detective not only wants to keep you all safe but also complete the capture of this villain and his cohorts."

"This is so complicated, Marissa," Georgi sympathized. "I didn't know he was trying to harm you more than he already has. I'm so sorry. All of this within a week...it's too much."

"But that's just it," reflected Roxanne. "What happened before Mitch died? What created this chain of events?" Pausing in thought, she decided to reveal more. "Mrs. Stockman, after I found your husband, I was mugged that day by someone who took my small waist pack off of me and knocked me down to the ground. Later, when the police drove me to my house, there was a hoodlum trying to break in. That very evening, Georgi was beaten by a thug who asked him what I found at the garden site. It may be that they were all the same person or maybe not."

Roxanne beseeched her, "What would warrant all of this activity and drive this brute to kill your husband? What was Mitch involved in that could have caused all these events?"

"I don't know," Marissa pleaded for understanding. Wringing her hands, tears streamed down her porcelain-like face. "Mitch had an ideal life. He mingled with wine connoisseurs, visited local vineyards, and helped a few wineries financially. I can't imagine why this happened. Can you, Georgi?" Marissa's cool exterior had completely cracked. The years of personal perfection and tight emotional control gave way to a deluge of grief.

Listening to her, Georgi's eyes welled up and with a sweet acknowledgment of their mutual affection for Mitch, they reached out to each other and grasped hands without a word.

Trying to excuse her recent attitude of indifference, Marissa explained somewhat meekly, "I'm so sorry I've been distant, Georgi. I just let Mitch have his space with his business, and he did the same for me. This summer, we each pledged to relax and spend time together. It would be like a second honeymoon. We were so looking forward to it." She gently patted her tears with a tissue and continued. "We were to resume our regular schedules in September. It seemed like the perfect plan."

Georgi tried to comfort her. "I understand, Marissa. We are all just living life. No one expected this…." Georgi looked at Roxanne for support, feeling helpless to make things better.

Roxanne aired her thoughts. "It seems like there is a huge missing link to this whole story. Someone might have known that Mitch wasn't returning to New London for two or three months. I have a hunch there is a connection to Long Island where people know you and Mitch very well. The whole story isn't here in New London. Heck, they've blackmailed you over your daughter. There isn't anyone here who knows about your daughter, is there?"

Marissa realized Roxanne's point. "Well, I don't think so. Vanessa has never been here."

"That's right," said Roxanne. "We don't have the whole story. I wonder how much more Detective Morrison knows because until now, we didn't know of your blackmail, and you didn't know of Georgi's."

Roxanne rose out of her seat. "Where is the detective?" She went to the boardroom door and cracked it open. A guard was outside. Stepping back in, she whispered to Marco, "I'm going to the loo," then she opened the door. The guard immediately stopped her advance.

"Sorry, ma'am, the detective asked that you stay here."

"Can I use the restroom, please?" Roxanne asked sweetly.

"Sure, down the hall, take a right, and it's on your left," he replied kindly.

She turned back, winked at Marco, and said, "I'll be right back."

Her petite form moved down the hallway, took a right, and came upon the elevator doors. She pushed the button, entered alone, and pressed for the lower level. She remembered there was a big meeting room downstairs. The elevator dinged. She could hear the detective's voice yelling orders.

Roxanne peeked out the elevator door and spied a broad six-foot-tall multi-stemmed palm tree. It had variegated philodendrons cascading over the large pot. Promptly, she scooted behind the plant. Hidden from view, she took a deep breath and listened.

An officer on a walkie-talkie reported into headquarters, "We've tracked down the man in a silver sedan, Detective."

"Take him down, now!" Morrison yelled urgently.

The attending officer affirmed, "Yes, sir!"

Morrison stood erect, the tension of the moment being the rod in his spine. Anxiously waiting, he loosened his collar further and paced again. With his jacket off, the sweat circles on his blue oxford dress shirt were evident.

"We have him, boss! Capture confirmed!"

Morrison lauded the officers, "Good job! Bring that damn bastard in here."

A cheer rang out in the room. The officers, detectives, and clerks on hand didn't hold back. Unusually buoyant, Morrison yelled, "Finally! Prepare to interrogate the hell out of this perp." Motioning to Jack, he said, "You're with me." Morrison felt his adrenaline surging. "We're on the final leg of a marathon, Peabody. Let's finish this."

As soon as she heard the man was captured, Roxanne quickly popped out from behind the palm plant. She pushed the elevator up button and hoped she would escape before Morrison saw her. She made it back to the boardroom without incident, and the guard opened the door. Roxanne smiled and went inside.

She whispered to the group, "They caught him. He's in custody!" They all silently cheered and quickly settled down.

Roxanne was now encouraged and gently asked Marissa, "If Georgi and I went to Long Island sometime, could we take you to lunch?"

"Oh, that would be wonderful, Roxanne," she said with relief in her voice. "Georgi was telling me while you were out that you have actively been trying to help the detective find this horrid man. I can't thank you enough. Really, I can't."

Georgi said coyly, "I have something else to ask you, Marissa." He held his hands to his chest in reverence. "I'd like very much to hold a memorial service for Mitch on this side of the sound. There are many people here who did business with him, learned from him, and adored his love of wine. I'd like to hold it at Vinho Verde, of course with your permission, to celebrate his life with those who admired him here. I don't expect you to come—"

Marissa interrupted him, "Oh, Georgi, that is so thoughtful of you. Of course you can. And I would love to come and meet his friends. Thank you." Her change of heart through the whole ordeal had softened her toward Georgi and New London. She took his hand and added, "Oddly, now we understand each other. Thank you."

The door to the boardroom abruptly opened and in walked Detective Morrison.

Stunned at his appearance, everyone in the room gawked at the detective. His hair had sweaty spikes that stood on end. His tie was half-cocked, his shirt was loose, and his eyes had an unusual steely focus as if he had just been in a wrestling match. It was very apparent he was stressed.

Unperturbed by their stares, Morrison made his mission known. "Okay, folks, we have the killer and his helpers in custody. Mrs. Stockman and Attorney Blum, I would like you to come with me and see if you recognize any of them. You will observe them through a mirrored window. They won't see you. Take a walk with me."

Marissa glanced at her attorney, then squeezed his arm. Barely audible, she said, "Jonathan, I'm afraid."

He put his arm around her shoulder and whispered, "It will be alright. It will be quick. We need to do this."

Marissa and her attorney left and when they returned, Georgi, Roxanne, and Marco silently sat, anxiously waiting to hear what happened. Choking back tears, she faltered, "I don't know them. To think one of them killed my husband and that boy...it's just dreadful." As her voice trailed off, Georgi came to her side with a tissue.

"We'll get through this together," he offered. Consoling her, he added, "Anything you need, I'll be there for you, anything at all." She crumpled onto his shoulder and wept.

The once distant and reserved woman with a stiff upper lip and crème brûlée crust had melted. The horrible events and the support she now was experiencing had softened her. Her new compassionate companions had sweetened her bitter blue-blood attitude.

Morrison entered the room and announced, "You have all been here long enough, and I won't hold you up any longer. Mrs. Stockman, Attorney Blum: please be available as I may have more questions. We still don't know the motive. I need to see this case wrapped up neatly. Do not leave the country."

Attorney Blum confirmed, "Yes, Detective, I'll be sure she doesn't, and I will have someone watch over her." Adamantly, he added, "Detective, please contact me with any news, day or night."

"I will," Morrison responded. "You can go home and feel safe and sound,

Mrs. Stockman."

"Oh, what a relief," Marissa whispered, hand against her heart.

Resolute, the detective added, "I will return the money to both of you as soon as possible. Just be patient."

Now relaxed, Georgi swished one hand into the air. "Oh, I don't care how long it takes, as long as it's returned. I'm alive, and a crazy man isn't after us anymore. I suddenly feel light as a feather and immensely relieved." His arms stretched out in a fan dancer move and everyone smiled.

Marissa added gratefully, "You've all been so kind. I did not know what you have been through. I'm so sorry. Thank you. I don't feel so alone anymore now that we've spent time together. It's such a relief. Thank you for everything." She turned to her attorney, "Let's go home, Jonathan. I think we can make the five thirty ferry, and I really need to hug my daughter."

Chapter 33

To help establish their innocence, the three persons of interest, two men and the girl, were ready to identify the third look-alike man being detained. Each had claimed they were paid well to pick up a package yet now realized they were only stooges, set up by the man named Mr. Silver.

Morrison felt that once they confirmed this third man as being Mr. Silver, he could move on to the final details, such as motive, and if there was any involvement by Georgi and Marissa Stockman.

Individually, each person in custody was escorted behind the one-way mirror and took their turn to identify the man who had set them up for the fall. The first two men — one was apprehended in the train station and the second, Mr. V, picked up the envelope at four p.m. — both positively identified the third man as Mr. Silver.

The young library woman was now ready for her turn to identify all the men in custody. She was very slim and wore tight black jeans, black boots, and her gray hoodie. She had a small silver nose ring, dark eyeliner, and milk-white skin. Morrison noted her black painted nails and a small yin-yang symbol on her wrist. Her stylish short black hair, on one side, swung to a point at her chin and was razor short on the other. Her demeanor reflected an attitude of 'Don't mess with me.'

In the lineup, Morrison placed all three men in their gray suits and added three civilian clothed police officers. All men were of similar features and build. They faced her and then turned so she could see their profile. She looked at Morrison and the officer next to him. "It's none of them," she said tersely.

The officer in charge of the lineup said, "Now take your time, little lady, and look them over carefully."

"Ask them to smile," she said dryly.

The officer grunted, "This isn't a beauty contest."

Bluntly, Detective Morrison ordered, "Ask them to smile, Officer." He did so.

"It's none of them," she stated emphatically.

"Why don't we have them speak to you?" the attending officer suggested.

Her head spun around to look at the officer directly. "I said, 'It's none of them.' He's not there. Look, I'm cooperating. Some guy gave me a one hundred dollar bill to push a book cart down the aisle and pull a green envelope to deliver to him. I put it under my shirt. All I cared about was making one hundred bucks." Her tough girl attitude was authentic. Morrison realized the blackmailer knew how to pick his pawns.

"I briefly met that man," she pointed to one of the men in the lineup, "outside the coffee house. He was in a silver sedan, and I asked him where was Mr. Silver? He said he was on his way to meet him. I gave him the envelope, and he drove toward Starr Street. It's that simple."

She fiddled with the zipper on her hoodie in frustration and then declared, "I want a lawyer. I'm invoking my Miranda rights and not saying another word." She stared at them with her darkly lined eyes. The swagger in her thin framed hips demonstrated her confidence of pushing the limits.

Morrison threw up his hands, left the room, and entered the next interrogation. For the third time, Morrison met with a man in a gray suit. He was clean-shaven, wore Italian shoes, fancy sunglasses, and had dark hair. He had the same build as the other two. Morrison opened, "You're telling me he calls himself Mr. Silver? And he looks very much like you? How do I know you are not him and just giving me a line of bullshit?"

"I'm nobody," the guy answered. "You can check with the food bank. I'm in there every other day trying to scrounge enough food for my family. I've been trying to find a job for months. I was laid off. I stand in the temporary job line every day. Mr. Silver hired me two days ago to be on call. He gave me money, one hundred dollars in advance, a nice suit and shoes, and treated me well. I didn't know he was shifty. He looked good, and it was easy money. Are you kidding? Who in my position wouldn't take the work? He called me today at noon to have me standby and pick up a green envelope after four o'clock outside the coffeehouse from a girl with a gray hoodie."

Morrison considered the other two goons in the rooms next door. "So you said he hired you off the street, cleaned you up, and asked you to drive around today and pick up an envelope at four fifteen, and you didn't ask why?"

"Yeah, I didn't care why. Silver said to meet him on Starr Street after I had the package. What's the big deal?"

Morrison ricocheted back, "What about the empty green envelope we found in the trunk of your car? The tracking device we planted in it led us to you. So where is the money?"

"Well, he fooled us both, didn't he?" the duplicate snarled back. He took a deep breath and continued. "Look, I gave the man the envelope, he had me pop the trunk as I sat in the car, he took something out, and evidently he put something in, then he left. I didn't know what was in the envelope and that he left it in the trunk. Hell, it's his car. I wasn't watching what he was doing. He told me I could have the car for the rest of the day."

Begrudgingly, he sighed. "Besides, a hundred bucks buys you peace of mind and no questions. I was sitting pretty until you guys showed up and slammed me on the hood."

"Come on!" Morrison emoted, "To put on this charade? What else was in it for you?"

"One hundred dollars and some nice clothes," the man lied. Morrison put the three men and the girl in holding cells until he knew more.

He strutted to his office and yelled, "Peabody, where is the red envelope with the money from the ferry office?"

Jack faltered. "Boss, we assumed the suspect had it in his satchel. Once we realized the envelope was not on him, we homed in on the transmission of the tracking device we put inside the fold of the envelope. I sent two officers to search the area near the tugboats, but the transmission died. You know the weeds are tall past the docks. I had them question everyone in the area." Officer Jack Peabody braced, ready for his boss's backlash.

If Dan Morrison could spit fire, it would have occurred right then. Unloading, he growled, "Who in the hell thinks assuming is a viable excuse in the police force on a homicide case? If those officers were paying attention, they would have found out right there and then that he did not have the envelope. Assumed cannot be used as the reason we lost a killer, Jack!"

Morrison marched the floor as his thoughts raced over what this blackmailing outlaw would do next. *You've left your imprint somewhere, Mr. Silver. I will track your ass down.* The detective's thoughts were interrupted by Sergeant Maggie O'Malley overseeing dispatch.

"Detective, they found Charlie Brass! He's at the Old Town Mill. He's been called in as an unresponsive man down."

Morrison raced to the scene with Peabody in his SUV. Chief Samson heard the call and arrived on the scene with the emergency medical service crew.

chapter 34

Charlie Brass was undoubtedly dead. His Greek fisherman's cap was pulled down over his face. He was seated, leaning against the historic Old Mill. He'd been positioned to look drunk and passed out.

Chief Samson stood beside Morrison, looking down at the untouched body. Upon closer inspection, the two men saw the notorious pattern.

"Morrison, is that a plant in his mouth? And look at the white flower in his shirt pocket. It's positioned like a decoration." The flat, white umbrella flower and lacy green foliage looked benign.

The detective commanded the officers, "Cordon off this scene with a tarp wall. I don't want anyone watching us."

Morrison spoke in a low tone, away from the crew, "Chief, this guy who killed Stockman is a serial killer. Charlie Brass is his third victim. The boy, Johnson Jones, was found at Riverside Park last night. He was wrapped in bittersweet vine. I have three men, who are look-alikes, in custody with a young woman. I just sent Roxanne, Georgi, and Mrs. Stockman home, thinking I had the guy. Obviously, I don't. I have mayhem instead."

Chief Samson stared at the corpse. "This is extreme, Morrison. A serial killer in New London and my wife is involved?"

"He's playing a bait and switch game with us," Morrison informed further, "using locals, street pawns, and coercion to throw the investigation off the trail. This mastermind is using the eighty-ten-ten, Chief." Sam knew exactly what he meant. *He's picked up his working crew off of the streets.*

Frustrated by the dilemma, Morrison watched the police and forensic crew preparing the crime scene for the investigation. Suddenly, his irritation sparked an unconventional decision.

Morrison ordered the crews, "Everyone, gather round." In a firm but quiet tone, he said, "Charlie Brass, ladies and gentlemen, is not dead until I say so. He is in critical condition. Does everyone understand?" He looked over the officers and emergency responders.

"Yes, sir," they all replied.

He continued, "We have a serial killer, and I need twenty-four hours before we declare Charlie Brass dead." Morrison scanned the area. "Forensics, make a plaster of those tire tracks and footprints on the edge of Mill Street. And where is this plant from?"

One of the crime scene investigators peered down toward the wooden water wheel turning in the flow of Briggs Brook. Deep in the gulley, a tall branching plant with white flowers grew along the embankment.

"That seems to be the plant," one of them claimed.

"Take a sample and compare it," Morrison commanded.

Chief Samson decided this was a good time to leave him to his investigation. "Morrison, if there is anything you think I need to know, give me a call, will you? And we'll keep this all in mind while we prepare for the president's arrival in two days."

"Sure thing, Chief." They shook hands and Morrison added, "I'm on this like a pit bull, and I'm not letting go until I have him."

"I know, Dan, and my wife depends on it." Chief gave him a knowing nod and walked toward his red and white SUV.

Morrison continued to observe the terrain. The Old Town Mill that Charlie Brass was leaning against was originally built in 1650 and established by Governor John Winthrop, Jr. This gristmill ground corn and wheat for all of New London County until it was set afire by the infamous traitor, Benedict Arnold in his 1781 raid. The gristmill, being a hub for their primary source of bread flour, was immediately restored by industrious colonists.

By 1957, Interstate 95 and the Gold Star Memorial Bridge were installed high above the Old Mill, which became overcast by their shadow. The mill was relegated like a troll in a storybook to dwell under the bridge.

In recent times, it was authentically refurbished, and the handsome water wheel continues to splash into the brook. Its elevated flume, wheel pit, and tailrace are still a masterpiece of timber and iron construction, though they no longer grind the grains.

Morrison's thoughts were gnawing away at the killer's motives. Why devise such a travesty? Reaching into his pocket, he fingered the 1964 Kennedy half-dollar his father had given to him as a teen. Always with him, it was part of his morning regimen, like his badge and his gun, with him every day.

Jack Peabody joined him. Morrison acknowledged his presence. "There was some planning in this, Peabody. Charlie Brass was set up to be the key player in this scene with the plant, the location, and the positioning. This was staged. This guy is one crazy son of a gun. And where is the envelope and the tracking device?"

"The officer who discovered Charlie said they haven't found it yet," Jack reported.

Carolena Sanchez, the forensic officer, had been examining the scene and identified the plant as a poisonous water hemlock. The weed had grown to six feet tall. "Detective, this is one hell of a killer," she said. "The plant is common near fresh water and can take down a cow! This guy knew its deadly qualities. He purposely had Mr. Brass meet him here for his demise. He's a cocky bastard!"

"Carolena, you're right. He's showing off. Look, there is a lot of information to tag and review here. When your team is finished, see that he's delivered to the medical examiner. Tell the M.E.'s office to call Peabody as soon as they know the time and final cause of death."

Addressing everyone on site, Morrison announced, "The rest of you officers, back to headquarters now. I'll be holding a meeting in half an hour."

Trudging to the vehicle, Morrison lamented, "Damn it, Peabody, this is not how I thought the day would go. You drive. I need to think." He reached into his pocket for his nicotine backup of cinnamon gum that kept him off his once comforting vice of cigarettes. Peabody silently drove to police headquarters.

Chapter 35

After a half hour passed, Peabody accompanied Morrison into the briefing room. It was full of officers. There were thirty men and women. The second shift had come to relieve the first, but no one was going home. They were being held over for special duty.

"Alright," Morrison began, "we have some nut job having a grand old time toying with us. He's not a street urchin or a common thug. I believe he's a professional with a strong motive, playing a twisted cat and mouse game with us.

"The perpetrator killed and possibly poisoned Mitch Stockman. He blackmailed Mrs. Stockman and their manager Georgi Algarve, so it seems. He mugged and harassed both Roxanne Samson and Georgi. He killed J.J., Johnson Jones. And at this time, Charlie Brass is in critical condition.

"Our suspect has been paying the youth and out-of-work men in New London to do his bidding. After interviewing these men, which he has dressed to look like himself, the only thing we do know," Morrison thundered loudly, "ARE THE PARAMETERS OF OUR IGNORANCE!" Several officers flinched.

He brusquely went on. "This guy is meticulous and one step ahead of us. He is a planner, but we don't know his motive. I want EVERY detail from the hotel, the car rental dealer, and the barbershop owner. I want every shop owner and individual on the street to be interviewed again. You know the drill: knock and talk, door-to-door. When this guy makes his next move, I want to be there!"

Visibly red in the face and with indignation, he added, "Folks, what we have here is a manhunt." Morrison slammed his fist on the table. "Our city center businesses are hounding me. The Long Island Ferry owners are furious. The mayor and now Homeland Security are breathing down my neck, and to top it all off, the president will be here in two days. The Secret Service knows of our efforts as we attempt to quell this situation promptly.

"I know how time-consuming this will be! I am instructing you, good men and women, to get me some leads, to apprehend this killer! ASSUME NOTHING!" he ordered. "You know the adage."

Morrison paused for a breath. "I do not want the TV news outlets to grandstand these deaths. I don't want to hear the words 'serial killer' yet. We will have the whole Associated Press down here if they get a whiff of this. DO YOU HEAR ME?"

"Yes, sir!" came the unanimous response, knowing full well how the press would interrupt their work.

Morrison continued, "This guy is a chameleon; he has mugged, harassed, and blackmailed to accomplish an agenda of which we have not yet determined. He has plenty of funding, as he is renting premium cars, has a collection of expensive suits, and bribes people easily. He is a generous smooth operator whom people believe and trust. I don't care what you have to do, bring him in! You know what to do, people. For God sakes, GET IT DONE!"

chapter 36

The *Mary Ellen*, a 260-foot multidecked car ferry, left its New London terminus and motored at fifteen knots through Long Island Sound. Marissa Stockman and her attorney, Jonathan Blum, caught the five thirty p.m. vessel to Orient Point, Long Island. They sat in the small twenty-seat bar by a window at the aft.

"I'm so glad Vanessa is safe," she whispered to her attorney. "I can't wait to give her a hug and know that everything will be alright."

Attorney Blum empathized but warned her, "Now that they have the criminals in custody, you can rest a little easier, but the detective still has plenty of unanswered questions. And consider what Roxanne said. Why did the killer go after her and Georgi? And what was he looking for at her house? Lastly, I want to know why he killed that sixteen-year-old boy." Blum paused to make his next point.

"Since you addressed that envelope to Johnson Jones, it made you look really bad. But worse, how could you bring a gun, no less, to an interrogation?" Blum huffed with exasperation. "Why didn't you call me when you were blackmailed? Honestly, the detective could have booked and held you for twenty-four hours if I hadn't been there."

With a hopeless tone, she conceded, "I know that now. I was afraid. All I could think of was Vanessa. It's beyond reason to think logically when you're frantic about your child's welfare. I wanted to protect us and make the blackmailer go away. In hindsight, I see it was stupid." She sighed. "But now I'm in more trouble with Detective Morrison." Nervously, she played with her wedding ring, and her voice quivered. "I never thought it would make me look involved with Mitch's death."

Trying to comfort her, Blum put his arm around her shoulder and whispered, "That's enough. They have the man and his minions. We'll get beyond this. Don't worry, Marissa."

***

Detective Morrison attempted to reach Marissa Stockman and her attorney by cell phone. He wanted to warn them, but the ferry was in an area out of signal range. He changed his strategy and contacted the captain.

One of Griswold's officers called him to the radio room. "Sir, we have an urgent call patched through to you from Detective Morrison on the secure line zero-one-niner."

"This is Captain Griswold on the *Mary Ellen*, calling Detective Morrison, over."

"Captain Griswold, it's good to hear you are in charge. We have a bit of a tangle here in New London. There has been another murder, and it looks like the killer has escaped us. I feel there is an excellent chance he could be on board your ship, sir. Do you have enough men to keep an eye on Marissa Stockman and her lawyer? Over."

"Copy that. Yes, I do, Detective. What shall I tell the men to do? Over."

"Keep a lookout for a man of muscular build, over six feet, mild-mannered, well-dressed, and friendly. Someone you wouldn't suspect. That's how he's been so successful, but he can flip like a switch. He has dark brown hair and wears sunglasses, Italian descent with a slight accent. Over."

"I will inform my crew. The bartender will have eyes on Mrs. Stockman. I'm not equipped for much else. Over."

Morrison added, "Listen, I've decided that you not tell Mrs. Stockman or her lawyer. See if anyone approaches them. If so, it's possible she is in danger unless, of course, she hired him. Over."

163

Griswold returned, "Copy that and why don't we have the police in Long Island meet the ferry and check everyone's IDs? I can also put the Coast Guard on alert, if needed. Over."

"Copy that and good luck, Griswold. I'm counting on you. Over."

"I've got your back, Morrison. Over and out."

Captain Griswold informed his crew on the top decks, one by one, ensuring no undue attention. His crew was well-trained, but this was unusual. Griswold went to his duffel bag and slipped a Taser gun inside his jacket pocket. He had it on board, unofficially, for scenarios like this. Deciding he should also patrol the ship, he had his first and second-in-command at the controls in the wheelhouse. He stationed the bartender, Marty, on Mrs. Stockman.

Marty Lamont had worked on the ferry boats for many years. He was muscular, a weight lifter at about 225 pounds and had boxing experience too. Griswold had always thought he was a good guy to have around in a pinch.

The captain made his rounds, graciously greeting the passengers. It looked routine, yet he utilized his peripheral vision to observe those around him. *Situation awareness,* he thought. In other words, watch your back and the full 360. When he was a kid, he intuitively learned it on the streets but when in the military, he learned it was a term that had a name. He had memorized the definition.

Situation Awareness:

Observing your surroundings as far as you can see and feel in order to understand how information, events, and one's own actions will affect goals and objectives, both immediately and in the near future.

He moved from stern to aft of the ship, from dinghy to dining area. He nodded at Marty; Marty nodded back. Griswold went to the upper exterior deck and saw a man leaning over the rails. "Excuse me," the captain said. The man turned and appeared bleary-eyed. He was clutching the rails; his knuckles were white. Suddenly, Griswold realized he would be sick! The man turned back to the rails and vomited into the sea. Griswold left him. He didn't fit the description.

Radioing the helm, he announced, "I'm going into the cargo hold now. I'll have my radio on. Over."

"Copy that, Cap. Chip is taking his dinner break down below. You'll find him there."

The captain went down the narrow metal stairs and lit his LED flashlight to scan the cargo area. The vessel was full, a typical big haul of agriculture, fish, and quarried material. Today there were sixty-six cars loaded. He walked up and down the makeshift aisles, scanning the pallet bundles, car cargo, and construction equipment being transported. He entered the room where Chip, who manned the cargo area, was eating his dinner.

Chip jumped. "Cap. I didn't know you were down here."

"It's okay, I'm just taking a walk. Sit down." Chip sat and chewed what was left in his mouth.

"We may have an unwanted passenger on board," the captain confided.

Curious, Chip asked "Do you mean a raccoon? A cat? A weasel? You know weasels are going all over the place now. If people don't like them as pets, they let them off in parks or wild areas."

"This is a different type of weasel. It's a man," Griswold said somewhat darkly.

"Oh?" Chip asked surprisedly. "Is it the one in New London?"

"Yes, we've been asked to keep an eye out. Have you seen a guy over six feet, dark hair, muscular build, Italian, and friendly?"

"No, sir," Chip assured. "No one is down here except Johnny and me. He was emptying the dumbwaiter."

"Okay, keep checking this floor and use your walkie to contact me if you see anything suspicious."

"Yes, sir, I'll get right on it." Chip put away his food and started walking among the cars.

It was another thirty-five minutes to their destination dock. In twenty minutes, Griswold would head to the bridge to take the ferry into port. He was looking forward to his evening dinner break, and his stomach grumbled in agreement.

Griswold repeated his rounds through the engine room and checked each floor once more. Without any incidents, he returned to the wheelhouse. His helmsman was maneuvering through Plum Gut, a major fishing area with strong currents, at around five knots. The areas off of Plum Island and the Race were where the water from Long Island Sound flowed heaviest. This day was mild with plenty of fishing activity but on days with rough water and the winds against the current, you could find eight-foot to ten-foot standing waves.

Griswold took the helm and on approaching the dock, he turned the vessel and inched it astern until it could be tied up at the berth at Orient Point, New York. Just as promised, the Homeland Security police were there to check everyone getting off the ferry. Since they knew who they were looking for, they bypassed all the women and children.

Marty, the bartender, reported to Griswold that the trip was uneventful, and Mrs. Stockman and her attorney had no visitors or distant admirers.

The crew was preparing to disembark with the leftover passengers when Chip reported to Griswold, "It's probably nothing, but Johnny didn't empty the dumbwaiter, and I can't find him. The dockmen are nearly finished unloading the cargo bay. I took one last look around and have not seen him. Have you?"

"No. I'll use the PA."

Chip offered, "Maybe he had a hot date and left early."

"It's just not like him, Chip," countered Griswold.

The captain announced on the PA system a request that Johnny come to the bridge. Then he asked Chip, "Let's quickly look for him again." As they descended the stairwell, they heard pounding sounds from one of the large life jacket bins.

"Get me out of here," a muffled plea was heard.

The captain flipped the latch, and out popped Johnny, all tangled in life preserver straps.

"How did you get in there?" asked Chip, completely bewildered.

"I don't know," answered Johnny, "but I have a massive headache. I noticed the latch on this cargo hold was open. I looked inside, and that's all I remember. Maybe the lid hit me on the head, and I fell in and the jolt locked me in." The captain and Chip looked at each other and then hauled him out.

"Johnny, have your head checked at the first aid station with Chip." Griswold would report the incident to Morrison and have the police continue to search the ship. He considered the likelihood of Johnny falling into the bin. His situation awareness was telling him, *Too much of a coincidence. It feels like a shark is circling us.*

Chapter 37

Marissa Stockman was at the end of the ramp waiting for her attorney. All the men were detained while women and children waited off the ship. Since she couldn't see him, she felt nervous. It had been a long day, and she wanted to get home to her daughter.

"Dear me, what's the hold up?" she said under her breath.

The woman next to her said in a strong Long Island accent, "Oy! What's the hold up? My husband was saying they're asking for passports to keep the New Londoners out of Long Island. Hah! I said, 'Honey, forget about it. Go to the bar and have another Long Island iced tea.'" She fluffed her bouffant hairstyle with her wickedly long manicured nails. Her twanging continued. "Then he ran to me and said people were talking suspicious-like. I said, 'Honey, we're in Long Island. Everyone here yaps like those little pocketbook dogs. Don't you pay any attention to them.'"

Marissa smiled and then laughed aloud, finding it all bizarre. She simultaneously realized it was the first time she had laughed since the news of Mitch's death. A surreal, momentary suspension of reality, much like when you're on a roller coaster and gravity releases its hold on you. For a few precious seconds, you're weightless, and you breathe deeply. Then just as suddenly, it drops you back into your seat, back to reality. Her memories came back. Back to what she knew was true: Mitch was dead.

The men waited in line to disembark as the police crew systematically searched the *Mary Ellen*, opening every door and locker. A man, finally released from the line, came through the gangway and yelled to his wife as he held up his ID. "See, I told you. They let me in because I'm from Long Island." The wife standing next to Marissa shook her head.

Several of the female passengers started asking questions. "What's going on? Where's my husband? How come we must wait so long? I have to pee!"

The wife whispered to Marissa, "Doesn't it remind you of yapping?" Marissa laughed again. Then in the next moment, she saw her attorney, and a broad smile of relief crossed her face. He looked at her surprisingly and was quite amazed to see her smiling at him.

"Let's pick up Vanessa," he offered. "Dinner is on me tonight. You deserve it."

Surprising him, Marissa took his arm. "I think that sounds delightful," she grinned, feeling a sudden relief from fear and hopelessness.

Captain Griswold was pacing the deck. The whole transition of searching and checking IDs was taking up a lot of time with no results. He radioed Detective Morrison with his suspicious incident report. After completing the call, he realized it was so late, he had run out of time to heat up his meal. His stomach grumbled again. *That does it for my sunset dinner on the upper deck. I'm resigned to Captain Crunch in a bowl of milk.*

***

An elderly, white-bearded man with thick eyeglasses limped off the gangplank with a bag and cane in hand. A police officer assisted his descent and checked his identification that he presented from the inside pocket of his tan trench coat. The gentleman tipped his hat and maneuvered his way past the crowd to an awaiting taxi.

He silently chuckled to himself. *It's simple to create an illusion and throw off suspicion.* The infamous chameleon, Mr. Silver, had transformed himself on the ferry. No one would suspect a weak old man gingerly going about his business.

169

Chapter 38

Roxanne went home to lie down on the couch. She was exhausted after the ordeal with Georgi and the money drop at the library, the arrest at the coffee shop, and the police station saga. Trying to relax, she nonetheless found she was too wound up. She skimmed through a book to take her mind off the day.

From her library, she selected *Deadly Promises of Poisonous Plants*. The author thought it a good idea to let everyone know how certain plants were dependable in making you sick or killing you. His dark sense of humor made Roxanne snicker. She found him oddly amusing like Edward Gorey, the artist who enjoyed poking fun at death.

Glancing through the book, it described the deadly yew shrub found in Mitch's mouth. It has been known to be an effective poison since the ancient times of Caesar. Many warriors and statesmen were prepared to drink a mottled concoction of yew leaves for an early death rather than be tortured or killed by the enemy. Roxanne murmured, "Oh my!" at the lethal confirmation.

The mysteries of horticulture continued. A serene image of a lovely English garden full of demure petals, leaves, and twigs suddenly devolved into the depths of a secret society of plants with bold and poisonous possibilities. *Everything is not as it seems!* She read on, enjoying the surreal adventure.

Mind-altering plants were suspected in an account reported in the *South Australian Register* in 1874. A purported man-eating plant in Madagascar, witnesses testified, attacked a woman.

> "…The tendrils one after another, like great green serpents, with brutal
> energy and infernal rapidity, rose, retracted them, and wrapped about

her in fold after fold, ever tightening with cruel swiftness and savage tenacity…"

Stunned at the account, Roxanne read on, laughing loudly. It was a complete fabrication in order to sell more papers.

The eccentric reporter had woven the whimsical on a loom of historical facts using threads of the hysterical. He splattered colorful irony throughout and sprinkled opium poppies and other noxious plants within. In other words, he was ridiculous.

Roxanne chuckled and enjoyed the much-needed escape and pondered, *Hmmm, what's this?* Poems of Devious Dirty Deeds.

Jealousy and Jimson Weed

She wants to be a swinger,
her lover hasn't a clue.
She wants to dance in revelry,
all the night through.

He wants her devoted attention,
to have her as his wife.
He tries to pin an apron on
to keep her in his life.

She steals away in evening time
to spark her inner light.
He finds her with another man
a dark and handsome type.

With strong and urgent desires,
his nostrils puff and flare.
His options leave no other choice
to keep his lover fair.

A murderous note he's hastily scrawled
now lays upon the ground,
with remnant seeds of Jimson weed
scattered all around.

He'd found a way to keep
and bind her to his heart.
He had her drink a deadly dew
so in death they'll never part.

Roxanne read the description aloud. "Datura Stramonium L., Jimson weed, Jamestown weed or Devil's Snare, is noted and nicknamed for contributing to the untimely deaths of many settlers in the early 1600s in Jamestown, Virginia, the first colony in America." Suddenly, a loud banging bolted her upright on the couch. Slowly, she leaned to peer into her backyard. Much to her relief, Sam was pounding his boots clean on the back deck. He was just arriving home from work.

Finding her with a book on the couch, he thought, *all seems back to normal.* Sam ventured an observation. "You're taking it easy, I see. Have you worn yourself out among the poppies and the peonies?"

She looked at him in a strange, uncomfortable way, like a cat with a mouse in its mouth.

Her appearance caused a watchful Sam to say, "If you are going to be sick, I'll get out of the way."

"No." She kept quiet, not knowing what to say. He didn't know the details of her afternoon, and she was still reflecting on the outcome. She debated internally with her own unsettled relief, trying to determine how he would react to the events of the day. "I've something to tell you," she said softly.

"Well," he surprised her, "let's wait until you have some food in you. I'm taking you to Captain Scott's Lobster Dock. Some fresh air will be good." She smiled, secretly glad she could put off telling him about her last mission impossible.

"I am feeling a little weak," she agreed. "Maybe food will give me the energy I need. What do the Brits say? I'm feeling a bit peckish?"

"Okay," he smiled, "let's take our 'Beauty' out for a ride."

172

In her best fake British accent, she declared, "That sounds just lovely!"

They climbed into their spacious 1947 hunter green Buick Super. The shiny chrome grill looked like it could eat the road, while the sizable whitewall tires made it a cushy ride. The engine purred as they drove in classic fashion on this warm summer evening. Prepared, Sam had selected some music and with his phone attached to a small portable speaker, he hit the play button and the song started. Smiling, Roxanne sang the Smokey Robinson tune called "Cruisin'". At the chorus, Sam joined in.

They passed Fort Trumbull's entrance and turned right onto Hamilton Street. At the very end of the narrow and lumpy road was Captain Scott's restaurant. It sat in an odd nook in New London, perched and squeezed between the train tracks and a marina on Shaw's Cove.

After standing in the self-serve line at the outdoor venue, Sam ordered and paid for a few of their favorites: clam fritters, scallop salad, and fresh fish sandwiches. They sat at one of the picnic tables away from the other diners. The sun was still high enough at six thirty p.m. to be above the sailboats that flanked the marina. A soft clinking of the mast lines and the lapping water sounds created the relaxing atmosphere Roxanne needed. A few seagulls soared above, calling for food, and murmurs of dinner conversations rose and fell around them.

As they finished their last few bites, Sam said, "I have a confession to make."

Roxanne perked up. "You do?" *That was my line,* she thought.

"The detective told me all about your ordeal this afternoon. That's one of the reasons I was home late from work." Sam had decided to hold off on telling her about Charlie Brass.

"Oh?" She said, relieved, "I was about to tell you...but I wanted to wait awhile."

He added, "I'm sorry to say all has not ended well. There has been a new development, and Dan says they have the wrong guy."

Roxanne lunged forward in her seat and whispered loudly, "How is this possible!"

Sam knew of the other diners. "How about we take a ride by the water and talk about this?" She nodded in agreement. They cleared the table, and Sam drove their noble sedan to the coastline. He parked with a view of the Ledge Lighthouse.

He squeezed her hand. "Listen, most importantly, you and Georgi are safe and sound. All the folks the police caught were just cheap pawns in this guy's game. It's the old eighty-ten-ten rule."

"What's that?"

Sam elaborated. "Cops all over the world share a theory: ten percent of the people in a busy marketplace, like downtown New London, would never do anything bad. They would never cheat, steal, or harm. Another ten percent of the people would do all of these and more without a second thought."

Sam leaned in to emphasize. "Now wait till you hear this. All the other people, the eighty percent, can be swayed, and this is where it becomes interesting. This is the group we are talking about. If you're a bad guy, you want to pick the right kind of people, the ones who won't be noticed. Eighty percent of people can be persuaded if given the right incentive. So this killer picked people off the street to do his bidding for a quick hundred dollars. He took advantage of their personal motives."

Roxanne's hands went to her head. "Oh my God!" Processing what he meant, she asked, "You mean local people, whom we may know, were helping this guy? I can't believe it!"

Stunned by the revelation, she stared out to the calm waters of the sound and to Ledge Lighthouse. The red and white square brick structure looked like a floating gift box in the early setting sun. All it needed was a big white bow on top.

Softly, she wondered, "Isn't it odd to witness such beauty while encountering extreme stress? It's as if there's a great irony being played out like a Greek tragedy. When things went horribly wrong, they blamed it on some vengeful god."

Sam turned the key to the antique Buick and engaged the gear. He drove down Pequot Avenue. Roxanne kept talking. "The Greeks figured the gods were manipulating their lives. They had no control until a hero like Hercules arrived."

As if in a misty trance, she said, "That's how I feel right now; I need a hero. I have no control of what is happening...." Her voice trailed off as she slightly shook her head in disbelief of her circumstances.

They passed the mouth of the Thames River. The sunset cast glowing colors of pink and orange hues onto a large sailboat. The colors reminded Roxanne of a tropical fruity drink and suddenly, she thought of Georgi.

"Sam, let's go see Georgi. I want to tell him in person that they didn't catch the real guy. I feel so helpless. I don't think I have ever felt this helpless in my life." Sam reached across to her and put his hand over her knee. And she placed her hand over his and held tight.

"Sometimes, this is what life dishes us: a problem we can't easily solve. We just have to wait, be patient, and trust that things will work out." Trying to comfort her, he added, "Let Dan run his investigation. It will reveal more details. Eventually, given time, you will see the results. Let Dan be your hero."

"I guess you see this at work all the time, dealing with fires, arson, death, and raw emotions," she admitted. "I've never been involved in a major problem. Here they are happening all at once. Murders, blackmail, muggings: this isn't normal!"

"For Dan and me, it comes with the job," Sam conceded. "You never get used to it, but you learn after many stressful times that it will pass. You manage your emotions when all hell breaks loose and people are falling apart, because everything they own has just gone up in smoke. You do what you can until nothing is left to do. And in every suspicious incident, like a death or arson case, you know eventually all will be revealed. It usually just takes longer than you would like."

Roxanne looked adoringly at Sam, appreciating the tone of his voice, his experience, and his hand in hers. They finally arrived at the Vinho Verde Wine Bar. They could see Georgi moving about inside through the large paned windows, framed by the vine of heart-shaped leaves and white moonflowers.

chapter 39

Day 4 – 7:30 p.m. - Vinho Verde Wine Bar

Roxanne and Sam quietly stepped inside the entrance of the Vinho Verde. Soft sounds of jazz filled the air, and they realized an event was about to start. Deciding to stay, they selected a secluded table near the door so they could observe the wine tasting and dinner Georgi was hosting. One waiter approached their table, and they placed an order for coffee and devil's food cupcakes.

Georgi's clientele were on the balcony overlooking the Thames and sipping champagne. Suddenly, in a gentle way, a light breeze fanned the thin muslin drapes into billowing shapes. Roxanne's gaze followed the movement upward to the small twinkling lights encircling the rafters. "Isn't this wonderful?" she murmured to Sam.

Soon enough, the waitstaff ushered the guests to their seats. At each place setting was a line of various wine goblets, linen napkins, and polished silver. Stepping forward gracefully, Georgi appeared, dressed in crisp attire. He wore a tailored shirt in a soft lime with sleeves neatly rolled to the elbow and dark gray slacks that gleamed with a silken sheen. The young wine aficionado took on his ready-to-serve pose as the waiters stood by, keen to attend to their twenty patrons.

Welcoming the group, Georgi announced clearly, "Good evening, everyone." He slightly bowed as if on a theatrical stage. "I want to start the evening by giving you a little *In vino veritas*, which means 'wine truth.' We have several offerings that we sell here at Vinho Verde that are on the high end of the *Wine Advocates* rating list." Georgi gestured quote signs in the air around 'rating list.'

"To be known as a great wine on the list, it must be rated ninety points and above out of one hundred. This is all in accordance with wine aficionados, such as Robert Parker, who have established this point system based on an agreement among the refined tastes of master sommeliers. We will be offering a few of these wines this evening during our tasting dinner."

"Let us start with our first wine from Bedell Cellars, growers on Long Island since 1980. Their sparkling rosé is a unique handcrafted blend of grapes grown sustainably on their estate. Delicate, fresh, and lively, it's a fun wine, like me," he posed like a jester, "yet with a serious edge." He then saluted, and the group laughed. "Please enjoy this *tour de grape* that consists of Cabernet Franc, Cabernet Sauvignon, and merlot."

The guests sipped the sparkling rosé, chatted, and nibbled on fruit and fine cheeses. Georgi noticed Roxanne and Sam. He waved and blew a kiss. They signaled hello, and Sam leaned toward Roxanne to tease her. "I'm really hoping he blew that kiss to you." She eyed him with a smile, and he winked at her.

Having given the guests time to finish their glass of rosé, Georgi prepared for his next presentation by ringing a bell to gain their attention. "Our next wine, everyone, is a gewurztraminer from Priam Vineyards of Colchester, Connecticut. It is quite delicious with our first course, a warm grilled salad of curried eggplant, snap peas, summer squash, golden raisins, fresh spinach, and feta cheese.

"The wine's characteristics are a crisp minerality and fragrant Alsatian style white; this means it is like a fine wine from the northeast region of France. This wonderful vino is very complex and full of fruit flavor with a floral, fragrant nose of ginger, honey, hibiscus, and white rose. You will find it evolves on the palate in aroma and taste, first with fruit, then minerals, to a dry, tannic finish with crisp lemon rind and spice. This lovely libation has won seven international and regional awards."

The guests followed Georgi's lead swirling, sniffing, and tasting the wine. He paused as his guests hummed their delight, then offered, "Notice how the curry flavors, the creaminess of the feta, and the wine interplay on your tongue as you sip and bite."

Georgi left them as they blissfully imbibed and mingled.

After his guests finished their first course, Georgi resumed with exuberance. "Now for our second course, I offer you our local seared Stonington scallops on a bed of spiraled summer squash tossed in Alfredo sauce with grilled asparagus.

"The first of two wines in our tasting earned the famed ninety-four points. It's the Descencia Botrytis Chardonnay from the Wölffer Estate Vineyard of Long Island." Holding the stem of the glass, Georgi shared his counsel. "This light golden nectar from the vine has classic aromas of ripe fruit, honeysuckle, flinty stones, wonderful yeast notes, and fine toasted oak to fill the nose." He demonstrated by taking a long sniff, and everyone followed his lead.

"When you take a sip," he encouraged, "you will notice a firm structure and creamy texture with a beautiful honey and toasted almond flavor and a rich seductive mouthfeel. There is a perfect balance of the ripe fruit and the fine skin tannins, all wrapped with fantastic acidity and creamy lees. This finish is powerful and lingers with great minerality and finesse. Chardonnay is the perfect match for rich fish dishes, risotto, creamy chicken, and an array of cheeses. It is best served at fifty-five degrees Fahrenheit.

"Our next wine option is St. Croix from Maugle Sierra Vineyards in Ledyard, Connecticut. This delightful red wine is selectively handpicked and cold fermented in small batches. Aged in American and French oak barrels, it delivers intense flavors with a smooth finish. This fruit-forward red wine finishes in a semidry style, revealing unique blackberry, plum, and currant flavors that show the delectable characteristics of the St. Croix grape. It is a succulent accompaniment to fine dining and the frivolity that follows."

Georgi did a quick spin like a lyrical dancer and held one arm out broadly, and his guests chuckled. "St.Croix," he continued, "is best enjoyed as a long summer sip with friends, fine seafood, and memorable sunsets, as you are now partaking."

Each guest chose their preference and enjoyed their delicious serving. He gave them time to imbibe and chat among themselves while he stole away to say hello to Sam and Roxanne. "You've never seen me do a tasting, have you?" he asked.

"No, and you are naturally fabulous," Roxanne praised him. "You're so knowledgeable, Georgi!"

"Thank you," he said demurely, then quickly changed character. "Oh!" he squealed. Sam flinched. "This coffee just arrived. It is roasted on Long Island, an organically grown product from Native Coffee Traders. Are you enjoying it and the dessert? I need to know!"

Sam nodded. "Yes, it's good, and Roxanne will order a case of the coffee since it's organic. And she wants the recipe for the cupcakes too." He raised his mug toward her.

Georgi gave her a quick hug and said to them, "I have to return to my audience." He glided toward the tasting table without hesitation and rang his little bell to bring them all to attention.

"My dear friends," he announced, "and we must be friends by now because we have spent a joyful hour together." The guests nodded in agreement all flush with wine, food, and merriment.

Bathing in the adulation Georgi continued, "We have two desserts and three wine selections for you to taste. I know very well that some of you love chocolate, and it is the only dessert for you. For those, we have devil's food cupcakes, all warm and delicious, and for those who want something light and lovely, I have a lemon cheesecake with blackberry sauce. In either case, we will now taste and determine which of the three wines you would prefer with your choice of dessert."

As the waiters poured a tasting of the three wines for each guest, Georgi described them. "The glass on your left is from Paumanok Vineyards who have been growing in Long Island since 1983. This red wine has been awarded a prestigious ninety-three points. The Merlot Tuthills Lane offers intense aromas of crushed blackberries, plum, fig, and luxuriously sweet vanilla. It is a complex, full-bodied red with rich, voluminous tannins and multilayered flavors of black fruits, earth, and sweet spice." The guests all sniffed, sipped, and murmured their opinions to each other.

With a hand on his hip, their flamboyant host continued. "This next wine is also a merlot, and you may say, 'Why Georgi, why two merlots?' And my answer is because they are both from Long Island and both are acknowledged by connoisseurs. The suave international man of wine, Mark Oldman, has recommended the Long Island merlots in his wonderful book, *Oldman's Brave New World of Wine.*

Georgi spoke exuberantly. "This next red is produced by Shinn Estate Vineyards on the north fork of Long Island and is called Nine Barrels Reserve Merlot. This fine wine exhibits refined tannins with elegant flavors of blackberry and black plum, as well as distinct aromas of violet and chocolate. Shinn Estate Vineyards and our next vineyard from Italy are two of the few successfully recognized biodynamic growers and winemakers in the world.

"Now, I can tell," he paused, "that some of you are thinking about a white dessert wine, and I have one for you. It's from Stefano Bellotti Vineyards in Piedmont, Italy." Georgi held the wine glass by the stem. "This is C'era una Volta il Passato, Vino Bianco, made with Moscato grapes."

Taking a long sniff, Georgi waved his hand in a gentle upward motion, encouraging his patrons to follow his lead. "This delicious wine has a sweet full nose and delicate aromas of raisin, full and dense." Taking a sip, he elaborated, "You will find rich flavors of figs and honey, yet not too sweet. This wine is delicious with dessert and highly-flavored cheeses. Please select your favorite wine to enjoy with dessert."

Their host extraordinaire sashayed to the bar and returned to proudly present the Mark Oldman book on wine. "There are many fine books about wine, but my favorites are the ones that are like a great bedtime story. There's an adventure where you are taken to faraway lands with wine and fine food. This book is full of fanciful prose, and just look at this fine gentleman on the cover!" he pronounced as his voice rose.

Georgi held the book so everyone could see Mark's picture. "Ladies, right away you notice him because he's dreamy. And look at his Cheshire cat smile. It's as if he's saying, 'How are you this evening?' And you say, 'I'm very well, thank you, now that I found you!' And then you just stare at each other and have your own internal conversation." Georgi looked around the table. He knowingly paused and added, "About wine, of course! What else?" His guests laughed loudly, delighting in his lightheartedness.

"Now that you have sipped plenty of wine, this is when *In vino veritas*, which means 'wine truth,' helplessly tumbles out of one's mouth. May I tell you all a secret?" Georgi requested. Some laughed nervously, while several nodded and said, 'Yes.'

"Sometimes, I find myself in a wine quandary, and I pick up Oldman's book with his handsome stare. What should I select for such and such a tasting? And somehow or other, after a nice little worldwide trip through his book, I have the answer. It's quite convenient to have on the shelf, ladies. You can pull down his book anytime, whenever you need a friendly smile, and dream of sipping wine in southern Portugal." The guests giggled and elbowed each other, as they watched their quirky host in a trance-like stare.

Georgi shook himself awake and said, "You are all welcome to peruse my book collection. And gentlemen, you will find many lovely women wine connoisseurs suggesting food pairings with wine selections. I will mention a few: Karen MacNeil, who has the fabulous books *Wine, Food & Friends* and her very successful *Wine Bible, second edition;* and Christine Hanna of Hanna Winery and her book, *The Winemaker Cooks.* And, of course, there are many, many more. Have fun searching for your favorite wine and pairing books for your own world tour."

His lively guests sipped the wine and devoured the desserts. One of them asked, "Georgi, how did you come to learn so much about wine? You're not quite thirty, are you?"

"Oh," he squealed, "one should never tell their age. It is always held against you." The suave sommelier tilted his head downward as his eyes looked up at his guests in a demure pose and winked. Several women nodded in agreement, as he offered a knowing smile. Then holding his finger to his chin, he thought a moment.

"I will tell you another secret. You see, wine is a tradition in my family. My great-great-grandfather carried to America grapevine rootstock from Portugal."

Georgi's story seeded a quiet in the room. "He crossed the rootstock with local American grapes and grew them on the hillside of his small acreage and bottled his own wine."

"Eventually, he passed his knowledge and small vineyard to my great-grandfather, who rather preferred being a sailor. This worked to his advantage when prohibition came along. You see, great-grandfather wasn't much for following the rules." Georgi paused and looked around the room. "To be quite frank, he was a regular pirate. He had a zeal for hiding booze and wine on ships, in root cellars, caves, anywhere he could. He was a very colorful character...."

"Like you?" a guest interrupted.

"No, not quite like me," he answered with a twinkle. He twisted his torso and offered a gallant pose. "Although, I did inherit a pinch of the pirate…I am a rogue compared to most," he chortled. "Can you see it in me?" The guests laughed loudly as he had given them a quirky vision to behold.

When the clatter of his guests subsided, Georgi resumed. "My family and all the children did what they could during prohibition by making lots of grape jelly to hide the fact that grandfather was making wine. So yes, wine is in my family. As time went on, when my mother met my father, he offered to move her to New York City, away from the farm and vineyard. She jumped at the chance to be a fashionable lady." Georgi swayed gracefully.

"When I was young, I was interested in being a wine aficionado. So, through family and education, I fell into this wonderful job. And now I ask you, how?" he said raising his voice and his arms. "How could I go wrong? I can be fashionable, talk about wine, and eat great food. I love them all!" He clicked his heels, did a cheeky turn, and swished away to replenish their drinks. They all giggled from the wine and Georgi's drama queen antics.

Quietly, Sam opened the door, and he and Roxanne slipped out unnoticed. Roxanne took Sam's arm and asked, "Do you think some of his family's old karma of pirates and bootleggers has come back to bite him?"

Sam chuckled, "I doubt it." He took in a long breath. "This guy who killed Stockman is a modern-day pirate with a grander plan, for sure. It's the level of risk he's taking that's disturbing and for what reason?"

They crossed Bank Street and peered into the darkened windows of New London's popular Hygienic Art Gallery. Iron streetlamps gently lit the interior. Their artist friend, Troy Zaushny, had his work on exhibit. "We'll have to come back when he's here," Roxanne murmured.

Sam's phone rang unexpectedly. "Yes?" he asked. "Oh hello, Morrison. What's happening?" The detective reported, and Sam listened.

"Well, I'm glad to hear it, and so will Roxanne. Thanks for the intel." Sam ended the call.

"He says they believe the thug is on Long Island. They have an undercover officer to keep an eye on Marissa and her daughter. We should all rest well tonight."

Chapter 40

Detective Morrison was finishing his morning shave while a Van Morrison tune, "Into the Mystic," played in the background. He looked in the mirror and wondered what this day would bring. *Maybe a lead will be waiting for me.* The reward of $5,000 for information on Stockman had been posted in the paper.

Morrison flipped his half-dollar in the air. *Dad, I need some of your Irish luck today,* he whispered. He pocketed the coin, strapped on his gun, and clipped his badge to his belt.

Arriving at police headquarters at six thirty a.m., he found that no leads had come in overnight. The second and third shift police force had targeted the train station, shipping piers, and local storefronts surrounding the murders. They had scoured for any new intelligence from the hotel, car rental, barbershop, coffee shops, and the Italian restaurant. Most officers this day were on duty preparing for the president's arrival in the secured area of the Coast Guard Academy.

While waiting for a clue to emerge, Morrison reviewed the forensic team's work of analyzing minute details from the crime scenes. Assistant Detective Peabody was scanning the ViCAP on the Internet, trying to develop and follow any leads. He had entered the killer's crime profile: extortion, murders, and poisons. Wanting to unearth the smallest clue, Morrison needed to make some headway. "Give me something, Peabody." His order was merely a wishful request. "I'm dying here for a lead."

Peabody glanced up from the computer screen. "Come on, boss, something will come up. I can feel it."

"I need more than a feeling," Morrison said, pacing the floor in front of

186

Peabody's desk. "This guy is covering all his tracks. I tell you he's a pro with a purpose, and subterfuge is his modus operandi. The problem, Jack, is this little city has a half-mile radius of tourist shops and train travelers, cruise ships and historic sites. Then there is the variety of young and old, prim and posh, and many diverse people who live and work here. With a busy day, hundreds of tourists and locals are meandering around the Whale Tale Fountain and downtown proper. We have to home in on this guy. Fine-tune our radar. Someone can go unnoticed, but there has to be a clue."

"You're right, boss," responded Jack. "Even though we suspect he is in Long Island, any lead will help us. It was easy for him to blend in here. Look, we have sailors' pubs and fine dining establishments, art and antique stores. And there are those few vacant buildings undergoing refurbishment. It leaves plenty of places for this guy to mix in, meet up, and do business. Then he slips out of here. We thought we had the guy in custody yesterday; otherwise, we would have been checking the people boarding that ferry last night."

Morrison ran his hands through his thick black hair. "If we don't solve this quickly and the press catches wind of what has happened, we'll be on national news. The media is harassing me for information, and I only have until tonight before I tell them Charlie Brass is dead."

Morrison stopped pacing and like a vulture waiting for meat, he leaned over Jack and his computer. "Jack, the downtown merchants want this wrapped up before it destroys their summer business. Our wonderful Sailfest and City Center organizer was very concerned. And then there was Mr. Platinum Spoon's wife. You know, the one who lives in that big house by the water? She approached me the other day, pleading that we find the murderer."

Breaking into an imitation of her abhorrent female tone, Morrison emoted, "Detective, I must tell you, downtown is on the verge of a great transformation! It's a destination for food, wine, theater, and the arts. How can we go out at night with a killer on the loose? Please, please catch him! I have guests for the summer, and we won't feel safe!"

Jack gawked over his computer screen at his boss who had just mimicked the woman and her mannerisms. Having never seen him this animated before, he added his opinion. "Boss, this dude is like a nasty cockroach that's run off into the shadows. We have to start looking under rocks in order to please everyone."

Morrison acknowledged, "Look, when a popular well-to-do man is found downtown dead in the shrubs, no one wants to hear of it. They just want it to go away. All these deaths are connected to Mitch Stockman and his wife. Why? Who is he? What is the motive? Right now, Mrs. Stockman looks guilty, and her acting like a victim could be her only cover."

"Boss, let's see if something comes up on the ViCAP. The computer geeks are still searching all the business files on Stockman's desktop in Long Island. They found nothing obvious on the surface documents, but they are digging deeper. We are waiting on forensic fingerprint and footprint analysis, and the medical examiner is doing her thing."

"That's it!" Exuberant, Morrison's hands went into the air. "I'm going to the medical examiner's office. Maybe the dead have something left to say about this."

Jack warned, "Boss, she's the new M.E. out of New Haven, and she's intense. I met with her for the first time last night after we delivered Charlie Brass. This lady's a real stickler for the details. I couldn't leave until I had told her the whole story of this case. She asked a lot of questions and said it helped her get into the killer's head so she can look for clues on the deceased that might otherwise be missed. Her name is Dr. Angela Storm, and her fascination with death freaks me out!" Jack's shoulders shuddered. "I don't know how she does it, hanging out with dead people. It gives me the willies. You'll want to have a cup of coffee before you go. You're going to need it to keep up with her and her creepy acumen of death."

Morrison smiled knowingly at Jack. "You're a rookie, Peabody. Give yourself a few dozen more bodies and you'll get past all this shuddering." He gave the twenty-something a friendly slap on the back and walked out the door.

Chapter 41

Traveling along Broad Street, Morrison drove to the edge of town near the Waterford city line. He pulled up to a nondescript, one-story brick building with twelve parking spots. He approached the familiar unassuming entrance and paused by the door. To his surprise, a new plaque had been installed. It read:

Let conversation cease. Let laughter flee.
This is the place death delights to be to help the living.
Medical Examiner motto

Morrison exhaled and uttered, "I need all the help I can get, and if death delights in it, so be it."

He was buzzed in the door by the medical assistant, who then led him to the examining room. He saw, standing over three dead bodies, an average-sized woman completely covered in full medical regalia: a white lab coat over blue scrubs, gloves, a breathing mask, safety glasses, and a hair cap.

Morrison approached her saying, "Dr. Storm, I am Detective Dan Morrison. My assistant, Detective Peabody, told me he has informed you of the details of this case."

With no formalities, Dr. Storm answered, "Yes, Detective, you're just in time. I have something for you." She snapped off her latex gloves and pushed the surgical mask down under her chin. Her safety glasses stayed in place as she approached a stainless steel counter, lifted a plastic baggie, and handed it to the detective. In it was a small square receipt.

He looked at it closely. Surprised, he said, "It's a vineyard receipt from Ledyard. Where did you find this?"

"It was in Mitch Stockman's inside pocket of his jacket, crammed into a corner as if something had pushed down on it."

Morrison murmured, "Well, I'll be damned...." Then he grinned.

"Dr. Storm, I don't know you, but you just made me very happy. I needed this break."

She lifted her safety glasses and flashed her golden-brown eyes and a wide smile. "Glad to be of service, Detective Morrison. You bring me the goods," she pointed to Mitch Stockman, J.J., and Charlie Brass on the examining tables, "and I'll find you the killer's mood, method, and motive, if I can."

Taken aback, Morrison asked, "What do you mean, mood?"

"Well," she said, "the killer, in this case, has no mood. He is swift and decisive. He is on a mission. I believe he is a professional."

"I'm impressed so far, but why do you think so?" he asked. He knew Jack had informed her of the goose chase they had been on through the streets of New London, but this was a quick conclusion on her part.

"I am cheating a little," she admitted.

Morrison looked at her sideways, thinking she certainly had his full professional attention. Otherwise, he could not distinguish her from any other female in her medical gear with a tight hair bun and scrubs that gave no definition to her form. So, while he gazed into her golden-brown eyes, she had his interest.

"What I mean," she said seriously, "is the fact I am considering not just Mr. Stockman but also young Johnson Jones and Mr. Brass. They were all quick deaths. Fast action that broke their necks so quickly, they were dead in an instant. Not everyone knows how to do that. In my fifteen years of work in New Haven, I have not seen such a determination to kill.

"The murders I see are usually messy due to passionate feelings of anger, lust, or disgust. These three murders are quick and clean. He's not using a gun or knife. Johnson Jones has no defensive bruising or signs of struggle, so he was caught off guard. Although, I do see deep bruising and muscle strain on Mr. Stockman that indicates he struggled initially, probably surprising the killer with a few quick moves of his own. But once this lethal machine had the upper hand, it was over quickly for Stockman. And for the killer, the moment of final superiority was pushing the poisonous plants into the victims mouths. If there was a small chance of life left, Mr. Stockman and Mr. Brass would have died from the poisoning.

"Detective, this is a warrior act signifying he has won." She took a breath and eyed the detective. He was handsome enough, dark blue eyes, groomed dark hair, slightly tan, in good shape, and strong hands. *He must be from here,* she thought. *He looks comfortable, a well-worn, 'get it done' type of guy. That's good. I can work with that.*

Morrison was considering all she said and was about to comment when she added, "Yet, this act, Detective, can also be considered a brazen yet subtle announcement. It may be a purposeful threat or taunt. He is basically saying, 'Don't mess with me.'" She paused and pointed to the bodies. "This killer is deadly serious. I believe what you have here is a devil of death, an assassin. I have studied much about this type of personality profile but never dealt with their carnage directly, as in this case."

Morrison put his hands in his pockets and shrugged. "What do you mean by taunt, exactly? Taunting who?"

"Why, taunting you, of course," she said in a matter-of-fact tone.

Morrison's eyebrows rose. He looked at Dr. Storm with sincere curiosity. Her eyes were direct beacons staring at him, and her even-toned voice conveyed undeniable intelligence, yet he now wondered if she was slipping into another realm.

"Why on earth do you think he is taunting me?" He stared at her in disbelief with a look saying, 'You've got to be kidding.'

"Oh, not you personally, Detective Morrison, but you as 'the cops,'" she explained, as her fingertips put quotes in the air. "As I said, he is brazen. He knows that if you investigate the properties of the yew shrub, Taxus baccata, and the second plant, water hemlock, Cicuta maculata, that was found on Charlie Brass, and you discover these are poisonous, you will wonder, who is this guy with knowledge of the plants pulled from the garden of his kill?"

Morrison thought, *Yes, who is this guy? A hunter in a concrete jungle?*

Dr. Storm went on. "I believe he is answering you back." Morrison looked at her as if she had read his mind. "He is saying, 'I'm the smartest mothereffer you are never going to meet!' This man is a classic narcissist. He thinks so highly of himself and his intelligence that his behavior will most likely remain cocky and extreme to the end. From what your Detective Peabody told me, this mastermind sounds like a diabolical James Bond."

Morrison's mouth hung open for a second, then he reached for a stick of gum in his pocket while his thoughts took over. *Damn, who is this woman? This dame is something else.*

While he considered all she said, he offered her some cinnamon gum, which she declined. She didn't realize it, but Dan Morrison was doing something else. He was pausing. He learned from his Irish grandfather that pausing was a practice that must be timed perfectly, a tool to use even if it made the other person uncomfortable.

"Pausing," his grandfather had said, "gives you the time to assess your own thoughts and consider the other person's point of view. Sometimes if there is enough dead air, they will squirm or offer more information. Pausing always tells you more about them."

"Detective," she said, lifting her hand, "please don't mind me. I say what I think, and you can take it or leave it."

"No, no," he responded. "I don't mind your candor. It's refreshing, actually.

You have a profiler's method to your thinking."

She offered, "Since I was young, I would voraciously read murder mystery stories. I've always wanted to know the why, the reason behind a mysterious death. I wanted to know the motive. Some are obvious crimes of passion that you can see in how someone is stabbed. These three killings are crimes of determination. For him: a job, a paycheck. Let's hope he has completed his mission, so to speak, with no further reasons to kill. That receipt may lead you to him."

Morrison held up the baggie. "Dr. Storm, you are an intriguing weather system, a real wellspring of information. I'll let you know how your theories turn out." She smiled and offered her ungloved hand, which Morrison shook. As he was leaving, he turned to glance at the plaque again.

> **Let conversation cease. Let laughter flee. This is the place death delights to be to help the living.**

Dan smiled to himself. *Well, Mitch Stockman, the avenging angel of death has come to our aid, and her name is Angela Storm! Now let's catch your killer!*

chapter 42

After his informative encounter with M.E. Angela Storm, Morrison returned to police headquarters. Peabody had a lead. A merchant on State Street at Thames River Greenery had encountered a man with Mr. Silver's description. The two detectives left quickly, arriving at the establishment in five minutes flat.

Thames River Greenery was a successful European-style storefront, selling chocolates, cheeses, coffee, fine wine and spirits, and a beautiful selection of flowers with full-service floral design. The owners were Fred and Charlotte, and they knew Mitch and Georgi as downtown business peers.

Over the years, Thames River Greenery had renovated adjoining turn-of-the-century buildings and had recently finished the second floor of their establishment to add a cigar lounge. Charlotte's brother, a cigar enthusiast, persuaded them to cater to the smoking admirers in town. Fred, a gentleman with fine tastes, and a wine and liquor aficionado himself, soon acquired a penchant for cigars also.

It didn't hurt that, historically, Connecticut was known worldwide for fine shade tobacco wrappers. Cuban tobacco seed was brought here in the mid-1800s and grown ever since.

Upon their arrival, Fred escorted the detectives to where they could speak privately. They passed through the old-world ambience of the tasting room. The dark wood interior enhanced a wall full of fine wine, champagne, port, brandy, whiskey, rum, and scotch. Candelabras were placed among the tasting tables, creating a cozy atmosphere. The men climbed the staircase to the second-level smoking lounge.

The tall wood-paneled room had vintage art and furnishings of club chairs, game tables, and a small self-serve bar, which recreated a bygone era of a men's club. Contemporarily, women also frequented the traditional smoking room to enjoy a good cigar. Private boxed humidors were available, under lock and key, for the recurring visitors. The time-honored scent of cigar tobaccos imbued the pores of every surface in the comfortable room.

Detective Morrison had known Fred for several years. He often asked his advice for the occasional gift or proper wine for a dinner party. Upon entering the relaxed manly getaway, he drifted on the cigar scent to a fond memory of his father and grandfather.

Often, the three would take a long drive. Young Dan would sit between them on the bench seat of his grandfather's old-time Cadillac. While the men smoked cigars with the windows down, Dan would snack on his grandfather's unusual treats of Necco Wafers, confectioned orange circus peanuts, or toasted coconut marshmallows.

Taking a deep breath, the detective returned from his fleeting recall and began asking questions. "Fred, tell me about this man in the gray suit that matches our person of interest."

"It was the Gurkha that caught my attention, really. The scent of a Gurkha cigar is impossible to ignore. We sell several of the daily smoking variety but as soon as I caught the aroma, I complimented him on his excellent taste and asked where he had acquired his. He replied in a slight Italian accent that it was a gift from his business partner, an advance for an upcoming job. I was astounded and commented that it must be some job for such a fine gift. He laughed and said, 'Oh, it is, my man. It is.'"

Morrison questioned, "Excuse me, but what is this Gurkha?"

Peabody was taking notes while leaning against a club chair and looked at Fred with a furrowed brow. The latter raised his eyebrows for emphasis and asserted, "This particular one is only the finest cigar in the world, my friend. When you catch the exquisite scent, you know you are among royalty."

Perplexed, the detective asked, "Royalty? Why would you say that, Fred?"

"The one he was smoking is His Majesty's Reserve Gurkha Cigar. They are the single most expensive line at $2,000!"

Stunned, Peabody lost his balance and slid off the chair as Morrison exclaimed, "What! $2,000 a box?"

"Oh no, that is $2,000 for one cigar!" Fred explained, then proceeded to educate. "His Majesty's Reserve is an aged, eighteen-year-old cigar, infused with Louis XIII de Remy Martin Cognac. So an entire bottle of Cognac is infused into a single box of cigars!" Fred mimicked a royal gesture for effect with a wave of his hand and continued. "They are wax sealed in a glass tube to preserve their freshness. There is no imitation."

Fred added with sincerity, "This man was well-dressed and similar-looking to the men in your photos here but more refined. He also requested a fine rum to enjoy with his Gurkha. I suggested the best I had on hand at the time, a twelve-year El Dorado rum. Your man was quite pleased. He remained for about an hour, sipping the rum and enjoying his cigar."

"When was this, Fred?" Morrison pressed. "He sounds like the elusive, Mr. Silver."

"Oh, it was last Thursday afternoon around three o'clock."

Peabody deduced, "Why, that's the day Stockman was killed. This wise guy might have been following him all day."

"It's obvious this Mr. Silver is very comfortable with himself," Morrison declared, "and that is exactly why he will make a mistake, and we will be there when he does. Fred, if you see him again, please call me." Morrison put out his hand. "Thanks, Fred, I didn't think I'd be learning about cigars and rum today, but you've given me fresh insight into your wonderful world of decadence."

Fred smiled and shook the detective's hand. "Anyone who can afford a

Gurkha can afford pretty much anything, anywhere, at any time. If this is your guy, he is high priced. Maybe there is more to him than just a local murderer."

Heading toward the door, Morrison nodded in agreement. "Thanks for the info, Fred. I'll see you soon." He turned to his colleague, "Come on, Peabody, we're on the hunt."

Once out the door, Morrison said, "Fred hit the nail on the head with that one, Jack. So what does a hit man of that caliber have to do with a Long Island wine aficionado?" Deep in thought and fiddling with his keys, Morrison added, "Dr. Storm found a receipt from a vineyard Stockman visited the day he was murdered. Let's get on the road and talk to these people Stockman met with that morning. With any luck, maybe Silver was seen there too. We'll start in Ledyard."

"Good," stressed Jack, "I've been itching to get off of the desk work. My eyes were aching from sitting in front of that computer." Then with a nod and a grin, he added, "And boss, I always wanted to try vineyard hopping. I just didn't think it would be with you."

Morrison gave him an impish sideways glance. "Who did you plan to go with? I could set you up with Mabel. I don't think she's had a date in all her sixty years. She could use a bit of dusting off."

Rather stunned, Jack returned, "Dusting off! She needs more than that." He shook his head. "I don't want those images, boss. Let's focus on work."

Chapter 43

Morrison and Peabody drove across the Gold Star Memorial Bridge into the town of Groton. After traveling ten minutes, they saw the blue Connecticut Wine Trail sign on Route 117. An open flag waved them into Maugle Sierra Vineyards. Ahead of them was a picturesque timber frame building nestled under towering pines, and beyond was a manicured vineyard that swept into a valley toward distant hills.

The detectives strode into the tasting room. The interior had high post-and-beam ceilings with a fireplace hearth made of large local stones. Several cozy seating arrangements offered views out to the deck and into the vineyard. A friendly looking man was at the wine bar setting up glasses for tastings.

"What can I offer you, gentlemen?" the middle-aged man asked from behind the bar. "You're my first patrons today," he smiled graciously.

Morrison presented his badge. "We are here on police business, sir. I am Detective Morrison, and this is Detective Peabody. Can you tell us about your association with Mitch Stockman?"

The man stopped what he was doing and placed both hands on the table. "Yes, I can." The stocky, bright-eyed vintner was visibly upset. He composed himself and continued. "God bless him. Mitch was a good man. I've known him for several years now. Last Thursday, we chatted, and he tasted several of our wines for an upcoming dinner event. We discussed which foods would pair well with the wines he selected. He seemed to be his jovial self."

Morrison asked, "And in your conversation, did you discuss his other business ventures?"

"Oh no," he replied. "We discussed wines of the world but not my direct competitors or his specific business dealings. He was a comrade in wine. I will miss him," he said sadly. "I would ask his opinion on our wines and suggestions for my business. But that was all. He was always a gentleman and offered ideas that might improve our standing. I truly respected his input, his worldly view of wines, and his spirited friendship." The man visibly choked up again. "We made arrangements to deliver the cases of wine that afternoon. He had several more vineyard stops and needed the room in his vehicle."

The detective showed him photos of the men in custody. "Have you seen any of these men or someone who looked like them?"

"No, I haven't," the vintner replied, quite shaken. "So you believe his death was intentionally planned, Detective?"

Peabody replied, "At this point, it seems like no accident, sir."

Morrison was disappointed. He had hoped the receipt, found by M.E. Dr. Angela Storm, would be the ember needed to ignite a firestorm of action. But now he realized the bereft winemaker had nothing new to offer. The detectives gave him their calling card and left the vintner in his peaceful setting, adrift in a fresh fog of mourning his friend.

Morrison and Peabody's footsteps crunched across the graveled parking lot. A stiff breeze picked up, and the sixty-foot pine trees groaned overhead. They both looked up and watched the top of the pines sway in circles.

"Jack, we're like fishermen in the open sea pursuing a predator, like in the movie *Jaws.*"

"Or is he circling us?" Jack countered. "This has been a strange case."

Morrison stopped gazing up at the trees and eyed Jack. "After days of tracking this land shark, all we have are his flotsam and a situation that stinks like last week's chum." He exhaled and shook his head. "You know, maybe all the answers are on Long Island." With hands on his hips, he mulled over his predicament.

Jack kicked a stone across the parking lot. "These murders, muggings, and blackmail seem like a game to this guy. What is the point of it all? Nothing adds up. What is his motive?"

"What we know is this: Mr. Silver has a mission," Morrison responded. "Dr. Storm said he broke the necks of all three men with precision, as a professional killer would do. Who would orchestrate all this? Money has to be the motive because there's someone spending lots of it, trying to pull this off. Stockman's wife is loaded, and I don't trust her."

Grabbing the SUV door handle, he said, "Come on, let's get back on the trail. We just have to keep talking to people. What's the next location on the list?"

Jack pulled out his phone for a map program. "The next stop is in Stonington."

chapter 44

Meanwhile, in New London on Bank Street, Reginald Crumberton, aka Reggie the Crumb, was manning his bench and minding his own business. Although it was a warm June day, he was wearing layers of clothes. His matted hair, scruffy beard, and missing teeth masked the fact he was only thirty-six years of age. His disheveled appearance gave one an instant impression of his station in life.

Suddenly, a kid swept in on a skateboard close to Reggie. "Hey, watch what you're doing, will ya?" Reggie yelled and spat to mark his territory.

The kid swirled round and came back, landing next to Reggie, asking slyly, "Hey, man, want to make a fiver?"

"What for?" Reggie asked, eyeing him suspiciously.

"Just watch that statue over there while I get something to eat at Eddie's."

"No!" Reggie barked.

"Come on, you can use the money, can't you?" Reggie's homeless status was clear.

"Of course, I can, but I'm hungry."

"Then I'll get you a sandwich and soda too," promised the kid.

"Plus the fiver?" demanded Reggie.

"Yeah, alright," the skateboarder conceded.

"Okay but hurry up. I haven't got all day!" Reggie pushed his agenda.

The kid swung his hair back and looked at him, inquiring, "Where you gotta go?"

"None of your bleeping business, Skater," Reggie thundered, then mumbled profanity under his breath. The kid sped off.

Reggie's daily circuit started under the Gold Star Bridge near Mill Street, where he slept nightly in good weather. He would walk each morning to the local community center for free coffee and breakfast and then he would sit on his bench, petitioning his case to passersby. Often, he collected enough change to buy some scrap of food. Later, he would walk to the soup kitchen on Montauk Avenue for supper. Reggie hummed to himself. *Lunch and a fiver, this is a good day.*

Reggie watched the Columbus Circle statue. Beyond it was the small bistro restaurant with a constant stream of customers stopping in for their favorite lunch. Reggie started stretching, yawning, and dreaming of the lunch he was having delivered. Then unexpectedly, someone caught his eye.

It was a petite blonde woman who jumped out of a large black truck. She looked around suspiciously and then surprising Reggie, she slipped under the police crime scene tape. She huddled behind a shrub for a minute or so, then crept and crouched low again. Reggie stood up. *Where did she go? What is she doing?*

He stretched and leaned to see her but no sign. *Well, I'll be....* Reggie scratched his head, then tugged on his whiskers. *That woman is up to something.*

Roxanne snuck in to water her charge, the Columbus Circle garden. She opened the green trapdoor to the water spigot and pulled out an expandable hose from under her shirt, then proceeded to attach. It was her mission to not allow these plants to die. *One death in the garden was enough. I have my priorities straight,* she told herself. *Dan may want me to wait, but these flowers can't.*

Meanwhile, Reggie started to wonder and mutter to himself. *Why is this kid watching the statue? What is this woman doing hiding in the shrubs? Who's the son of a gun behind that murder? Dag nab it!* All flustered, he balled up his stuff and stormed off, mad as the devil. Just then, the kid skated over. "Hey, you're leaving?"

Reggie turned around as fast as a bullet, grabbed the kid by the neck, and breathed strongly into his face. "I don't know what you're up to, but I don't want anything to do with it. Give me that sandwich." He grabbed the bag from the kid and huffed off.

"You crazy old man," the kid yelled.

Reggie whipped about. "I'm not old, you stupid kid. I'm homeless and one day, you'll know the difference, you idiot, because you'll be just like me if you keep listening to stupid people making you deals and promises they can't fill. Now give me that fiver!"

"What did you see?" the kid said, holding the fiver in the air out of reach.

"Some lady was jumping in and out of the shrubs. That's all. Now leave me alone." Reggie grabbed the five-dollar bill and left.

Roxanne slinked under the crime scene tape and returned to her truck. The kid spied her as she drove by and then made a phone call.

"Hey, Mr. Silver? Yeah, a lady in a black truck was there and just left. Yeah, she's blonde. Sure, I'll catch up with you later."

The kid stepped on his skateboard. *That was the easiest hundred bucks ever. Reggie just did me a favor. Life is good.* Kicking off on his board, he glided over the disjointed asphalt on Bank Street. His destination was the city boardwalk. And his next order of business was carving the street, hanging out with the guys, and pulling moves or slides wherever he could.

chapter 45

Morrison and Peabody were on their way to Stonington Vineyards by 10:00 o'clock. Peabody read from his laptop, "It says here the vineyard is situated on fifty-eight pastoral acres and was established in 1987. The visionary owners were the founders of the Connecticut Wine Trail. Southeastern Connecticut offers a maritime microclimate for growing grapes, not unlike Bordeaux, France, due to the proximity of the Atlantic Ocean.

"Okay, boss, they offer award-winning wines and seven days of tastings. Are we trying any?" Morrison gave him a raised eyebrow that meant obviously not. Peabody added, "Who knew there are so many vineyards around here? This is my best day on the job; it's like a trip into paradise."

"Jack, enjoy your momentary daydream of wine and roses because it's the murders you have to wrap your head around today." Jack became somber as Morrison kept his focus on the three dead bodies in Dr. Storm's morgue.

After traversing the country roads, Stonington Vineyards appeared. It was a lovely modern building with patios and a gazebo to view the undulating vineyard. The men walked into a refined tasting room of contemporary architecture and met with the vintner and a few of the staff. They tried to determine the timeline of Stockman's last day alive, if there were any signs of suspicious activity, and if a man with Silver's description had been there. Having discovered only Stockman's arrival and departure time, the men moved on to their next interview.

At 11:00 a.m. the rural route took them to Jonathan Edwards Winery in North Stonington. As they turned a corner, a picturesque scene of bright white buildings with red roofs came into view. They were seamlessly interconnected in a traditional farmstead layout of New England architecture. Enveloping the buildings were broad lawns, graceful flower gardens, and sweeping vineyard fields.

Even though it was work, the detectives were now getting used to this new experience of vineyard hopping. They entered the tasting room, asked for the manager, and questioned the staff.

All had given the same impression of Stockman being an upstanding friendly individual who was a wealth of information on wine and willing to help out the business in any way he could. They were not aware of Stockman's private investments or any personal contacts.

Lastly, the elusive Mr. Silver was not identified. The friendly staff assured they could not imagine it would be the last time they would see Mitch Stockman as they helped him load his trunk with cases of their wine. The detectives, short of hard leads, made their way to Mitch's supposed last stop, Saltwater Farm Vineyards.

On the meandering drive, Morrison pondered aloud. "The vineyard business, Jack, seems to be a small world within a big world. The farming, growing, and harvesting is an undertaking and then they transfer over to processing equipment, stainless steel tanks, and oak barrels before the wine ever hits a bottle! Then they reach out to the world to sell their wine. These folks are so busy and hardworking. I don't see how they have time to be part of a murder."

Suddenly, an odd form came into view. "Are you sure we are in the right place, Jack? I don't think a hangar is what we are looking for."

"It is, actually," Jack confirmed as he did more research online. "I'm reading a write-up in *Ink Magazine*." Paraphrasing, Jack said, "The Connerys converted the 1930s World War II hangar into a winery. The property had evolved from a 1600s farmstead to an airport and then in 2003 to their vineyard.

They have a hundred acres, six grape varieties, and a vista of Long Island Sound.

"And look at this, boss," jokingly Jack teased, "it's a destination for weddings. You can check it out for when you meet Mrs. Right!"

Morrison wrinkled his face. "I certainly don't see you jumping on that bandwagon. So leave me out of it, will you?" Jack smirked, enjoying a tug on his boss's personal preference of bachelorhood. Morrison had revealed he had seen enough marriage destruction in his police work and didn't know if it was worth the complications.

Upon entering Saltwater Farm's tasting room, they first noticed the impressive architecture of the hangar; a huge thirty-foot ceiling arched overhead. The interior was a sleek construction of steel, wood, and stone. Its spacious layout had two levels and a large outdoor deck with a broad panoramic view of the vineyard and water. The detectives approached the tasting table and asked for the owner or persons who might have waited on Mitch Stockman. After many questions to the vintner and staff, and by showing the photos of the men in custody, a wine server realized he did see a man much like those in the photos.

"He ordered a bottle of wine and sat by that corner window," the wine server explained. "I noticed him because he seemed to be watching the vintner. Now I realize he may have been keeping an eye on Mitch, who met with the vintner over there," he pointed to a table.

By one o'clock, the men left the tranquil vista of Saltwater Farm Vineyard and sat in the SUV. "Jack, we've confirmed that Stockman was being watched. I wonder if Mr. Silver followed him all the way from Long Island. We have Stockman's movements from eight a.m. to twelve thirty p.m. when he arrived at the Vinho Verde. There seems to be a half hour or so missing in the timeline."

"Maybe he just drove around," Jack offered.

"I doubt that," Morrison answered. "Stockman's schedule was pretty tight. If he had something else on his agenda, we need to discover what it was."

Jack sifted through his notes with names, dates, and time frames. "I'll go over everything at headquarters, boss, and add these timelines on the boards. We'll keep narrowing it down. Someone knows this homicidal maniac; we just need a break."

As they drove away, Jack lightened his mood. "Boss, most people on the vineyard circuit would have had a few glasses of wine by now, and we haven't tasted a drop." He pretended to be disappointed and faked a frown.

Morrison laughed and added with mocked sincerity, "You can return when you're off duty, and I highly recommend the riesling with pepper jack cheese."

Jack tilted his head quizzically and chuckled, "You sound like Georgi!" They laughed knowing they were ignorant of both wine and cheese.

Upon returning to police headquarters, they checked for any new leads and buried themselves in phone calls and research over the next two hours.

Jack piped up, "Hey, boss, I have another lead. The computer forensic team in Long Island just called and found information on Stockman's desktop. It looks like he had a vineyard partner on Long Island who died a year ago, a man named Lester Williamson. Stockman owned a percentage of Williamson's vineyard, yet upon Stockman's death, the ownership reverted back to Williamson's wife.

"And there is more! Another partner to this vineyard is a man named Morelli. He's an international liquor distributor with local ties. He has a summer house on Long Island. So that's two more on our list to interview: Morelli and Williamson's wife."

Relieved, Morrison heralded, "Finally, something for us to go on!" It was after three thirty when he called Detective Jason Reuben at Southold police headquarters on Long Island. They both attended the police academy in Connecticut and had worked several years together before Reuben took a job on the force in Long Island.

Keeping his official protocol intact, Morrison greeted his friend. "Hello, Officer Reuben, it's Detective Morrison. I'm hoping you can check on two people for me on this case we are trying to crack."

Reuben responded, "Of course, Dan, that's what we're here for. Give me the details."

"A guy by the name of Morelli, he's an international businessman with a home in East Hampton. Also, check on this woman who owns Williamson Wines — Madeline Williamson. Her deceased husband, Lester, was partners with the deceased Mitch Stockman and this guy Morelli. I'll send you the write-up I have. Question her on their business dealings and relationships with her partners. If you sniff out any abnormalities, let me know."

"I'll interview them both in the afternoon," Reuben responded, "after I take care of some other police business. I'll contact you afterwards, and we can catch up over a burger and a beer. It would be good to see you, buddy."

"Thanks, Jason. I'm happy to provide and upgrade it to a surf and turf." Morrison, grateful for his comrades, found the priority of work always taking over his friendship time.

At four o'clock, after a full day of work, Morrison turned to Jack. "How about we grab a beer down the street, Jack? We've done all we can today."

"Sure thing, boss. After a day of visiting wineries, all I want is a beer." Morrison chuckled. The off-duty detectives walked the two blocks to Bank Street.

***

Since the 1700s, the bustling commerce of Bank Street had kept the bars open. Originally, they catered to sailors, whalers, and dockhands during New London's seafaring era, where legendary stories were layered upon each other like barnacles on a pier post in the Thames River. The 'City of Steeples' now beckoned those to Bank Street for fine dining, bistros, and beer gardens on decks overlooking the water.

Morrison and Peabody entered the relaxing interior of the wings and beer establishment and sat at a long, polished bar. The pair soon had their favorite brew in hand, a New London local beverage called Safe Harbor, created by the Thames River Greenery partners, Charlotte and Fred.

"I love this beer," declared Jack as he took a slug of the hop-heavy brew. "Aah, I think I'm a beer snob." He watched Morrison tip up his bottle. "Boss, the added bonus to this beer is the long-legged beauty on the bottle. We have something lovely to admire while we quench our thirst." They both smiled.

Dan finished his beer. "That tastes like another, Jack." Music from the Lovin' Spoonful's title song beat over the sound system, "Hot town, summer in the city…."

Clinking his refreshed brewski to Jack's, Dan offered a toast. "Before it gets any hotter in this city, here's to catching our killer, Jack."

"Tomorrow, boss. We'll get him tomorrow." Jack took a slug.

chapter 46

THE PAST - East Hampton, New York

Music by The Doors boomed over the speaker system of Arthur Morelli's luxury home in East Hampton, New York. The title song, "Riders on the Storm," echoed in the lyrics. It was about a killer on the road.

Stationed atop the widow's walk of his luxury summer home, Art Morelli stared out at the stormy sea. Dark clouds were looming on the horizon with a promise of heavy rains. He found the beat of the music and the strong winds exhilarating. His shirttails flayed about. His bronzed, weathered skin tingled, and his bushy gray hair stirred in the blustery weather.

This feeling of being alive high above the widow's tower was thrilling. He gripped the railing and rode the wind. The crashing sounds of the waves roared through him, surging into his heart of sixty-eight years. He felt like master and commander of a tall ship, high on adrenaline and negative ions.

Morelli, the son of a self-made, wealthy international spirits distributor, sucked in the sea air like a great fish. But it was the briny mix of life and death that vitalized him. He had crafted yet another lethal method to add to his family empire. Morelli's lifelong dream of securing ownership of the world's best wines was his constant end vision. Long Island's terroir and vineyards excited his secret desire to dominate another region of wines in the world.

The Morelli family had been well-known as international distributors of wine and liquor since 1945. Working in his father's business for decades, Art compulsively searched the world for the best of the best in wines. He invested in vineyards, while his father watched proudly. As a matter of course, Art finally inherited the Morelli Distribution enterprise at the age of forty-two. But by then, his greedy, crass behavior in the wine industry had him snubbed by the elite winemakers and connoisseurs.

Wine is patience in a bottle. Art Morelli was like many powerful men — impatient for results. He reconciled that wine growers and vintners were not cut from the same cloth as he. It took years to grow a vineyard and create a fine wine aged to perfection. Morelli's mindset was, 'Let everyone do the work for him.' He craved the power of an industrialist. So this mogul found another tactic: buy, don't grow; reap, don't sow.

His plan was to acquire controlling interests in established award-winning vineyards using ghost holding companies, assumed names, and umbrella corporations. Owners in vineyards and wineries were not aware of his involvement. He targeted growers who had a successful wine but still struggled with the cost of growth and overhead. Many growers often sought investors. Morelli's motive was to capture and grow his family business using this modus operandi. His spiel: to provide our discerning clientele with the finest of wines. His goal: invest, then own. Now one investment was about to be fermented, from fruit into wine and vineyard.

Morelli recalled with mirth his last conversation with Mitch Stockman. It was as clear as yesterday. He had made an overpriced offer to buy Mitch's holdings in the famous Williamson Wines of North Fork.

Mitch responded with disdain, "I will not have Lester and Madeline's vineyard fall into your hands. For God's sake, he's only been dead for a year, and you're hovering over Madeline like a salivating wolf. Her vineyard is fine without your heavy hand."

By way of being absolutely clear, Mitch huffed, "Let me remind you, for one, I don't like the way you do business, and no matter how high your offer goes, I will never agree to put my percentage of Williamson Wines with the likes of you. A silent partner is all you will ever be. I wish Lester had never responded to your investment offer. That is what put him in the grave with a heart attack, God bless him."

"Now, now, Stockman, don't disregard me so quickly," Morelli cautioned. "Eventually Madeline will tire of her duties as a business owner and will have visions of relaxing on a beach in the south of France instead of here in the Hamptons."

Mitch pursed his lips in disgust. "Your vision of being the controlling mogul who manipulates with strong-arm tactics will never see the light of day as long as I'm around."

Easily arranged, Morelli reflected with psychopathic fervor.

Mitch criticized him and charged, "The way I see it, you already have enough controlling advantage to unbalance wine distribution in New England. Your competitiveness is on the verge of becoming a monopoly."

Morelli starched his words. "Oh no, my friend, you misunderstand. My intent is a finer appreciation than you realize. I want to enhance the standards, upgrade the quality of wine across the board, and eliminate these low-priced wines. Of course, in the meantime, a fine profitable business venture doesn't hurt."

"I don't consider you my friend, Art," Mitch retorted. "Your father was my friend and respected mentor, and he was grievously mistaken to give you control. I suggest you take a look at his business handbook. I must decline your lucrative offer."

Morelli scoffed, "Well, don't let the bird in hand fly out the window. At least consider it."

Mitch stood strong, staring Morelli down. "I told Lester I would take care of Madeline. It is not just a business venture." Mitch noticed the air had chilled and decided to throw Morelli a bone. "Before I do anything, I need to do more research on the Morelli Corporation holdings. And you need to give Madeline more time, Art. She is not ready to sell."

Mitch knew Art Morelli was bad news. He had a funk about him like a bad wine cork. Having seen his greed firsthand on several occasions, Mitch knew the man was blinded by power and could not care less about the vineyard workers, vintners, and wine.

Morelli comprehended Mitch Stockman was not about to let go of Lester's award-winning vineyard. He knew Mitch was devoted to the grape and the people of the vine. Morelli met many men and women with this passion that could not be bought. Williamson Wines would have to be acquired another way. Mitch Stockman would be taken out of the equation.

An easy deed done by Silver, Morelli gloated, commending his advocate for a swift execution. He had the sense of sailing in the wind atop the widow's walk of his home. He mused, *Now Stockman is gone, and I am free! Free to play among the women and wine! Free to dance in the moonlit vineyards!* His wild imagination and adrenaline had him running naked through the undulating rows of Williamson Wines, soon to be in full possession.

***

The fresh news of Mitch's death had Morelli slyly visiting Marissa Stockman in the guise of a sympathetic vineyard owner. Knowing she was unfamiliar with Mitch's business affairs, he offered, "If there is anything I can do to relieve your stress, I will. I'm here for you. I can help you get through the harvest season. I'll review Mitch's books and files and assist you anyway I can. You can unburden yourself on me."

Marissa graciously appreciated his concern for her. "Oh no, everything is in New London. The business is going to Georgi. Mitch knew I didn't want anything to do with it." Morelli's eyes widened when he realized he was done with her. His eagle-eye focus on Lester and Madeline's vineyards was still a moving target.

The ruthless Morelli's next arrow was now aimed at the business files Mitch may have had on him. Mr. Silver had not found them in the condominium or at the Vinho Verde Wine Bar. Nabbing those files before Georgi eyed them was paramount to eliminating suspicions of his business practices. He would assure Mr. Silver's quiver of arrows remained fully stocked so he could complete the clandestine operation.

chapter 47

MITCH'S LAST DAY – 8:00 a.m.

On the day of his murder, Mitch Stockman arrived in New London at 8 a.m. on the vehicle ferry, the *Mary Ellen*. He drove off the ferry in his Mercedes-Benz SUV and traveled eastward to Ledyard and Stonington for several vineyard appointments.

Enjoying the fresh morning air, he walked through the vineyards, looking for the promise of the juicy jewels that would feed his thirst in the months to come. He lightly bantered with the vintners and tasted their selections.

Before opening a bottle, Mitch would look it over for its general appearance, legibility of label, and size of air space. As a discerning buyer, he held the wine bottle up and looked through its neck to observe the vintage's clarity and at the conical punt on the base to detect the wine's brilliance. Once poured, he deeply breathed in the bouquet, hoping to be enticed to taste this fresh decant.

Pressing the glass to his lips, he cherished that moment, the very moment that promised instant gratification. On tasting, he savored, then assessed, the balance between sweetness, acidity, and astringency. He was determining whether it was vinous and invigorating with a sufficient bite. Satisfied with his choices, Mitch purchased several cases from each location — some were to be delivered and some loaded into his SUV.

His next destination was Stonington Borough, which occupied a point of land that projected into Little Narragansett Bay. Mitch adored the escape he felt upon entering the Borough, like arriving into another era of time. He found the historic charm embraced him as tall branching trees swept over the narrow streets filled with the sweet scent of the sea. He drove past grand sea captains' homes, period houses, and colonial architecture exhibiting old-world regalia. The large granite stoops seemed to welcome him and pledged exquisite interiors within.

Mitch had read that during the American Revolution in 1775, Stonington Borough was barraged by a British fleet that the residents stalwartly fought off their shores. Two hundred years later, a replica of the attack ship, the *HMS Rose*, was built in 1970 and later modified and used in two films, *Master and Commander: The Far Side of the World and Pirates of the Caribbean: On Stranger Tides*.

These corridor streets of Stonington Borough now welcomed the owners of sailing yachts, kayakers, boaters, and diving day-trippers. Fishermen still worked the waters for Stonington scallops, lobster, and fish right from the bay and the sound.

Yet on this day, the handsome wine expert had a special mission planned. Mitch drove down Water Street, passing the boutique shops and savory fare restaurants, parked the car, and strolled with a spring in his step into a jewelry store. The shop owner was anticipating Mitch's morning visit.

"How are you, my friend?" asked Orlando the owner. Reaching out his hand, he clasped Mitch's with both of his. Excitedly, he announced, "Your wife's ring is ready. The size is now a perfect six and a half. She will be so surprised!"

"Thank you, Orlando. I'm looking forward to giving it to her. Marissa would have found out about it if I had it resized in Long Island. She knows everyone, and my surprise would have been ruined. I'm grateful my friends at the Water Street Café here recommended you."

"I have the ring in the safe," Orlando said by way of assurance. He stepped into the back room to retrieve it and while he was absent, the bell on the door jingled as another customer entered. Mitch noticed a well-dressed man in a tailored silk gray suit, dark turquoise tie, and expensive Italian shoes. The gentleman nodded to Mitch.

"Good morning," he said with a slight, nondescript accent.

"Good morning," Mitch responded.

The gentleman asked, "Would this be the right place to have a diamond bracelet resized? My fiancé is so petite, it is falling off her wrist."

Mitch understood what the man was asking. *Could the jeweler be trusted with an expensive item?* "Oh yes, Orlando is a certified jeweler and has been here for many years. He just resized an anniversary ring for my wife."

The gentleman thanked him and waited. When Orlando returned, he saw the new customer and said, "Mitch, please come into my office." Then he told the customer, "I'll be with you very soon, sir."

Mitch stepped behind the counter and slipped into Orlando's work area that housed large magnifiers, special lighting, and a bench meticulously lined with instruments of the trade.

"Here, take a look at this," Orlando said, handing Mitch the magnifying glasses he wore. "See, on the back it says, 'Forever My Love.'"

Mitch was pleased. "I'm so glad you suggested inserting a special message. She is going to love it."

Orlando laughed. "Mitch, my friend, this ring is seven-point-nine carats! There is plenty of room to inscribe on the back of such a rare pink diamond like this! Oh my my! In all my life, I have not seen anything like it! I did my research and found there is only one mine in Australia. It's called the Argyle, and it produces some of the best flawless pink diamonds. There is the famous Pink Star from this mine that is fifty-nine-point-six carats and was auctioned for over eighty-three million dollars. *Buono fortunata*! You have honored me by letting me work on your one-of-a-kind treasure. *Multo grazie*, thank you."

"Well, this one is quite smaller, just shy of a million," Mitch stated. "I was *buono fortunata* to have found it for Marissa; she will enjoy showing it off." Mitch smiled broadly, "I thank you, Orlando, for having it ready in time for our anniversary."

Just then, the shop bell rang. "It's a busy morning," Orlando exclaimed and stepped to the doorway of his office to see who else was there. "Oh, he is gone," Orlando murmured.

"I think he will be back," Mitch declared. "He said he needed to resize a diamond bracelet."

"Very good," said Orlando. "Here is your receipt, Mr. Mitch, and I wish you all the best."

Mitch put the receipt in his inside pocket, then had a thought, "I'll be right back...hold onto the ring." He ran out to his SUV, opened a cooler, and grabbed a bottle of wine. Returning, he offered it. "Orlando, this is one of my favorite wines with pasta, shrimp, and a fra diavolo sauce. It's a lovely Lu Rappaio Primitivo, an Italian zinfandel."

"*Grazie*, thank you," Orlando nodded with honor. "And here is your ring in its lovely case."

Mitch slipped the ring box into his inside jacket pocket, shook hands with Orlando, and was off. Sitting in his vehicle, he patted the ring in his chest pocket. He adjusted his rearview mirror and saw the man in the jewelers cross the street and step into a silver sedan. Mitch started his engine and continued to the end of Water Street for a quick look at Stonington Harbor. He admired the Old Lighthouse Museum and parked at the point. The high tide surf crashed on the granite boulders that retained the big shoreline view out to Watch Hill, Rhode Island, and beyond to the Atlantic Ocean.

Mitch made a call to his next stop, Stonington Vineyards, to say when he'd be arriving. He was unaware of the man in the silver sedan curving round the parking lot, observing him, and slowly leaving.

***

Evening of Demise

Mitch Stockman strode down Bank Street whistling a tune. The evening's wine dinner at the Vinho Verde had gone extremely well. He felt confident that while he took the summer off with Marissa, he could leave the business in Georgi's capable hands.

Arriving at Harlow Towers, Mitch met up with his friend Tony for an espresso at the bistro on the ground floor.

Under the stars and on the patio, they enjoyed their coffee and enthusiastically encouraged each other's businesses in New London. The new Coast Guard Museum was about to boost tourism and their incomes too. When Tony bid him a good-night, Mitch stood up, stretched, and took in a deep breath.

Fancying a short stroll, he admired the up-lit face of the Columbus statue and stepped across the sidewalk. He circled the dimly lit garden to the back of the statue in shadow. He looked up into the canopy of the grand old tree whose scraggly branches caught muted light and appeared like widow's fingers grasping for the stars.

While Mitch stared upwards, he suddenly felt off balance. His mind tried to catch up to why he was falling.

He reached out as he pitched forward and found himself against the back of the statue where he braced himself against the stone, staying on his feet. Swiftly, he realized someone had shoved him, so he pushed off the statue towards his assailant.

Pivoting perfectly, Mitch surprised the attacker with a left hook that sent the aggressor reeling backward. The dark figure was at a disadvantage.

The two opponents were still in the shadow behind Columbus's sixteen-foot stature when the mugger came back at Mitch like a bull. He tackled him at the waist, bulldozing him into Columbus's marble foundation. Mitch hit the back of his head yet fought with all he had. The foe, the illusive Mr. Silver, was now at an advantage. He swiftly turned Mitch toward the statue, pinning him with his knee. Then with hit man precision grabbed his head and twisted his neck. Mitch went limp.

Morelli's advocate rifled through Mitch's pockets, then cursed. He quickly grabbed a handful of the yew shrub that Mitch laid in and stuffed the toxic plant in his mouth, ensuring his death. Frantically, he scrounged around in the dirt to find his bonus. Loudly, a passing car's sound system broadcasted the song "Mercy" by Shawn Mendes. There had been no mercy for Mitch Stockman on this night.

Chapter 48

Georgi, a self-professed neatnik, was at Vinho Verde cleaning, dusting and being frustrated. He was trying to stay busy while he waited to hear if Detective Morrison had caught the actual killer.

Motivating himself to feel better, he turned on his sound system and played "Safe and Sound" by Capital Cities. When he noticed the studio album title, *In a Tidal Wave of Mystery*, Georgi snickered at the irony. "Welcome to my life," he murmured.

Intent on his hygienic practices, he decided to clean and ran a disinfectant cloth over the stainless steel prep area of the bar. To the beat of the music, he sang and danced as he moved the cloth over and around the cash drawer to the storage area below it.

Unexpectedly, his hand encountered a slim, hard edge deep in the cubbyhole. Quickly bending down, he saw nothing, so he reached into the recess. Surprised, he pulled out a black laptop computer.

"Uhh, this is Mitch's!" he gulped. Opening it, he suddenly felt like an intruder into Mitch's private sanctum. A back and forth banter ensued in Georgi's mind between curiosity and fear. Finally, he stopped his mental and emotional rumination, turned off the music, and made a call.

"Roxanne!" he yelped into the receiver. "I just found Mitch's laptop under the bar! What do I do?"

Rubbing her ear, she put him on speaker and yelled at the phone. "What? Oh my God, Georgi! We may finally have a break. I'll be right there."

Roxanne raced for her purse, ran out the door, and took the five-minute drive from her house to Bank Street. She wished and hoped along the way the whole thing would be over with soon.

On arrival, she urged him, "Go ahead, what are you waiting for? Open it up, Georgi! See what's in there!"

He stared at the laptop, immobilized. "I'm scared. What if we don't want to know what's in here? What if we we're intruding?" He whined, "I'm so confused, uhh." His will was withering.

Roxanne pressed him, "We have to know now!"

"I'm so nervous. I'm wound tighter than a string. Do you think this is the right thing to do? Shouldn't we call Detective Morrison?" he implored.

"No!" she said loudly, and Georgi jumped. "Let's strum that string and find out what's in this damn laptop! Then maybe we'll know who's playing with us and what to do. If we give it to the detective now, we may never know what's inside," pleaded Roxanne. "Don't delay, Georgi. We've come too far. Think, will you? Mitch would want us to find his killer."

Georgi moaned, so Roxanne added with a motherly influence, "Let's imagine we are Mitch's private investigators. We have to help Detective Dan. He has nothing to go on, and this guy has been hiring local people off the street and in the library to do his dirty work. He uses decoys in gray suits and silver sedans. In the end, Dan has no leads, just people who are paid a hundred-dollar bill here and there to drive a car or pick up an envelope."

She attempted to appeal to Georgi's compassionate side. "Poor Dan has nothing. Everyone is breathing down his neck. We have to help him," she beseeched him with her best attempt.

Georgi had listened intently. "Oh, the killer is marrying his mistakes, blending the group to make a finer wine."

"What are you talking about?" Roxanne was baffled by his response.

"Well, it's like wine, darling," Georgi countered elegantly. "A vintner can start with an initial wine that may come out too acidic. But if blended with a sweet, say fruity wine, they call that marrying your mistakes. You put an average wine with a good wine, and sometimes you get a great wine. So that's what this mastermind has been doing. He takes some average people off the street and pairs them with his smart plan. He's made an ingenious diversion and a series of calculated tricks to confuse the cops. He doesn't get caught, his pawns do, and they know nothing. It's a perfect blend."

"Oh," Roxanne uttered dryly, now remembering to whom she was speaking. "Okay, you view the world through rosé colored glasses" she found herself quipping, yet she was exasperated. Her hands animated her words as her voice swelled. "I'm talking about the antics of a murderer, and you attribute it to winemaking! I give up!" She looked toward the ceiling hoping for help from any willing angel.

He loudly interrupted her quiet prayer. "Of course, it's all about the wine, darling! However else shall we see the world?" Teasing her, he gestured with one hand rising slowly into the air, as if holding a helium balloon. Roxanne's eyes followed his hand upward. Then, as if released from its tether, his hand gracefully floated downward and dramatically. He tapped the enter key on the keyboard of the laptop.

Sure enough, Mitch had his business files here. Some were labeled vineyards and vintners, others were labeled distributors, and some were labeled wine favorites. Then he came across one file labeled Morelli International Distributors. Georgi's forehead crinkled. "I don't believe Mitch liked him much," he muttered. Applying his instincts, he pressed the key to open the file. It had several subdirectories of multiple documents, links, and images.

Georgi clicked one, and up came a Morelli site describing the company with its marketing methods and such. "They are one of the top four distributors in the world," he clarified.

Roxanne wondered aloud. "Why would he bother to have all this information on Morelli Distributors?"

Georgi narrowed his eyes and winced, as if in pain. "This looks suspicious. Maybe we've gone far enough." He rubbed his temple, recalling the blow to his head. "Let's call the detective," he urged.

"Georgi!" Roxanne yipped. "It's time you grow the balls of a bull!" She made a fist.

Georgi squealed, "Oh!" and his eyes grew large.

She accused him, "Don't look at me with eyes like crème bombes!"

"Oh ho ho!" Georgi exclaimed. "If I had crème bombes, we would be eating them with a good pinot noir from Burgundy, France," Georgi teased. Crème bombes were one of his favorites, individual chocolate cakes with a white custard center.

Dramatically, he tapped the keyboard again. "How's this?" Another file opened and zoomed forward on the screen. "Uh, look! These are all the companies that Morelli has holdings in. I thought he was only a distributor. Why does Mitch have all this detail on him here?" Georgi was now intrigued.

"See what else there is," Roxanne pressed.

Georgi clicked the keys without hesitation. "Here's Williamson's Wines, vintners on Long Island, one of Mitch's favorites...." Georgi's voice trailed off, then he murmured, "It's a shame Lester died."

"He died?" Roxanne exclaimed. "When? I'm not taking any death for granted."

"Oh!" Georgi gasped. "Just over a year ago. Oh my!" His face became morbid like Melpomene's, the Greek muse of tragedy. "Do you think it's connected?"

"Yes, I do," Roxanne answered emphatically.

Georgi hypothesized, "Mitch could have been onto something about Morelli."

"Who owns that vineyard now?" she posed.

"His wife Madeline, I think," he responded.

"Look it up!" she commanded.

Georgi searched for Williamson Wines. "Here is their webpage. I'll go to the tab that says 'About Us.'" Georgi read a historical review of the owners and the vineyard.

"It says here, 'Lester and Madeline Williamson have owned their vineyards of fifty acres in the north fork since 1980. Lester developed the land into vineyards, which were originally potato fields. In 1988, vintners from Bordeaux, France, were invited to advise the North Fork vintners on how to work with their climate and terroir. They reviewed which grapes were the best varieties and how to trim the vines and leaves for the best sun exposure. The goal was to harvest more mature fruit for a complex and flavorsome wine.

"'In 1995, Williamson Wines started winning awards for their wines, first with a reserve merlot, then expanding to their chardonnay, sparkling rosé, and cabernet. Sadly, Lester passed away a year ago, and Madeline oversees vineyard operations with her sister, Camilla.'"

"Is that all?" Roxanne asked.

"That's all, other than photos and their wines for sale," Georgi answered.

"Well, that's not enough information," she declared.

Georgi leaned back in his seat and stretched. "This doesn't make sense. Mitch wouldn't have all these files on Morelli for no reason." He clicked back to Mitch's files, opening one attachment after another until he found a Morelli Distributor's holdings list. "Here it shows Williamson Wines, and that Morelli is a twenty-five percent silent owner with a stipulation of reimbursement plus earnings. That's it!" Georgi jumped off his seat and raised his arms.

"I think we've found something that links Morelli, Lester, and Mitch." Roxanne proudly beheld her new private eye protégé.

"Uh, I forgot!" Georgi admitted, "Mitch invested in Lester's vineyard in the early 1990s. And he mentioned that in 1997, Morelli had made Lester an offer to help him financially. Lester took the offer and later wished he had not, as

Morelli was disagreeable and trying to force marrying his Finger Lake wines with Lester's." Georgi's curiosity and adrenalin were in full flow. "Let's find out what else Morelli owns!" He scrolled through the screens, searching further into Mitch's notes.

"Look, Mitch has listed all the vineyards where Morelli is the owner or major shareholder: Italy, Spain, Portugal, Chile, Argentina, California, Oregon, plus the Finger Lakes in New York. Wow! Mitch went to a lot of effort to figure this out. This means Morelli's distribution can be sourced from the companies he owns rather than equally among the wines he represents as a distributor! Mitch found evidence that Morelli can manipulate wine markets. No wonder he documented all this research."

"Georgi, do you think Morelli found out that Mitch was suspicious of his business practices? And maybe there's a connection to Lester's death? We have to be careful. This is much bigger than we could have imagined. Now, we really need to talk to Dan!" Roxanne readied to make the call.

"Wait!" Georgi shouted. "Look, Mitch writes here he suggested to Lester that they speak with a lawyer and find a loophole to set up a trust for the fifty percent share Lester owned and protect it. Williamson's Wines was looking like Morelli's next target for takeover."

"Wow!" Roxanne called out. "We are finally onto something, Georgi."

Jumping off his seat with hands on hips, Georgi paced the floor, strutting in his naturally fashionable way. Thinking aloud, he speculated, "But it doesn't make sense that they bothered you and me because we don't know anything. And why the blackmailing and killing? I'm confused."

Sitting again, he read on. "Mitch has in his notes that he never imagined Lester would die at sixty-four or that the greedy monster Morelli would stalk a vineyard owner. Early in the year 2001, Lester had to lie to Morelli to appease him. He led Morelli to believe he may sell his controlling interest to him. Yet in 2009, after one of Lester's vintages won a ninety-six point acclaim, Morelli tried again to buy him out. Lester refused and became disgruntled with Morelli's push. Morelli was unable to a buyout.

"After Lester's death, Mitch says he hired a private investigator and did his own research on Morelli. He wanted to prove if Lester's death was suspicious, even though it was deemed a heart attack."

Georgi leapt off the chair and shook his hands as if electrically shocked. "Oh my God, Roxanne! All Morelli wanted was to take the spoils like a pirate. This slimeball is a land shark in Bermuda shorts! What are we to do?" he pleaded.

The image of a suntanned man smelling of musk cologne in Bermuda shorts ran through Roxanne's mind. She shook her head to release it. Struggling to understand the scale of Morelli's operation, she expressed the now obvious. "No wonder this is complicated."

Horror began to sink in when she realized the worst. "Georgi, how did this man acquire all those vineyards? Did any of their owners die? Is he able to hide what he is doing under 'legal business practices?' Are these professional criminals? It's time to call Detective Dan!" she spouted.

"But wait," Georgi urged, holding up one finger as if to say 'give me a minute.' Deep in thought and eyes stationary, he stared up at the large hand-hewn beams overhead.

Roxanne looked up too, then back at Georgi, then to a statue behind him. *That statue looks like Georgi,* Roxanne mused. *Oh, silly me. It's Dionysus, the Greek god of wine.* Becoming impatient, Roxanne stared at him in suspended anticipation. "Yes?" she said loudly. Georgi's Dionysus stance came to life and circled about, pacing the floor as his shoes resounded on them. With an edgy tone, she animated, "These pine planks haven't seen this much traffic in a hundred years. Come on, this is serious, Georgi! We have enough information to bring to Detective Dan now!"

She was interrupted by a loud stomp as Georgi's heel hit the floorboards. "I have it, Roxanne!" He marched toward her grasping her shoulders. "We're going to Williamson Wines in Long Island!"

"What! Why?" Roxanne gasped.

"We have to talk to Madeline, and we have to do it in person. And we have to go now!"

"Now? I'm not going now!" she protested.

Georgi dramatically leaned toward her and said warmly, "But darling, you must. It is the only way we will find out why Mitch and possibly Lester were murdered. Why I was beaten up, and why you were mugged, and why there is a dead boy named J.J."

Roxanne's eyes grew wide as she listened to Georgi's strategy.

"We can leave immediately," he urged. "We'll take my car, and we'll pretend to be going on wine business. It's not even nine thirty, so we can board the ten o'clock ferry and be there by eleven thirty. We will arrive at Madeline's by noon or so and catch the return ferry at three p.m. You'll be home in time for dinner, I promise." He laid his hand over his heart.

Roxanne's eyes narrowed. "Georgi, what's gotten into you? We can't just take off. What do I tell Sam? And what about your business?"

"I'll put a sign on the door, 'Closed — Will Reopen Soon.' Everyone knows about Mitch; I need not explain. And Sam, well that's your department. Where does he usually think you are?"

"Oh, gardening of course."

"And do you garden all day long?" Georgi asked, tilting his head knowingly.

"Sometimes...." her voice trailed off as she considered this clandestine caper running wild in Georgi's head. "Is this a good idea?" She was tentative about following Georgi's lead. She was the one often dragging others along on hers.

Georgi responded, "We don't know exactly, but that's the point, isn't it?

We need more information to definitely prove Morelli is behind all of this."

Continuing to sell his idea, he added, "How about this? You are doing a consultation for someone, and you'll be back for supper. That's no lie! You are consulting for me!"

"Oh, Georgi," she hummed, reasoning that meeting with Madeline may be helpful, and at the moment, they only had a list of unverified theories. And sure, Dan could investigate them, but maybe one more piece of information wouldn't hurt. Decidedly, she said, "I'll do it! What do we need to bring?"

Georgi listed, "I'll bring the laptop and office items," and suggested, "why don't you run to Muddy Waters for coffee. I'll pick you up at their front door in five minutes."

Roxanne made a beeline for the door, then stopped, turned around, and wondered aloud to him, "Who are you, and what did you do with the meek and mild Georgi?"

Smiling broadly, he held up his fist. "Balls of the bull, Roxy!" She laughed and left.

chapter 49

Roxanne was waiting at the curb with goodies in hand as Georgi pulled up in his burgundy PT Cruiser. With the drink tray balanced on her lap, she hung on tight as they swerved past the historic red brick Union Train Station and the waterfall of the Whale Tail fountain. With great anticipation, they arrived at the ferry terminal building.

Georgi had texted and confirmed with Madeline Williamson that he was coming for a visit. While he put his car in the lineup, Roxanne ran into the ferry office to buy the tickets with his credit card. Returning, she hopped into the car just as they started to load the ferry. The dockhands waved them aboard.

"I hope we know what we're doing, Georgi." She gripped his hand, and he held hers tightly. They looked at each other and laughed. He squeezed tighter and said, "Don't worry, Roxanne. We'll be back before anyone notices we're gone. This isn't *Thelma and Louise*."

Her eyes grew wide, and she cried out, "Georgi! We'd better be back!" He giggled at his own gusto.

***

Neither of them knew that their clandestine mission was being watched by one of Silver's stooges who, at this moment, was on the phone reporting their whereabouts.

"Yeah, hey, Mr. Silver. Ya told me there would be another Benjamin in it for me if I found out something new. Well, I've got it for ya. That guy in the PT Cruiser and his blonde lady friend just boarded the ferry to Long Island. Just thought that would be bonus material for the both of us."

Silver snickered, "*Buono*, good job, boy. That'll get you a Benjamin."

With a click to end the call, Silver's flunky raised his fist, cheering his own windfall.

***

Once the PT Cruiser was parked in the belly of the ferry, Roxanne and Georgi took their goodies to the top deck and sat on a bench in the open air, admiring a beautiful 360-degree view. Being three stories above the water they overlooked New London, Groton, and the Thames River. They nibbled on their crisp tarts and sipped coffee.

"Isn't this nice?" Georgi asked, cozying up to Roxanne's shoulder.

"Yes, we're so high. And look, you really do notice several of the church steeples from here."

Towering spires of granite, brownstone, brick, and wood pierced the sky. Roxanne explained to Georgi, "The original namesake of the city will always be 'The Whaling City,' but many, including whale enthusiasts, were pleased to coin a new one and so 'the City of Steeples' has been proposed. We'll see if it passes the muster."

"No matter what the muster says," Georgi added, "I like it. It elevates the city to higher ground." He nudged her, pleased with his intended pun.

Nearby, competing for air space and a paradox to steeples, a twenty-first century feature scraped the sky. On the roof of a 1950s building was a crowded metal tower with a collection of computer age antennas, satellite dishes, and cellular components. Roxanne looked at it as a necessary eyesore.

Continuing their gaze across the panorama, colorful tugboats were lined along the shore, ready for work. In the background, the Gold Star Memorial Bridge massively spanned the Thames River into Groton.

Roxanne exclaimed, "Everything looks different up here on the deck. See the obelisk and Fort Griswold over there?" she pointed. "There's a lot of history crammed into this area. I guess that's why the new water taxi is doing

232

well as a sightseer's dream ride."

One could see the Groton Monument obelisk rise up near the green acreage of the fort's river battery. A small tunnel inside the mound allowed one to peer out, like the revolutionists, through a stone archway to the sparkling river below.

Fort Griswold was the second landing of the turncoat Benedict Arnold's troops. In a 1781 massacre, Colonel Ledyard and eighty men were killed after they surrendered their weapons. The museum at the base of the obelisk honors this memory with many artifacts from the farmers and colonists.

Announcements crackled over the ferry's loudspeaker, and the horns bellowed for takeoff. Jolted by the abrupt sounds, Roxanne giggled.

"Whoa! I'm not used to all this excitement!" Standing up, she clutched the rail to watch their departure. A surreal shift occurred in Roxanne's vision as the ship slowly moved away from the dock. Looking over the rail, she watched the water swirl and foam gather far below under the engine's surge. A cloud of diesel fumes puffed through the air and passed by her, making her feel a little dizzy. Simultaneously, she was blinded as the boat turned toward the bright southeast sun. She gripped the railing tighter. The mixing of new sounds and sensations with the impromptu adventure had her feeling off. She focused on the shoreline.

A fresh breeze moved across her face as Georgi came to her side. "Isn't it lovely?" he mused happily.

"I'm just finding my sea legs," she revealed. "Being a gardening girl, I'm more comfortable standing on soil than moving water."

"Don't worry," he encouraged her, "you will steady in a minute. And I promise you, when we are in North Fork, you'll be immersed in gardens and vineyards." He nudged her. "Look over here." As cargo ships, sailboats, and motorboats glided along the river, Georgi pointed at a black navy submarine mounted in its dry dock.

"Oh my," Roxanne resounded, "I've only seen them slink by in the sound. It's a huge boat out of the water!" Strolling across the deck, they caught a view of the impressive Coast Guard's tall ship, the *Barque Eagle*, on display at its own dock. Consecutively, the New London City Pier had the grand 1840s whaling ship, the *Charles W. Morgan*, available for tours.

Georgi spotted the wall of cannons facing the sound at Fort Trumbull. "Those cannons look ready to fire. We probably could use those on our side." He nudged her humorously. Roxanne recalled her angry thoughts of war just days earlier. *So much has happened since then...and it's not over yet,* she mused.

The breeze was blowing Roxanne's hair about. She looked at Georgi. "So what's the story? Not one hair on your head is out of place!"

He smiled. "The ancient secret is aloe vera gel to set my hair, and the modern secret is hairspray to hold it."

"Aloe vera? That's a good tip." She considered, "If people really understood how dependent we are on plants, they might give the planet a little more respect instead of taking it all for granted."

"Oh, look!" someone called out. Rapidly coming into view and hugging the shoreline was the brilliant white octagon spire of New London Harbor Lighthouse. "It's so handsome from here, and look at the lightkeeper's house," Roxanne admired. "I wish everyone could see this view. It is totally different from driving by it on the road."

The ferry continued advancing toward Neptune and Ocean Beach. As it headed into Long Island Sound, what at first appeared to be a tiny lighthouse in the distance came into full view once they were upon it. The majestic Ledge Light rose as the four-story guardian between the Thames River and the sound.

Roxanne confided, "Lighthouses represent hope to me, Georgi, so let's hope we are motoring toward a new future where we can return with solid evidence for the detective to break this case."

Georgi added with vigor, "Evidence that catches that heartless killer."

Roxanne looked up into Georgi's blue eyes and saw a determination she had not witnessed before. It was confidence. He was starting to believe in himself, and it looked good on him.

"Fresh breezes, Roxanne. Soon we will have our lives back." He cupped her hand. "Don't worry, Thelma, we'll be fine."

She sheepishly smiled, hoping he was right. She looked back at New London. *Here I am on a secret mission. It's a good thing Sam's busy with the president's visit today. At least I'll be back by supper.* She sighed and convinced herself. *Sam will understand.* Roxanne looked out over the water. *All I want is peace back in my life.*

Although encouraged by the hope of new evidence, she knew the possibility of peace was held delicately on the wind of their journey. This positive desire propelled her across sparkling waters toward sandy shores with vibrant vineyards and land sharks in Bermuda shorts.

chapter 50

In one hour, the motorcade for the president of the United States would arrive on the grounds of the Coast Guard Academy in New London. Connecticut's governor, senators, and numerous officials stood by, ready to greet the president and shake his hand in an official photo opportunity. News was being made, and the press were waiting to report it.

***

Meanwhile at police headquarters, Detective Morrison was up to his neck with three murders, buying time before releasing the information on the death of Charlie Brass and planning to withhold the connection to Mr. Silver. The president was leaving by one p.m., and the detective was very concerned to maintain a static state of suspended reality until the president's plane left. Morrison's hope was 'nothing new, no emergencies, no urgencies, and definitely no murders.'

Assistant Detective Jack Peabody was fielding calls in response to the $5,000 reward offered in the newspaper and poster notices for information on Stockman's demise and the whereabouts of anyone suspicious. Morrison expected they would be busy all day interviewing these informants. Meanwhile, one of the research experts investigated Morelli International Distributors on the computer.

Looking forward, Morrison was anxious to hear from his colleague on Long Island, Detective Jason Reuben, and his results from the interviews with Mrs. Williamson and Mr. Morelli.

***

The unlikelihood of Morrison ever discovering the background of Mr. Silver was high. Having worked in the undercover field for decades, Silver was an infamous secret silencer. His job was to assure covert success. In the past, Silver had been in the Italian Secret Service but had become a double agent and gone rogue in an undercover project called Operation Gladio with the Military of Defense. The job was far-reaching into the depths of an international underworld. He was what was known as a ghost: a legendary invisible hit man that could appear anywhere at any time and extinguish anyone.

Once Gladio dissolved, he slipped into civilian life yet stayed connected to the underworld where he was known for his talents. Eventually, he met Art Morelli.

Silver's special skills and complete discretion were rewarded well by Morelli and with an open-ended expense account, his lust for the good life was satisfied. With each triumph, his ego grew, and he relished the ease of manipulating unsuspecting targets. Most of all, he prided himself in his obscure trademark of death. He had gained from the forests and fields the secret knowledge of poisonous plants. Coupled with his intelligence and multiple methods of annihilation, he could assure a final take down with a handful of weeds.

Chapter 51

After traveling over an hour, the ferry captain announced they were passing Plum Island Lighthouse. Once it came into Roxanne and Georgi's view, he jumped from the bench and crooned, "Ooh, couldn't we hold a lovely party there? I love buildings made of stone. It's so handsome and strong."

Roxanne teased him, "All you think about is dressing up and entertaining. You're so funny!"

More of his dramatic flair emerged as he used the rail to steady himself and used his other hand expressively. "You know, it's in my genes! When your family makes wine, you have to come up with ways to enjoy it. That means having people over, eating some great food, and having fun. That's how I enjoy life. The party is in me; it has to come out! It's the only way I know how to be." He batted his eyelashes, leaned toward Roxanne, and added in a lower tone, "I'm lucky I'm paid to do this."

"If you were paid enough," she offered, "you could buy the island. I heard it's up for sale."

A sudden jolt went through Georgi as he straightened and considered the option. A little fairylike glimmer crossed his face. "I'm going to look it up." He pulled out his phone and zeroed in on the details of the building's history.

"It says here, 'The light from this striking two-story granite home is fifty-five feet tall. In 1826, Plum Island was originally purchased for ninety dollars, and a light was placed atop a thirty-five-foot stone pillar. In 1869, the current lighthouse was built. Refurbishing of this antique beauty is being considered by the town of Southold.'"

Georgi smiled, having enjoyed a momentary dreamscape. He read further, "Oh, the government owns it now," he said flatly, "and they want a million dollars. Forget it! I would have gladly paid ninety dollars." With a wave of his hand, he dismissed the whole idea.

Roxanne pointed to the water. "Look at all the fishermen!" Their boats were anchored in the churning waters, adroitly positioned in Plum Gut, between Plum Island and Long Island, where it was known for great fishing. Roxanne pulled out her phone and started taking pictures. Georgi smiled at her, knowing these were the first of many now that she was becoming used to the camera option.

The ferry captain informed over the speaker system, "Gardiner's Island is to our left in the distance. It is still owned by the Gardiner family, but the current population is ospreys, seagulls, and swallows."

"Oh, Georgi," Roxanne exclaimed, "I have an interesting story you might like. It's a love story about Gardiner Island."

"Do tell." With a hand gesture, he swiveled toward her. She had captured his full attention.

"I read this in a book about Connecticut history and the famous Griswold family. The Gardiners, who settled the island in the 1600s, had made a deal with the notorious Captain William Kidd, allowing him to stash his treasure on their shores. It was reported he unloaded chests of gold, emeralds, rubies, and diamonds. Kidd offered Gardiner's wife a bolt of gold cloth for their goodwill. But Lord Gardiner secured extra payment by secreting away a diamond in a well bucket, and the buccaneers were never the wiser.

"The diamond stayed in the family coffers. Now fast-forward to the early 1800s when a sailing party of young men and women, organized by Sarah Griswold from Old Lyme, was becalmed far out in Long Island Sound.

"As the day wore on, a sudden gale swooped in from the west and forced

239

the group into a safe cove at Gardiner Island. The rain poured so fiercely, they immediately raced toward the house to take refuge. Drenched and shaken, the housekeeper took them in to dry their clothes. Soon the handsome, young Lord Gardiner made an appearance."

Georgi interrupted, "Stop right there. I'm imaging the handsome, young lord and the drenched party." Georgi's eyes were raised to the sky. "Okay, I have them pictured. Go on." His hand flitted at her as he beamed with excitement, waiting for love to enter the story.

Roxanne smiled at his amusement. "This young man's name was John Gardiner, the seventh lord of the manor, and he had dry clothes brought for Sarah Griswold and her group and insisted they stay for supper. Of course, as one thing led to another, music and dancing followed. The charmed refugees stayed the night at the manor and left in the morning, bidding their new friend farewell. Although Sarah sailed away, John Gardiner's heart had become smitten with her.

"Sarah was a spirited beauty and the granddaughter of Governor Matthew Griswold. Soon enough, John Gardiner came to court her, and beached upon the shores of the Griswold home in a splendid barge of his own. In family lore, they say he presented her with Captain Kidd's diamond in hopes she would take him seriously and marry him. It sealed the deal, and they were married in 1803. They settled back on Gardiner Island to where the wind had blown her to her destiny. And two great families from Connecticut and New York were united," Roxanne smiled.

Georgi sighed, "Oh, that was lovely, Roxanne. Pirates and diamonds and love, oh my! I doubt Captain Kidd ever missed that diamond with all the booty he had. And just think what a perfect gesture to promise your love."

Just then, on the opposite side of the ferry, the duo spotted Orient Point Light. They crossed to the starboard side to watch it go by. The black and white sparkplug beacon was perched on a rocky outcrop.

"Roxanne, look!" Georgi loudly exclaimed and pointed. "A black sea monster is rising out of the water!" Several rounded black humps were emerging on the surface. As they stared in anticipation, Roxanne was ready to shoot a picture. The monster took full form when three scuba divers became apparent. She laughed and slid the phone back into her pocket. "I thought we had a winning chance of capturing the Loch Ness of Long Island Sound!" she said playfully. "And look, now I see their red diving flags."

Georgi's brow furrowed in thought. "Oh, we could have called her Sound Ness," he snickered at himself.

Nonetheless, all these distractions eased the stress and tension that underlay their real mission. Georgi and Roxanne were anxious to be on land. Finally, announcements crackled over the loudspeakers, asking the passengers to prepare to disembark. The ferry was carefully hitched to the dock, and the pair drove off.

chapter 52

The presidential convoy left the Groton Airport at eleven a.m. sharp. All personnel were stationed and at the ready along the entire route to the Coast Guard Academy. Streets and access roads were closed, and ten lanes of the Gold Star Bridge were closed to the customary heavy summer traffic. The Coast Guard was manning the waterways of the Thames River, and drones were flown to survey the entire area.

The president, in his heavily fortified motorcade, was secure in one of three blast-proof limousines. Escorting him was a gaggle of SUVs, an ambulance, and many other unseen assistors.

The black fleet came upon Route 32 and was about to turn into the Academy when a crowd of people came into full view. Connecticut College's campus had a throng of protestors that traditionally pitched themselves there to rally and raise all types of grievances, for a moment in time, to the current president.

Once through the Coast Guard Academy gates, a beeline was made to the commencement hall.

***

At eleven thirty a.m., Georgi and Roxanne traveled toward Williamson Wines on the north fork of Long Island.

"After we pass through the towns of Orient Point and Greenport, we will enter Southold," Georgi informed.

With the windows down, Roxanne relaxed and watched the scenery roll by: small beaches with windswept grasses, little cottages, large homes, and a mansion or two. Restaurants and marinas dotted the roadway and water's edge.

A sea hawk swooped in for a fishy prey, then alighted atop its huge nest of babies perched on a high post in the salt marshes.

"I didn't know it was so beautiful here," she gushed admiringly. "I guess I imagined the hustle and bustle of New York, but it's nothing like it and quite charming. Oh, and look over there!" she said, surprised. "Huge lavender fields, they're gorgeous!"

Georgi announced, "That's Lavender by the Bay. We're passing through Marion now." Acres of the lavender's purple haze mesmerized Roxanne.

Georgi's eyes twinkled. "It is lovely, but wait until you see my favorite part — it's heaven on earth!"

"It will be hard to beat that," Roxanne swooned. They passed their first small vineyard with young grapevines, newly trained on cables and connected by posts. Georgi broke into tour-guide mode.

"That's Peconic Bay on the left, and Long Island Sound on the right. We are riding the sandy bar of the north fork. A fork of land between these two waterways and the Atlantic Ocean is behind us. This is what makes Long Island's landscape unique for growing good grapes."

"Tell me more," pressed Roxanne. "This gardener needs to know the secrets of viticulture."

Georgi, now blissfully enraptured by his favorite subject, happily continued. "The influence of the Atlantic air cools the vineyards during the summer heat. Long Island Sound and the bay warm them during the winter's freezing temperatures. Grapes have an issue when it gets too moist. Fungus can develop. So the dry winds that blow across these flat beach lands help prevent humidity naturally. In every vineyard, the key is soil. It must be well-drained. This soil is sandy and coarse, so it's perfect. Too many nutrients are not good. The vine needs to strain in order to produce a tasty grape.

"Are you still interested?" he interrupted himself.

"Yes, of course, go on," Roxanne encouraged. "It helps me comprehend not only the process of growing a vineyard and winemaking, but maybe why someone would murder over the business."

"Okay, now when it comes to pruning," he rattled on, "you can achieve a better grape with a lower yield, so even heavily producing vines are trimmed hard. That allows better airflow through the vineyards and a sweeter grape when matured properly. This also makes the tannins, the bitter astringent element in the skin and seeds, better.

"Tannins affect the taste, color, and mouthfeel of wine. It truly is the land, the air, the vine, and the vintner that collectively make a great wine. Remove one and you have nothing drinkable.

"This is exactly why Long Island wines and Williamson Wines are great," he explained. "It was Lester Williamson's tender hand, insightful instinct, patience, and willingness to experiment that made great wine. He took risks, but he listened to the earth, the plants, and the weather. He developed an inner wisdom through practice, practice, practice.

"It was Lester who invited Mitch to the legendary 1988 meeting with vintners from Bordeaux, France. Mitch became so inspired that he told Lester he wanted to invest in him so he could institute the practices and ideas of these prominent and knowledgeable experts. All Mitch wanted was Long Island to have a great wine. Mitch knew Lester's past years of trial and error, so he invested in his passion and Williamson Wines. In 1995, Lester won America's finest with his Reserve Merlot."

"Georgi, now I understand Mitch and Lester's partnership better. Their perseverance is impressive, as is the humbling labor required to maintaining a vineyard. With so much effort, no wonder they became deeply attached and committed. The horticultural knowledge and the vintner's experimentation is all on the hopes to create a great wine." She nudged him. "You're quite the expert too. You're like a fine wine — you finish well!"

He smiled broadly. "I finish well? I must be rubbing off on you," he joked.

"You're spouting wine terms now."

Unexpectedly, he watched her as she studied him a moment. "What is it?" he beamed.

"Your hair is so damn perfect!" she quipped. His impeccable pompadour was still in place. He checked it in the rearview mirror, happy with the result. She flipped down her overhead mirror and was flustered by her own wind-tousled tresses. "It's time I start using hairspray," she announced and quickly pulled a comb out to restyle her blonde bobbed haircut. Once satisfied, she finished and flipped the mirror back.

"Okay!" he announced as he waved his arm across the windshield, "I present to you the first of many vineyards along the wine trail of the north fork. Welcome to my nirvana!" Roxanne gawked as one vineyard entrance after another invited them in for wine tastings. Gardens with multiple annuals trumpeted each destination with a colorful display.

A variety of alluring architectural wonders went by, some formal and old-world, others ultramodern with a few whimsical cottage charmers. Long glorious rows of green grapevines were meticulously trimmed, stretching along acres and acres that trailed into the distance.

"Oh my, this is my nirvana too, Georgi! Look at how they celebrate and work with nature! The gardens, flower displays, and look! They even have roses at the ends of the vineyard rows!"

Georgi smiled broadly. "I knew you would be glad you came. And you're so observant because the roses are an early warning system for the grower. Roses show the presence of plant-sucking aphids or mildew on the leaves. The roses are checked regularly and if they see pests or fungus, then it is time to protect the whole vineyard from an influx of problems to come."

"Wow, I didn't know about the relationship of roses and grapevines. Gee, now you're teaching me about gardening!" Roxanne smiled to herself and asked, "Why do you think roses have thorns?"

Georgi pondered the question, then asked, "Is it because they don't want to be picked or eaten?

"That is one theory, but another one is thorns help them clamber for the sunlight by hooking on to other plants so they can bloom and reproduce."

"That's like us," Georgi said matter-of-factly. "We're trying to put our hooks into some facts and clamber for our own light on the subject of Mitch and this whole mess!" Roxanne shook her head at his weaving of metaphors.

"Look, Madeline's is just ahead. You'll like her," Georgi exuded with certainty. "She is connected to the earth like you, hands-on with nature. She is at the forefront of knowledge with viticulture. She runs their property as certified sustainable, meaning safe to the environment. Her sister, Camilla, runs her own smaller vineyard and is an expert on biodynamic farming methods. Together, they are pretty impressive."

"Gee, it would be nice to meet Camilla, too."

"Oh, we will. Madeline said her sister will be there." Georgi tried to quell the dread rising inside him. "I'm feeling really nervous now. How are we going to tell her why we're here? I don't want to dredge up sad feelings in her, but it can't be helped."

Roxanne offered her advice. "We have to be gentle and simply explain what we've discovered." Trying to soothe his apprehension, she added, "If Madeline can enlighten us about Mitch and Lester's partnership, it may help us solve this debacle. I really hope she can tell us more about Morelli too. Right now, he is our mystery man. And think about how Dan will be so pleased if we find evidence for him."

"I guess this will be tough but worth it." Georgi smiled sheepishly. "It's a sure test for my cojones."

Roxanne smiled, "This whole experience is a test. We have to take this all the way. We're in deep, Louise!"

"Ha! Yes, we are, Thelma! Look at us: we're on the road, we took a boat to get here, and now we'll catch a murderer, I hope." Georgi gripped her hand as they both wished for the best.

chapter 53

Day 6 – Noon

Roxanne and Georgi arrived at the large, framed vineyard entrance and drove under an iron archway. It was artistically monogrammed 'WW' with filigrees of grapes and leaves curling and swirling. Fields of old gnarly trunks were topped with bright green grapevines and laid out in row upon espaliered row. The harmonious flow allowed Roxanne to breathe deeper as she took in the scene. "This is amazing," she whispered, not wanting to disturb her moment of utter calm.

They parked in front of the elaborate cedar shake buildings. Extensions of enclosed porches and large patios overlooked the vineyard. A pair of French doors welcomed them to enter, while plants of lavender bordered the path with blooming hot pink Knock Out rose bushes. Annabelle hydrangeas were preparing to bloom in the distance, while flowering drifts of yellow lantana, bright blue scaevola, and pink petunias offered ongoing cheerfulness through the garden beds.

Roxanne exhaled. "Peacefulness pervades here."

The French doors to the porch flung open, and there was Madeline in a casual summer skirt, wedge heels, and a loose, flowing top. Her sandy hair was in a casual updo. Her arms opened wide to greet Georgi.

"So lovely to see you, darling." They kissed cheeks, and Georgi stepped back. "Madeline, this is my dear friend, Roxanne."

"So nice to meet you, please come in." Madeline escorted them through the main room with lofty ceilings and a spacious wine bar. They arrived at a table that overlooked the vineyard. A woman entered with a platter of olives, cheeses, crackers, gherkins, crudités, and a chive dip. She placed it down and greeted them.

"This is my sister, Camilla," Madeline introduced. "She has a wonderful pear cider here from her vineyard. Would you like a glass? The alcohol is light, only four percent."

"Yes," Roxanne and Georgi chimed. Camilla poured.

"I'm so interested, Camilla, in your biodynamic practices," Roxanne exclaimed. "Can you tell me more about it?"

"Why, of course." Camilla's light brown hair fell past her shoulders and softly swooped to one side. She wore capri pants, a casual summer top, and flat sandals.

"We plant, fertilize, and do certain work according to the cycles of nature, based on temperature, time of year, and the moon's position. We make our own natural fertilizers and compost to keep at bay certain pests and fungus. Everything we do is utilizing a method developed by Rudolf Steiner, an Austrian philosopher. Many farmers are using these methods and finding the soil improved, insects greatly reduced, and the crops superior.

"I'm trying to encourage Madeline to incorporate some of these practices, but she feels they are too esoteric. Yet, she does see how well it works in my vineyard and notices the wine. Biodynamic wines are less allergy inducing too."

Madeline spoke in French while pointing to her lips. *"Ma soeur, tout le monde est le bienvenu à leur propre opinion."*

Georgi interpreted for Roxanne, "My sister, everyone is welcome to their own opinion."

Madeline raised her glass and said, "Cheers, to our friends."

They sipped, and Georgi cooed, "Ooh, the pear wine is so delicate and refreshing, Camilla. I love it." He took a deep breath, sighed and then reached for the appetizers.

Madeline noticed his sigh. "Georgi, how are you doing? I'm beside myself about our dear friend, Mitch. I have visited Marissa twice. I'm so sorry. He was Lester's best friend, and he'd been so good to me, making sure I had everything I needed to keep the business going. Look how they are both gone in a year. It's heartbreaking. I don't understand what happened. It's just terrible. How could this happen? Who did this to him?"

"Oh, Madeline, it's so hard, and you know of this because of Lester. And my dear Roxanne, well she found Mitch." Georgi hung his head and was overwhelmed with emotion. He used a napkin to dab his eyes, and Roxanne spoke up.

"I'm so sorry, Madeline, for the loss of your dear husband. We actually came to bring you news of something we discovered and wanted you to be the first we tell." She paused briefly and continued. "Georgi came across a file in Mitch's laptop. It looks as though Mitch was doing research on Morelli International Distributors. Morelli has been investing in vineyards around the world, and we were wondering how much you knew about this."

Madeline gave a still, dead stare to her sister. Camilla asked, "What are you saying?"

Georgi explained, "It's possible, is it not, that Morelli might have thought Mitch's thirty percent ownership of your vineyard would be available to him after his death? Maybe he thought he could acquire it by negotiating with Marissa. Mitch's files say that Morelli tried to repeatedly buy him out, and Lester, but they both refused. I don't know if you knew that."

Madeline informed, "Lester and Mitch were so good about running the business, I let them be in charge, and I handled the wine tastings and renting to private parties and weddings. I didn't know."

Georgi continued, "At some point, Mitch must have become disenchanted with Morelli, and he made arrangements with Lester. First by assuring you received Lester's fifty percent ownership and then Mitch placed his thirty percent into a trust to protect it from Morelli. I just read the files. You and Lester were the executors if anything ever happened to Mitch.

"I'm sorry, Madeline, but what I am trying to say, which is so hard to say, is that Mitch researched Morelli's domination of small to medium-sized vineyards around the world. Mitch was concerned for you and wanted proof. Morelli purchased other successful vineyards, like yours, with award-winning wines. It looked as though he strong-armed many and to some...well, unfortunate things occurred."

Georgi looked grief stricken as he explained. "Madeline, my dear, I'm so sorry but frankly, I think Mitch was suspicious that Lester did not die from just a heart attack."

Madeline's hands went to her face, then to her stomach as she doubled over. Camilla quickly reached for her sister and hugged her. Realizing the possible horror that Lester could have been murdered was overwhelming. In a low undertone, Madeline uttered, "This is so bizarre."

Dismayed, she explained further. "Art Morelli is in our business and in my life. He has tried to wine and dine me. He's been offering to help me, wanting to invest more into the business. He says he wants to relieve me of the workload. He said I could partially retire. I was actually considering it." Suddenly, she had another realization, and her demeanor changed. "I think I found something you need. I'll be right back." She left and quickly returned.

"This is Lester's." She presented a computer memory stick. "I recently found this in the bottom of a strongbox Lester kept in the wine cellar with receipts and a few business papers. I didn't realize he had anything worthwhile in there. This was in an envelope inside the box with a note. 'In case of emergency, view this with Mitch.' I didn't know it was there or I would have told Mitch, and now it's too late." Her voice trailed off as she started to sob.

Teary-eyed, Georgi hugged her. "I'm so sorry." After a few moments, she regained her composure.

Georgi sat by her and made an offer. "Madeline, Roxanne and I are working with Detective Morrison in New London on Mitch's case. There is so much that has happened that I won't bother you with the details. But if you don't mind, I'd like to take this memory stick to him for the investigation."

With tissues in hand, she said, "Of course, dear." Then she suddenly became aware of the likelihood of Georgi's theory. "You get that bastard, Georgi, or I'll kill him myself." With a bereaved sigh, she said, "You'll have to excuse me now. I'm too upset to continue." Madeline hugged Georgi and said good-bye to Roxanne.

"Georgi and I are returning directly to New London on the ferry, Camilla," Roxanne gently informed. "We'll call you with any new information. I think we have what we need for the detective." Camilla nodded while holding back her own tears. Georgi and Roxanne saw themselves out.

Once outside, Georgi softly moaned, "Oh, I feel horrible." Tears rolled down his face, and Roxanne dabbed them with a tissue. The fresh air, flowers, and sunshine did not penetrate his sorrow.

"Georgi, let's go. We have to keep moving and stay focused. Let me drive for a while. Okay?" Georgi gratefully handed her the keys. They drove straight away on Route 25 toward Greenport.

Roxanne looked at her watch. "We have an hour before the ferry leaves. Let's stop in front of this ice cream stand and look at the memory stick." Georgi agreed. They opened Mitch's laptop and plugged in the stick. Up popped Lester's files of his dealings with Morelli.

Roxanne reviewed the notes Lester made and paraphrased aloud to Georgi. "Lester says he had a bad feeling. Even though Morelli was friendly, he felt excessively pressured. Lester regretted letting him invest in his business. He didn't like the idea of adding Morelli's choice of grapes to his wine blends.

"He says here he didn't want to bother Madeline with his concerns. So he just put everything in these notes as he tried to figure out what to do. He says they suspected Morelli, so Mitch helped him arrange the trust that protected his business for his family.

"He researched other Morelli holdings. He created a spreadsheet that showed Morelli at the top and any possible subsidiary companies listed below. It was a difficult process but through his vintner connections and word-of-mouth, Lester verified these connected enterprises. Morelli would pretend to help a family by investing in their vineyard until he could control it. The more Lester researched, the more he felt Morelli was acting like an international monopoly, trying to own and control the wine prices and distribution.

"He told Mitch his concerns, and together they made a plan to protect Williamson Wines. The pattern was obvious: Morelli was building an empire constructed on the hopeful dreams of vineyard owners while pillaging for his grandiose schemes of supreme market domination."

Roxanne added, "Lester followed all his details and data with a haunting phrase. 'Mitch, if something happens to me, take care of Madeline and investigate that bastard Morelli.'"

Roxanne's voice became unrecognizable as she belted out a clarion call. "We have to call the detective now!"

Jolted by her fierce toll, Georgi yelped, "Call him! Call him now!"

Chapter 54

Day 6 – 1:00 p.m.

"**D**etective Morrison here."

Roxanne had the detective on speakerphone and started the conversation off casually. "Oh hi, Dan, it's Roxanne and Georgi. We are here on Long Island to meet with one of the vineyard owners." Unable to maintain the farce, her tone changed, and her voice sped up. "We discovered hard evidence here in North Fork that connects Morelli International Distributors to Mitch's death and possibly Lester Williamson's."

Morrison stood stunned, feeling as though she had just spun his mind. Trying to catch up to what was said, he realized her words had deep significance.

Roxanne continued to blurt on. "This morning, Georgi found a laptop Mitch had left at Vinho Verde under the cash register. We looked at some files and came here to talk to Madeline, Lester's widow. She gave us a memory stick she recently found. We opened it, and it confirmed Mitch's research on Morelli. It's very incriminating, Detective!"

Morrison reeled from relief and disbelief. The responsibility he felt for Roxanne's safety was monumental, and she didn't seem to comprehend the gravity of his duty to her husband, Chief Samson.

"Roxanne," Morrison thundered, "I swear to God, you're nuts! What are you doing? These people are really dangerous! Do you know the president of the United States is easier to manage than you? I know this because your husband is handling his visit to the Academy now!"

She looked at Georgi with raised eyebrows and mouthed, "We're in big trouble." Georgi crinkled his face, wondering how seriously in trouble. He pulled out a lavender handkerchief and patted his forehead.

Sternly, Morrison instructed, "I want you to stay right there. I am sending a pair of local officers to escort you to New London." He took an obvious deep breath, then growled the words, "Where are you exactly?"

"We're at the Magic Fountain ice cream stand in Mattituck in Georgi's PT Cruiser. But we have to make the three o'clock ferry," she whined, looking at the time.

"Just stay put. We'll get you on the ferry but with an escort. Do you hear me?" he asked, completely frustrated.

"Yes, I hear you. We'll wait, but I'm afraid for Madeline at Williamson Wines in Southold."

Trying to respond gently, he said, "I'll send an officer over there too. Okay?"

Softly, Roxanne said, "Yes, Dan."

"Good," he said and hung up.

"We have to wait here for the police," Roxanne confirmed.

"Oh, he's mad at us!" Georgi said, not amused. "I thought he'd at least be grateful for all our hard work."

Staring longingly out the window, Georgi read the Magic Fountain's ice cream list. "Can I have an ice cream? It sure would make me feel better."

Roxanne smiled, noticing the little boy inside the grown-up. "Sure thing. I'll treat and have one too." Roxanne gave him the money and while he was in line, she further explored Lester's files on the laptop.

Finally, Georgi returned with the ice cream. Roxanne enjoyed a dish of coffee Heath bar, and Georgi had black raspberry chip. After several bites, someone knocked on the window. Georgi's mouth was full, and Roxanne looked up with a spoon in her mouth.

"Ms. Roxanne?" a man asked. "Detective Morrison asked us to escort you and Mr. Georgi to the ferry. Are you ready?"

"Uh, I was expecting the police," Roxanne protested.

"We are, ma'am," he answered as he quickly flashed his badge. "We are in plain clothes so we don't draw any undue attention."

"That makes sense. Do we follow you?" she asked.

"No, we will follow you, ma'am."

She put her ice cream in the cup holder and drove toward Greenport. A police car suddenly went past them with flashing lights on.

Greenport was dotted with fancy bed-and-breakfast inns, restaurants, and charming shops. Georgi admired the tasteful window decorations and large flowering pots at the store entrances. "Oh, they have some ideas I could use," he mused. "Marco would love it here," he dreamed.

Once at the ferry terminal, they waited in the car lineup and finished their ice creams. The plainclothes officers followed them onto the ferry. In the canteen area, one officer stayed with them while the other scoped out the ship and decided the second-floor open deck was the most secure.

The officer instructed, "Ms. Roxanne, we'll have you and Mr. Georgi sit outside here on the forward exterior deck, if you don't mind. We will be posted inside and have an eye on you at all times to keep the area secure."

"Oh, that sounds fine," she acknowledged. As soon as their escorts stationed themselves indoors, she poked Georgi. "Don't you feel better? Isn't it nice to know you have your own bodyguards?"

"Oh yes!" Then he mimicked a posh accent. "Mr. Georgi is quite pleased to have his own bodyguards." They laughed, relaxed, and stood at the railing overlooking the water. This smaller deck was located at the bow. The larger upper deck was behind the captain's wheelhouse and faced the aft of the ship. Lucky for Roxanne and Georgi, the small number of passengers on board at this time gave them the privacy they and their undercover escorts needed. From their secure perch, they gazed toward their future again as the boat traversed Long Island Sound's expansive waterway.

Georgi turned back to look ashore. He observed blue flashing lights on the

Orient Point dock. "They sure have plenty going on around here in Long Island. I thought this was a sleepy tourist town. Boy, was I wrong."

She joshed him with a nudge, "Maybe they're escorting someone important."

He smiled and then was distracted. "Look at the Jet Skis behind the ferry." They both moved to the starboard side and leaned out to look behind the boat. Two Jet Skis were speeding toward the ship, taking advantage of the ferry's wake. The curling foam of white water offered a substantial ramp for the WaveRunners. Applying crisscrossing maneuvers, the Jet Skiers high-jumped the waves and deftly became airborne. "Wow, look at them go!" The water acrobatics kept the two entertained as the boat moved further away from shore.

Roxanne's hair was whipping around and once again, she noticed Georgi's hair holding steady. "I need a new hairstyle for water travel," she teased him, "but if I put that amount of gel in my hair, I would look like a wild emoji or a manga character!"

Georgi laughed. "Once I get it right, I don't want it to move the rest of the day." His hand puffed his hair like a 1950s actress, then he struck a pose. Roxanne rolled her eyes and pointed to the view looking toward Plum Island. The fleet of fishing boats had grown, vying for a freshly caught dinner.

Finally, the two decided to sit on a bench and relax. Simultaneously, they heaved a happy sigh. Both were feeling more confident than they had in the week since Mitch's death.

Unknown to them, from every angle, their future was about to radically change.

chapter 55

While Georgi and Roxanne relaxed in their safe zone, a gentleman in a gray running suit suddenly approached them. He had dark hair, a shadow of a beard, dark eyes, and a fine form. Their jaws dropped, stunned by his good looks. His handsome presence induced them to stand up.

In a soft, smooth, hypnotizing accent, the fellow spoke. "Roxanne, my dear, what did you do with the diamond you found?" He leaned toward her in a demanding way that was mystifyingly precocious.

"What? What diamond?" she stuttered confused.

"The one I lost in your garden, sweetie, next to Mitch." The hot breath of Mr. Silver warmed her skin as he pressed against her and cinched her arm. "Don't play the fool with me, Blondie. I'm not a patient man."

"Leave her alone, you brute!" Georgi pounded on his back. The man pushed him aside easily.

"I don't know about any diamond!" protested Roxanne, trying to push him away.

Georgi warned him, "We have security guards. Get away from her!"

"Those men are with me, you idiot," the villain seethed through his teeth. He motioned the thumbs up sign to the guys, and they gave it back.

"Oh no!" Georgi wailed.

The man barked at Roxanne, "This is your last chance, my dear. Where's the diamond? Do you have it on you?" He attempted to check her pockets, making her feel disturbingly invaded by his hands. She swatted him with vigor, using all she had to fight him off.

"Leave us alone. I never found a diamond!" she answered angrily and attempted to push him off balance, but his solid form did not budge.

He growled, "You've been all over that garden, sneaking around in it. Where is it?"

"I never saw it," she yelled. "I don't know what you're talking about!"

His annoyance peaked. "Don't be coy with me, sweetie. Maybe a cold swim will refresh your memory."

Roxanne screeched, "Don't you dare! If I had it, I'd give it to you."

He lunged forward. "Then tell it to the fishes!" In one swift motion, he scooped her up and tossed her over the rails into the water twenty feet below. Roxanne screamed the whole way down.

Georgi screeched, "You're crazy! You're a madman!"

"Yes, I'm mad," he hissed. His eyes looked to be on fire. He frisked Georgi, who yelped in pain from the man's forceful maneuvers. He found Madeline's memory stick and pulled it off Georgi.

"Hey, that's mine," Georgi bemoaned.

"It's mine now, you buffoon, and your laptop too. Here, have a drink on me." He lifted Georgi up like he was a toy.

"Oh no, oh no, oh no!" Georgi hollered.

Holding him horizontally in the air, the man grunted, "*Arrivederci,*" and threw him over the brink. Georgi plummeted into the choppy water below.

***

Meanwhile, Detective Morrison received a call from the Long Island police officers. "Detective, Madeline Williamson is secure in Southold. But we did not make contact with Roxanne Samson and Georgi Algarve."

"What?" Morrison roared furiously. "What is going on? That woman is going to drive me to drink."

The officer continued, "They weren't at the ice cream stand, so we sped off to the Orient Point Terminal. The ferry had just left when we arrived. The manifest had them listed as driving onto the ship."

Morrison issued, "If anything happens to them, I don't know what I will do. What is the name of that vessel?"

"The *Mary Ellen*, sir," responded the officer.

"Okay, hold there at Orient Point. I'll contact the Coast Guard," Morrison informed.

"Copy that, sir. We'll wait to hear from you."

The detective called Coast Guard Sector Long Island Sound, who manages operations on the waterway. They patched him through to the Coast Guard station in Montauk, New York.

The call was answered, "Captain Harelson here."

"This is Detective Morrison in New London. I have a hot one." Dan explained the situation, then asked, "Can you radio ahead to the *Mary Ellen* and have the captain secure Roxanne Samson and Georgi Algarve until you get there? I want you to board that ship and take control of it. There is a possible assassin on board, and these two are his target. They are in imminent danger."

"Yes, detective, we are in Gardiners Bay, five nautical miles away. We're on it right away." Captain Harelson ordered his crew of the response boat to respond immediately and prepared the crew of the motor lifeboat to back them up. Captain Harrelson radioed the *Mary Ellen* and spoke to Captain Griswold, informing him of the details and to prepare to be boarded.

***

Having been plunged deep into the churning waters from a twenty-foot fall, Roxanne and Georgi were both scrambling for the surface in the cold fifty-eight-degree water. Roxanne broke the surface and gasped for air. She was grateful to be a good swimmer, but the waves had four-foot swells. Looking desperately for Georgi, she kicked off her shoes to remove their weight. She spotted him surfacing and yelled as loudly as she could, "Georgi, over here! Are you okay?"

260

He was coughing up water. He gurgled, "No." The bobbing waves made it difficult for them to see each other.

The ferry was moving further away when finally, people on the upper deck spotted them. "Man overboard!" they yelled.

Chapter 56

The elusive Mr. Silver immediately grabbed the backpack with the laptop in it and bolted past the doors where his comrades once stood. He slid down the staircase into the belly of the ferry. Suddenly, he heard a walkie-talkie. "Code Red – be on the alert for anyone suspicious."

A deckhand rounded the corner and was blindsided instantly by a punch to the head that knocked him out cold. The walkie-talkie continued announcing as Silver listened. "Locate a five-foot-two-inch blonde, middle-aged woman named Roxanne Samson and a five-foot-ten-inches, slim, twenty-nine-year-old man named Georgi Algarve. Bring them to the captain's wheelhouse immediately!"

Silver opened a life jacket storage bin and pulled out a stash of items for his escape, then shoved the deckhand into the bin. He rapidly removed his clothes with an athletic Velcro maneuver and revealed his wet suit. He loaded the laptop into a waterproof bag and latched it to his diving belt. The memory stick was placed in a secure waterproof pocket. He slipped into his fins and then lifted on a scuba tank backpack.

Silver set his diving compass and slipped into the water. In record time, he was submerged. His two accomplices, the men pretending to be plainclothes policemen, had moved to the canteen for drinks and an alibi.

Captain Griswold's crew was several steps behind Silver's reclamation operation. Having heard 'Man overboard,' Griswold informed his crew to implement rescue procedures and caught sight of Roxanne and Georgi through his binoculars. Griswold radioed Coast Guard Captain Harelson and reported,

"Two persons are overboard zero point two nautical miles off our starboard side. We are attempting to rescue."

When Griswold saw the Coast Guard boat in the distance bearing down, he ordered his crew to stand down and prepare to be boarded. The Coast Guard's precedence in this whole procedure was customary.

***

Roxanne hollered to Georgi, "Hang in there. I see a boat with flashing lights." She swam toward him using a stiff breaststroke. The waves helped bring her closer. She could see he was dog-paddling and having serious trouble keeping his head above the waterline.

She yelled, "Georgi, kick off your shoes and wave your arms in big circles." She attempted to swim closer, but the strong undercurrent now seemed to work against her. She panicked. *I can't get to him.*

"Look at me," she yelled. "I'll keep swimming to you."

The Coast Guard's response boat, a twenty-five-foot high-speed craft used for search and rescue and law enforcement, swiftly approached them. Roxanne shouted, "Help!" and waved her arm. The vessel slowed down and flung out life rings. Roxanne grabbed hers quickly. Georgi couldn't swim to his and was being swallowed by the waves. He went under. Roxanne kicked toward him, but he was gone. "Georgi!" she shrieked. His head bobbed up, he took a breath, and he went back under. "Oh no!" she pleaded.

Looking to the rescue boat, she saw a guardsman in a wet suit dive in after Georgi. Retrieving him quickly, Georgi came up sputtering and coughing. The rescuer kept a hold of him until another ring was thrown out, and the diver caught it. Georgi's savior gave him a slap on the back. "Hang in there, buddy, and let us do all the work." He stayed behind Georgi, making sure he was secure and alright.

The guardsmen hauled them both aboard. Wet, cold, and fatigued, the pair was led inside and given towels and dry coveralls to change into. The officer in charge quickly asked what happened and for a description of the men involved. The response boat approached the ferry. A second Coast Guard boat, the forty-seven-foot motor lifeboat used for law enforcement and Homeland Security, arrived to assist.

Crews from both boats boarded the ferry. Their tasks were to systematically search the boat and the water for the men and find any telltale signs of the predator that had thrown the two overboard.

The response boat with Roxanne and Georgi raced toward New London to deliver them to the emergency medical service crew and authorities there.

Approaching the pier, they could see the Coast Guard Cutter Chinook waiting with two response boats and an emergency fanfare of red, white, and blue flashing lights. Ambulances, fire trucks, and police cars were prepared for any required need.

Roxanne was horrified to see all the commotion. "Well, this is it, Georgi," she motioned to the crowd. "This is all for us. I'll be grounded for a year and leashed to the porch!"

Holding her hand, he apologized. "I'm so sorry, Roxanne. It's entirely my fault. I talked you into this, and the killer took our evidence. We have nothing." Wet and forlorn, he looked hopeless.

"Don't you worry, Georgi. We're alive, and that's all that matters. Nothing else matters. Do you hear? We are in one piece." She gave him a hug, wiped his tears with her blanket, and kissed his cheek. "A nice hot chocolate with scones will make everything better. I'm so proud of you. And don't forget that, no matter how mad anyone gets." Her thoughts drifted to Detective Morrison and Sam. *They're going to be hopping mad.*

The paradox of the morning's peaceful departure was not lost on Roxanne as the response boat slowly approached the dock. The boat rocked as it maneuvered its turn and reversed. She felt dizzy again as time on the water seemed to move in slow motion.

Once they were roped to the dock, everything sped up as if someone hit the fast-forward button. Men jumped on and off the boat. Georgi and Roxanne stood up, jolted by the activity. The duo looked like prisoners in their baggie gray jumpsuits and damp hair. The water had destroyed Georgi's perfect coiffure.

Soon they were hand delivered to the EMT and ambulance crews. Detective Morrison and Chief Samson, in uniform, raced forward. Sam grabbed Roxanne away from an EMT, squeezed her right off the ground, and kissed her. Then he set her gently down.

He whispered into her ear, "Are you okay? You could have drowned."

"I know," she said, "but I didn't. Thankfully, I'm a good swimmer." She smiled sheepishly up at him. The paramedics continued monitoring them both. "I'm really okay, guys," Roxanne protested, as she didn't want any more attention. "Check on Georgi. He's the one who nearly drowned."

Georgi piped up, "I'm alright, but I need to talk to the guy who saved me. Is he here?"

They brought the young Coast Guard rescue swimmer forward, and Georgi put out his hand to shake his. Pumping his arm enthusiastically, he raved, "You saved my life, you know! I would have drowned if you hadn't jumped in when you did. Thank you! Thank you so much! I'm forever in your debt!"

The rescue swimmer, now in his duty uniform, responded, "*Semper paratus*, we're always ready, sir, I just happened to be the guy there today. That's all, sir."

"Sir, don't call me sir," Georgi admonished. "You saved my life! Call me Georgi. You and your friends are welcome to the Vinho Verde anytime. You have lifelong drinks on me!" His arm went up and down as Georgi continued shaking his hand.

The rescuer finally retrieved his hand. "Thank you, sir, I mean Georgi, but what is Vinho Verde?"

"It's the wine bar on Bank Street here in New London. Bring a date, and I will impress her. Not that you need that, you're already impressive," Georgi giggled.

The guard smiled. "I will bring my friends, but right now I need to get back to work." He stepped away with a salute. Georgi saluted back with a broad smile and clicked his heels, immediately remembering he had lost his shoes.

Morrison arranged with the Coast Guard to hold Roxanne and Georgi in his vehicle. The pair waddled in their oversized jumpsuits to his SUV parked in a strategic position. They both sat in the backseat as the ferry boat arrived.

With the windows down, Morrison and Sam stood outside the vehicle to talk with Roxanne and Georgi while keeping them safe. Uniformed men were everywhere. Orders were being yelled; walkie-talkie radios were transmitting voices with static. All were at the ready to capture anyone suspicious as they came off the arriving ferry.

***

The national and local presses, having been previously released from the presidential visit, were now in the process of broadcasting the breaking news happening nearby on the Thames River. Their satellite transmission trucks had all moved to cover the events.

"We are on the scene and reports have just come in…The president of the United States had no sooner left from delivering his commencement speech at the Coast Guard Academy when all departments were called to an active scene at the ferry terminal in New London.

"It appears two people were accosted on the ferry from Long Island and were thrown overboard into the cold waters of the sound. Quick action resulted in a rescue by the Coast Guard of Montauk and New London. We are here on the scene live and will update you as more information comes in."

chapter 57

Mr. Silver's adroit getaway into the waters of the sound was flawless. His choreographed diversion of WaveRunners weaving over the ferry's wake assisted with his ruse. And the scuba divers near Orient Point Light were ready to support him underwater, if required. Additionally, the active summer boat traffic easily deflected the nature of his covert operation.

Quietly, like a water snake, Silver slinked, traveling with the water currents in the sound. His fins swiftly delivered him to the agreed coordinates of a fishing boat in Plum Gut. His well-equipped accomplice hauled him aboard. Easily, he was whisked away.

The various sailing and leisure boats in the sound remained oblivious to his silent endeavor until a sudden activity of flashing lights and blaring sirens from a Coast Guard boat sped toward the ferry.

The fishing boat Silver occupied motored along the west edge of Plum Island toward Bostwick Bay off of Gardiner Island. There they met with a polished classic wooden Chris-Craft. The 1948 motor purred as Silver boarded with his salvaged items. They sped toward East Hampton, New York, to dock where a car awaited on Old House Landing Road.

Silver was satisfied he had fulfilled his mission for Morelli; the laptop and memory stick were secure. Lester and Mitch had gone too far trolling personal vintner channels and using private investigators to collect the data. But the incriminatory evidence of Morelli's worldwide scheme would remain in-house. He knew Morelli might not acquire Williamson Wines, but at least all his holdings were safe from scrutiny. The self-appointed winner snickered to himself victoriously. *Non scommettere contro un uomo che non perde mai* (Don't bet against a man who never loses).

Soon, Silver would meet up with Morelli in Cuba and would be grandly compensated for his tireless work. Yet he lamented, *Se solo avessi avuto il diamante* (If only I had attained had the diamond)! Un grande premio. Sarebbe stato bello. *Una ciliegina sulla torta. È un peccato.* (A great prize. It would have been nice. A cherry on top. It's a shame.)

chapter 58

Detective Morrison directed Roxanne and Georgi. "The passengers are about to come ashore. I'd like you two to point out the men who abducted you."

"We weren't abducted," they chimed. "We thought they were police," Roxanne said defensively. "They had badges and said you sent them as plainclothes officers."

"I know," Morrison expressed with a sigh. He explained further, "They must have been following you all day. There's obviously a lot of money behind this job." He shook his head. "Damn, this is bigger than any of us could have imagined." He pointed toward Jack Peabody.

"Detective Peabody has been researching Morelli all day, and I had an officer on Long Island contacting him this afternoon. On the surface, Morelli looks spotless and starched, like all white-collar criminals. So we contacted the FBI. They are on the investigation too."

Morrison was interrupted by people and cars readying to off-load from the ferry. Each person was required to submit identification, and the cars were being searched. Suddenly, Roxanne recognized the vehicle the two phony undercover officers had driven. As it moved down the ramp, there was a blonde woman behind the wheel.

"That's the car," Georgi shouted, "silver with tinted windows!"

"But how can that be?" asked Roxanne. "Who's the blonde?"

Morrison spoke into the walkie. The officers pulled the car over, and the woman came out with her hands up, looking terrified.

"They have my boy," she whispered to the officers. She looked over her shoulder. "They made me drive their vehicle off." She burst into tears. "Find my son. Please! Find my boy."

The officers took her aside. "Stand here with us, ma'am, and watch for the people who have your son."

Georgi was scanning the crowd. Then he saw the imposter, without his jacket and tie but with rolled up sleeves and tousled hair. He was walking off the ferry holding a two-year-old boy in his arms. The child had a lollipop in his mouth.

"I think that's him!" Georgi said pointing. Morrison yelled an order over the walkie to the officers. They rushed in and grabbed the man with the child.

Racing to the woman, Morrison advised the men, "She's the victim here, officers. Just have her stay for questioning." Liberated, the mother reached for her boy, hugging him and sobbing into his shirt.

Roxanne examined the boat. "There, Dan!" she yelled. "The front end of the ferry — a man jumped off!"

"Eeeww," Georgi sounded disgusted, "he just plunged into the briny cocktail of the Thames."

Chief Sam's head cocked as he smiled. *That's Georgi for you.*

One of the coast guardsmen on the docked rescue boat saw the man plunge into the water. He raced to the closest water access and jumped in, nearly on top of him. The thug surfaced with his fists swinging. Another guard leapt in, swamping the assailant. Both guardsmen lugged him to the dock's edge, holding his neck and feet. Additional servicemen grabbed him up and out of the water and cuffed him in one swift, simultaneous movement.

"But where is the third guy?" Roxanne asked.

The detective and Chief Samson entered the SUV and sat in the front. Rolling up the windows, Morrison answered, "It was reported that a deckhand on the ferry was knocked out and woke in a cargo bin. The perpetrator left behind clothes and a duffle bag. The Coast Guard is scouring the ferry and searching the waterways.

"It's possible he had others working with him for a swift escape. We are looking for him in Long Island too. Don't worry, we'll get the bastard." Morrison's determination was evident.

"Oh, what a relief," Georgi expressed as his hand went to his head and then to his heart. He fell back in his seat. "This is more drama than even I can take."

"Take a deep breath, Georgi." Roxanne held his hand. "It's okay. It's all over, and we survived." Then she laughed. "This truly was like a Thelma and Louise adventure, except we didn't do anything wrong." Morrison and Sam looked at each other in disbelief.

Georgi flashed a sideways look at her. "Ah ha! Oh my God, we were threatened, manhandled, and thrown off a boat. Yet, we are still alive!"

The realization washed over them in laughter. Tears of joy streamed down their faces. Roxanne snorted and Georgi giggled, both laughing at each other laughing.

He squealed, "Stop, I'm going to pee my pants!"

She chuckled. "You could have done that when you were in the water!" An ongoing belly laugh ensued that they couldn't seem to control.

Morrison eyed the chief, who said knowingly, "You know what is happening, don't you?"

"Yeah, I've seen it," Morrison replied nonchalantly. "Nervous laughter. People become ridiculously elated when they realize they are okay after a traumatic event."

The men shook their heads incredulous. "They're hysterical," Sam remarked. "They can't stop even though it's inappropriate."

Morrison noted, "It's a good thing they are in the car with the windows up, or else they'd be carried off to the loony bin by the EMTs!"

"Considering their antics," Sam offered, "we should take them to the psych ward for an evaluation and leave them there for a while. We have the authority, don't we, Morrison?" The detective rubbed his chin with serious consideration and smiled slyly.

Hearing them, Roxanne pinched herself so she could stop laughing. Georgi watched her go through these motions and crossed his legs while giggling.

Morrison flicked his head toward the door and nudged Sam with his elbow. "How long do you think they will carry on?"

"I don't know, but I think it's time we walked away," answered Sam. Both men opened their doors and left the SUV.

As they strode toward the task force, Morrison reported, "With these two men in custody, the FBI involved, and some questionable practices of Morelli, this case is coming together. It's Mr. Silver that has me concerned. He's damn unpredictable."

Sam gave Morrison a friendly slap on the back. "Dan, I'm looking forward to getting my wife back." Their acknowledging glances spoke volumes. It reminded Sam of one of Morrison's unusual cases. "Remember when the circus came to town and you had to investigate the strange death of that naked woman found in the elephant pen?"

Morrison raised his eyebrows high. "That was a doozy! And what about that weird guy Lenny the lip-locker years ago? All those nine-one-one calls for a 'man down' from bars on Bank Street. Whenever you told me it was the same guy pretending to be unconscious and luring the sailors to give him mouth-to-mouth resuscitation, well, that was beyond my imagination!"

"Yeah," Sam added, "until we caught up with his ruse. He had a system of rotating through the bars, and finally he was banned from them all."

Dan says, "I think the sub-base still has his face up on posters saying, 'Beware of Lenny the lip-locker!'"

Sam chuckled. "Yeah, and I heard someone listed on it the names of the guys that were tricked for a kiss!"

Dan laughed. "So, Sam, we'll just add today's events to the list of strange and amazing!"

As Roxanne watched Dan and Sam walking away, she suddenly remembered the danger on Long Island. She jumped out of the car and raced toward them. "What about Madeline and Marissa?" she puffed.

Georgi was quickly behind her. "And Camilla?" he piped.

"We sent officers to gather them up immediately," Morrison replied. "The police have been searching Madeline's property and have just begun to find cameras and listening devices. I expect the entire place was bugged, including her phone lines and Internet. They were likely listening with a scanner to your cell phone call with me, which explains how they pulled this all off. The women are fine, a little overwhelmed, but they're okay."

"Oh!" Georgi clutched his chest. "Another heart attack avoided," he crooned.

Morrison informed Georgi, "We have your car, so now I need the laptop and Madeline's memory stick. My men will review the files for evidence. We need to verify the possibility that Lester and Mitch were both murdered by Morelli's assassin."

"Ohh, no!" Georgi wailed.

"What now?" Morrison asked as he gawked at him impatiently.

"That horrible man took Mitch's laptop and the memory stick!" Georgi gulped.

"What! All of our evidence?" Morrison nearly burst an artery.

Roxanne tried to allay the sudden tension. "I can help. I have a confession to make." Sam looked at his wife and hoped beyond hope that she wasn't going to say something that would put Dan in the hospital.

Looking at both Dan and Georgi, she said, "I copied the laptop files when we were at the Vinho Verde this morning. I put them in a secure file that I have on the Internet. Since I've been managing our NLBC garden blog, I learned how to do this with photographs."

Georgi leapt out and hugged Roxanne. "Thank you, thank you. We are saved! At least we have something. But wait! That brute took Madeline's memory stick off of me. That data really could have sealed the deal on Morelli."

"Well, that's not all." Roxanne paused.

"Don't be evasive now," Morrison said. "I need all the help I can get."

She continued, "When we were at the ice cream stand, I copied the memory stick files to my online account too."

Now it was Morrison's turn. He wrapped an arm around Roxanne and gave her a kiss on the top of her head. "Now that's my kind of woman," he said, smiling at Sam.

Gleefully, Georgi proclaimed, "There detective, I knew you had some chaptalization in you."

"What's that?" all three voiced.

"Sugar added. It's a winemaking term for when one adds sugar to the grape juice before fermentation. It makes the wine sweeter." He smiled knowingly. "In other words, it's nice to see your sweet side detective."

Sam shook his head and stepped toward Roxanne. "My dear, I think you saved the day." He gave her a kiss. She smiled and glowed in the adoration.

"Dan, I can email you the files now from my phone."

Morrison immediately forwarded the files to the FBI. Then he turned to Roxanne and Georgi. "Okay, Wonder Woman and Spider-Man, you two are officially and permanently off the case! Chief, you are my witness."

"I am," Sam said grinning. Then he looked deeply into Roxanne's eyes and said, "Now, that's it, that's all. No more snooping, whispering, wondering, or worrying. Let's go home, shall we?"

Georgi saw Roxanne cross her fingers behind her back. "Yes, dear," she said with a chirp. Georgi caught her eye before saying good-bye. He realized there was something left unsolved.

chapter 59

DAY 6 – 4:30 p.m. - Morelli's Escape Plan

Mr. Silver had called Art Morelli from the Chris-Craft getaway boat and told him the deal was done. He had Mitch's laptop and Lester's memory stick, and they would meet in Cuba. Grateful that the fiasco of confiscating the evidence was over, Morelli arranged for his helicopter to be ready for takeoff. Hurriedly, he packed a bag to leave his Long Island home for good.

Morelli and his henchmen boarded his private chopper stationed on the front lawn of his grand summer home. They were airborne instantly. Morelli took in a final glance of the widow's walk where he stood a week earlier. His Sikorsky helicopter zoomed toward the East Hampton airport.

Before landing, Morelli had the pilot circle around to scope out the landscape. They saw no police or unusual activity. Having made a call to his pilot, Morelli's Learjet waited on the tarmac for him. His chopper landed. Morelli raced to the Lear and boarded as his helicopter left.

The jet pilot was cleared for takeoff. He taxied down the runway and was soon in the air. Art Morelli reclined and gave instructions to the pilot.

"Take me to Cuba, Maurice. We have friends with cigars and rum waiting for us."

"Yes, sir."

"Maurice, have the flight attendant bring me a Wild Turkey on the rocks, will you?"

"Yes, sir."

The self-satisfied mogul stretched out in his recliner, feeling like he was on top of the world.

A moment went by before a silken, female voice spoke. "Wild Turkey on the rocks, sir." She handed him the drink from behind on his left. He took a long sip of the superior bourbon and put his glass on the coffee table.

Her sultry tone now made him an offer. "I have something else for you, sir."

"What's that?" he murmured, looking out the window.

She dangled an object in front of him. "Would you kindly put these on?" A pair of handcuffs came into view. "I'm FBI Agent Myers. Arthur Morelli, you're under arrest for your connection to the murders of Mitch Stockman and Lester Williamson."

Behind him, a gun clicked in his right ear. He heard a man's voice. "And I'm with Interpol, Morelli. Today, you're the turkey on the rocks!"

chapter 60

The day after her unintended swim in Long Island Sound, Roxanne attempted to return her life back to normal. It was a quiet morning and a pleasant day.

Sam asked, "What do you want to do today, honey?"

"Oh, nothing special. I'm just planning to rest, relax, and maybe do a little gardening," she said casually.

"Okay then, shall I go into work or call out for the day?" he asked.

"Oh no, you go in. I'll just putter around here," she answered.

"Good, I'm glad to hear it." He dressed in his uniform and was out the door in no time.

Roxanne stepped outside to admire her garden. Her tomato and herb bed was coming along well. The rhubarb was ready to harvest. Overall, she felt the garden looked good. It had stayed at peace while she traveled a long weary road, playing cat and mouse with an evil man.

Her thoughts meandered to Georgi. She decided to visit him to see how he was doing the morning after almost drowning. Jumping into her truck, she took the waterfront route along Pequot Avenue to Bank Street.

As she drove aside the Thames River, she rejoiced at the freedom she felt. Serenity had a place in her life again, and everything looked fresh and new. She passed Mitchell College's campus and the waterfront beach. Green Harbor Park came into view, and she looked over the small garden site she managed with the New London Beautification Committee. Roxanne thought of her friends fondly and looked forward to telling them her tale.

Even though her world seemed normal again, there was one last nagging issue. She mused, *Maybe Georgi will help me.*

It was just nine a.m., and the tarts were still available at Muddy Waters Café. Roxanne made a quick decision and delivered the goodies to Georgi at the Vinho Verde.

She found the door wide open and so were the windows that overlooked the deck to the Thames. She stepped inside and looked around. She heard his familiar footsteps coming up the stairs from the wine cellar, and Georgi appeared.

Roxanne greeted him, "How are you?"

"Fresh breezes, Roxanne, fresh breezes have rolled in, and I feel good." He did a James Brown dance move across the floor with flair.

"I brought you something," she said, "so we can celebrate our freedom."

"Oh, you're so sweet," he cooed. They sat on the outdoor deck. A ferry air horn sounded. They looked at each other knowingly while munching crisp, flaky tarts and sipping hot coffee.

"You know, Roxanne," Georgi's voice was rising with each word, "I was wondering what that man was talking about when he asked you about a diamond."

"I don't know. I thought he was just crazy, but he was obviously dead serious."

Georgi pondered, "But I was thinking, it doesn't make sense that you were mugged and shortly after, some man was at your house. And what about the guy who beat me up, asking me what you found?"

Roxanne stared out at the water. "Well, I don't know anything about a diamond, but it seems likely the killer thought I found it in the garden. Soo…," she eyed him impishly, "maybe it's still there?"

"But the police were all over Columbus Circle," Georgi reasoned. "You yourself said they took a hundred pictures and went through it with forensic precision. They would have found it. Or maybe it's in police custody, and they never told us. What do you think of that?"

"After all we've been through, don't you think Dan would have told us about a diamond? Besides, no one knew there was a diamond involved." She touched his arm. "But I have another idea. Why don't we just take a quick look to satisfy our curiosity? How about it?"

"I have someone coming in two hours. Is that enough time?" he asked.

"I think so. It's just to search under Columbus's feet in the garden," she smiled.

"Okay, Thelma, are we mining for diamonds?" he asked coyly.

"Why not? Don't they say diamonds are forever?" she declared and stood up. "We are finally on a peaceful quest."

Georgi blinked and, in a flash, he pictured Roxanne as the heroine embracing a palm frond atop the Soldiers and Sailors monument in the Parade Plaza, a symbol of peace.

"Yes," Georgi said, transfixed on his image, "a peaceful quest will be refreshing."

***

Roxanne parked her truck at Columbus Circle near the bistro. Gone was the yellow crime scene tape. While Roxanne stood on the edge of the garden, she tried to imagine what had occurred.

"If the murderer knew Mitch had a diamond, he might have threatened Mitch for it first."

Georgi continued the thought. "So let's say Mitch fights him and in the scuffle, the diamond goes flying."

"But diamonds are small," added Roxanne, "and could easily be lost in the garden or street."

"Mitch could afford a big diamond," Georgi boasted. "He's richer than you know."

279

"Why would he have a big diamond?" asked Roxanne.

"Well, he did mention it was his wedding anniversary in a month. Maybe it was a gift for Marissa," he surmised.

"Okay then, let's look carefully," she said. "Let's do it like the police and section an area off. I'll start here, and you start there," she suggested. While looking under every plant and along the surface, she moved the soil with her feet.

"We are just repeating what has already been done," Roxanne mumbled as she lifted the lid on the green ground box. Finally, they stopped their search.

With hands on hips, Roxanne tried to imagine a flying ring as Georgi stared at the sidewalk on the edge of Columbus Circle and Bank Street. "What's that for?" He stared down into a circular grate.

"It's where excess rainwater goes so the sidewalk doesn't flood," she answered.

"Oh, do you think a diamond could have dropped into it?" Georgi asked.

"Well, it's pretty far from where Mitch was found. I guess we could check." She went to her truck and grabbed a couple gardening tools. She pried the grate open with a shovel. They both peered down into the wet darkness.

"Here, let me turn on the flashlight feature of my phone," Georgi offered. It brightly lit the watery pit, but it was difficult to determine the water's depth.

"I'm going to put my hand down there," Roxanne said.

"Ooh, isn't it nasty?" Georgi asked, squeezing his nose.

"It's not sewage; it's just water runoff," she explained.

"Oh, okay," he conceded while still wrinkling his nose. Kneeling, Roxanne put her arm in, and her hand came out with nothing in it.

"Oh, that's too bad," Georgi sighed.

"It's too deep. I'll be right back." Roxanne went to her truck and took out a floor mat and grabbed a bucket. She put the mat on the ground and laid on it. She told Georgi to be ready to pass her the bucket as her cheek pressed against the mat. Then to Georgi's surprise, she slid into the opening headfirst with her shovel in hand. Disgusted, he grimaced with horror.

"Hold my legs, Georgi." Her order echoed from underground. "Sit on them." Overwhelmed, Georgi did as he was told but was well aware that to anyone passing by, the scene of her down the hole while he sat on her legs looked bizarre. It taxed even the limits of his eccentricity.

Concerned, he pleaded, "Hurry, if you can. People are going to wonder what we're doing. They may even call the police!"

"Let them, Georgi!" Roxanne's voice boomed defiantly from the hole, "We're on a mission!" Her shovel scraped below the dark water along the bottom. "Hand me the bucket," her voice resounded, and he did so.

She loaded several shovelfuls into the bucket. "It's full of gravel. I doubt it's here."

Georgi helped her up. Once on her knees, she stuck her hand into the bucket and wiped over the mud-covered rocks. With no results, she stuck her hand in and felt around. A larger rock was among the others, and she pulled on it. A sucking sound released it from the mud. Georgi winced, repulsed by her operation.

She smoothed the mud off, noticing it was different somehow. "Oh my God! This isn't a rock!" she exclaimed. Quickly, she pried it open, and a huge, glinting, pink diamond appeared.

"OHHH!" they both squealed. She closed the ring box, grabbed Georgi's arm, and hurried him toward the water spigot. Roxanne knelt and turned on the water to wash the ring box.

She excitedly whispered, "Pink diamonds are rare and expensive! I can't believe it was here all along!"

"Oh, Roxanne! I can't believe you found it! I couldn't be happier! I never, never, never would have gone down that horrible hole! You're amazing!"

Roxanne stood up and pulled Georgi toward her truck. Celebrating, they jumped up and down hugging each other.

"We're amazing!" She smiled. "Okay, now that we found it, I'll call Dan and ask him to stop by."

Georgi's forehead creased. "Alright, but I'm not sure how he'll feel about us slinking around. He told us we were off the case."

"Don't worry," Roxanne assured cheerily. "This is good news. It's lost and found, not murder and mayhem!"

Chapter 61

Detectives Morrison and Peabody arrived at Roxanne's truck, wondering why they were congregating at the tailgate of her truck.

"Hello, you two," Morrison started. "I'm curious why we are here, but let us first give you some good news. You tell them, Peabody."

Pleased to inform, Jack stated, "Last night, the FBI and Interpol captured Morelli. He was trying to escape to Cuba on his private jet."

With great relief, Roxanne and Georgi collapsed dramatically against each other.

Roxanne leaned in toward Morrison and loudly whispered, "Dan, those men are crazy! They were almost the death of us!"

With compassion, Morrison understood. "I know, Roxanne, and those men affected our whole police force too. Jack is my witness. It was as if we were training for a triathlon, mentally and physically. But most of all, I don't know if I could have lived with myself if you two were harmed any more than you were." He gave her and Georgi a knowing smile.

"I know, Dan, but let's face it. Georgi and I went a little too far with our private investigation work." Georgi nodded in agreement. "We would have stayed home if we had foreseen the outcome of landing in the waters of Long Island Sound. And it was so embarrassing. All those men and women who know me as the fire chief's wife, and here I am involved in a big fiasco! It's not a good look."

Morrison laughed. "It will be in the ledgers of New London's history; another tale we will account and retell, again, and again."

"Oh, please no, I don't want to be one of those silly stories." Roxanne knew there was nothing she could do about it. This was one of those tales that would go around the story circuit for years to come.

"Let me tell you," Morrison added, "after talking with the FBI's profiler, the observation was that Morelli's a classic, gluttonous narcissist. Although, they haven't caught Silver, as yet, they say his antics are a combination of military training and greed, a sadistic hit man who obviously takes pleasure in showing off his intelligence to taunt all of us."

Roxanne interrupted, "This is why I couldn't leave this last piece unsolved. I needed to know why he was after me. I'm an innocent nobody who found a body. I have no connection to Mitch. So I needed to know why I was mugged, and why he went to my house? So I did some digging, literally."

Looking at her queerly, Morrison wondered what she was up to now. He realized she was like a genie in a bottle, always fighting to escape and solve her own problems. "Roxanne, does this have to do with this bandana on the tailgate? Because I told you, you're off the case."

She nodded. "That man you call Silver," Roxanne explained, "yesterday, he asked me what I did with the diamond."

Both detectives exclaimed, "What diamond?"

"That's right, what diamond?" Roxanne referred to Georgi to back up her story.

Georgi reenacted the events on the ferry with fervor. "That beast was yelling at her, manhandling her, searching her pockets, demanding that she give him the diamond. I was pounding on his back." Georgi demonstrated in the air. "This was right before the ogre threw her in the water!"

Reliving the scene, Georgi became even more animated. "Then he turned on me! Lifted me over his head and threw me. Down I went into the water." Georgi gulped air as if he was going under again. Then ending his story, he swiped his brow with relief. Then, as if mimicking a stage performer, with a presentational swoop of his hand, he offered Roxanne to take her turn.

Taking her cue, she continued. "I told that handsome goon I didn't know about any diamond. So, then I started figuring, if he was that obsessed with thinking I had it, what happened to it? So I commandeered Georgi here to help me." She put her hand on Georgi's arm. He was now beaming with excitement.

Roxanne stepped toward the bandana. Carefully, she unfolded it until a dirty black case was presented. "I thought maybe we could find the diamond." She opened the case and exposed a sparkling pink diamond ring of seven-point-nine carats.

"Whoa!" Morrison and Peabody exclaimed with shock.

"Well, I'll be!" Jack said. "That's some booty!" Peabody eyed the diamond like a pirate. "It's magnificent!" He leaned toward Morrison and said under his breath, "That's some rock, boss. How come our forensic team didn't find it?"

Morrison looked at Jack, raising his eyebrows as if to say 'don't make us look bad!'

Roxanne explained, "Dan, I know you told me to stop looking into things, and I did promise Sam, but I was curious. I figured this had to be the reason the guy came after me. He thought I found it and kept the diamond for myself."

Roxanne pointed to the Columbus garden. "Georgi and I searched the areas your forensic team did, but when Georgi asked about the catch basin over there on the edge of the sidewalk, I thought why not look? So we used my tools and floor mat, and I went right in there, headfirst, while Georgi held my legs."

Baffled, Morrison ran his palm over his forehead. "It's a miracle you found that ring. I have to hand it to you two, you're quite a team. And you didn't tell me about it! You had to keep playing the secret agent role to the end. Didn't you, Roxanne?"

"Dan, I didn't want to bother you after all we had been through. And it was just a hunch I wanted to follow through. Please don't be mad at me. We were just lucky. It hasn't rained since Mitch was found, otherwise it could have been swept away."

Suddenly hit by the memory of Mitch, Georgi became a little misty-eyed. "Look at all we've been through in a week. Mitch died trying to protect Lester and Madeline's wine business. He tried to fight off that hit man and save Marissa's ring. We would be nowhere if I hadn't found that laptop he left behind. Somehow, we've survived everything." Georgi felt grief and gratitude for Mitch.

Roxanne gave him a sympathetic squeeze and told the detectives, "Georgi thinks Mitch planned to give this gorgeous ring to Marissa as an anniversary gift. You need it as evidence, don't you?"

"Yes, we need to document its involvement in the case." Morrison shifted in place while thinking through the sequence of events. "This ring would have been an extra bonus in Silver's pocket. Without a doubt, he thought you found it. No wonder he went after you with such determination."

"Will you give it to Marissa, Dan?" Roxanne asked.

Georgi instantly responded, "Can I make a tiny request, Detective?"

Dan was unsure. "Well, what would that be?"

Georgi whispered in Roxanne's ear. Her eyes grew wide, and she nodded.

"Can I trust you two?" Morrison asked.

"I promise," Roxanne raised her right hand, "we are now harmless."

Georgi made his request. "Could I be the one to present the diamond to Marissa? Mitch and I were good friends, and I feel closer to her now. I'd love to be the one to surprise her."

"Yes, of course you can, Georgi."

Jack Peabody was intrigued by his boss's response and looked at him a little differently. He seemed to be softening.

Detective Morrison spoke sincerely, "We would not be where we are in this case without you two. In the end, you made my department look great, especially by finding this ring. It's another piece to the puzzle and helps answer all the shenanigans these goons were putting us through: committing three murders, disrupting our entire community, and fixating on siphoning money from every opportunity. You two are the unspoken heroes. Silver is a professional hit man, but he never anticipated the likes of you."

Jack chimed in, "It's because he thinks he's so smart that he will eventually be caught."

Morrison asked, "Is there anything else I should know about before we leave? A basement hideout, another secret?"

"No." Roxanne and Georgi shook their heads to assure him.

"Alright then, you are both relieved. Consider this my official thank-you."

Georgi saluted, and Roxanne curtsied and winked. Morrison looked at Jack curiously. He had a smirking grin on his face. Jack lifted his hand to his cheek, and the huge pink diamond glimmered on his finger. Batting his eyelashes, the feminine pose had them all roaring with laughter.

Chapter 62

Silver's Chris-Craft getaway boat landed at a dock in East Hampton, New York. He rendezvoused with a man who would transport him to his next destination. The driver supplied a change of clothes for Silver and drove him directly to a private helicopter pad. A chopper was waiting to whisk him to a New Jersey airport where a charter jet had been arranged to take Silver to Cuba.

A rush of adrenaline surged through Morelli's advocate as he finally boarded the jet with his bag of recovered goods, the laptop, and the memory stick. He scanned the deluxe interior as a beautiful flight attendant welcomed him. She asked what he would like to drink.

Testing her, he said, "Corton-Charlemagne Grand Cru."

"Yes, sir, I have a bottle chilled and waiting for you. Mr. Morelli insisted we have it on hand." She made her way to the galley. Silver watched her sultry figure stroll to the rear of the jet. "Hmm," he hummed. The engines roared. She returned, and he watched her gracefully pop the cork off the bottle and pour him a glass of the fine vintage.

"Why don't you join me?" he purred. "No one should drink alone."

"Oh my, I'd be delighted," she demurely accepted and returned to the galley to take a glass from the rack.

While watching her, he tipped his glass, savoring it, and then drank it down entirely.

She returned, and he offered, "I will pour for you." She sat across from him and smiled alluringly, admiring this mysterious man who was handsome, tan, and well-dressed.

Mr. Silver finished the pour of the pale, expensive wine and reached out to hand it to her. His arm started to shake. He looked at it curiously, then at her in disbelief. His expression changed as he realized he'd been drugged. Helplessly, he watched the hostess reach under her skirt for a Beretta M9A3 from her thigh holster.

The last words he heard were, "Let's celebrate, Mr. Silver. I'm Athena, a bounty hunter working with Interpol. Today, I'm disseminating Bacchus' vengeance for wine crimes. I took a page from your playbook, you schmuck, and laced your glass with mandragora."

Silver slumped in his seat. The mandrake root or mandragora was an ancient powerful sedative that had been slipped into the wine of warriors since 200 BC.

Chapter 63

The Vinho Verde Wine Bar

A few weeks later...

Georgi hosted a memorial service for Mitch Stockman at the Vinho Verde. Many of the vintners, growers, and vineyard owners from the southeast region of Connecticut attended. New London's local business owners and restaurateurs also came to give their respects. Madeline Williamson and her sister Camilla had accompanied Marissa Stockman and her daughter Vanessa from Long Island. Ferry Captain Matthew Griswold and his wife Antonelle joined Detectives Morrison and Peabody at their table.

Roxanne looked around the room. Georgi had beautifully decorated with large bouquets of elegant white flowers all around. There were fragrant peonies, white lilacs, lilies, tall delphiniums, and greens of lemon leaf and asparagus fern. Smaller bouquets of short cut tulips, lily of the valley, and sweet peas adorned each table. Background music was provided by Georgi's friend, Christine Tulis, who elegantly played a large Celtic harp. A small podium was set in the foreground with a microphone for those who wished to speak at the service.

The vintners were first to come forward. Effusively, they stated their great appreciation for Mitch's friendship, love of wine, and support of their businesses. Each one said Mitch had helped them through low sales and offered good advice on wine and finances.

Camilla, Madeline, Marissa, and Vanessa sat with their arms around each other, listening to the lovely accolades.

Marissa said a few words. "Thank you all. I had no idea how Mitch touched your lives, as he obviously did. My heart is so full. I am grateful to all of you for sharing another aspect of my husband with me. His love of wine went further than I realized — it went straight into your hearts.

"Now I understand his great love of wine, his wonderful business partner Georgi, and this delightful wine community he fostered. I hope to know you, his friends, so you might also become mine.

"I have to say that our dear friend Lester Williamson was also a victim of this unfortunate greed. I want to honor him here on behalf of his wife Madeline. We are forever friends.

"Detective Morrison, I thank you and your department for diligently pursuing the case and exposing the men who were responsible for Mitch's death. I feel vintners worldwide owe a debt of gratitude for your assistance in uncovering his insidious operation.

"It's an honor to Mitch and Lester that you utilized their research to take down an international conglomerate that was trying to take over and manipulate the wine industry worldwide.

"And lastly, yet most importantly, thank you, Georgi, for all you and Roxanne have done to serve justice. Without your help, I don't know what would have happened. With much gratitude, I thank you all for coming."

As she was about to step away, Georgi moved forward and asked Marissa to stay by his side. "Marissa, please excuse me for using the vintner term, but I know you will agree that Mitch was a 'star bright' man. He would score points above many other men. He had a great vinosity, a flavor to his personality that was pleasing but not overpowering. There is one thing that Mitch wanted to do for you, but he didn't get the chance. He obviously loved you very much and held you dear in his heart, above wine I might add. Mitch had planned to take the summer off to be with you. There was something he wanted to give to you to express his eternal love. Here it is."

Sitting in Georgi's palm was a beautiful bright pink box. Surprised, Marissa looked at Georgi and said, "What is it?"

Georgi explained, "Mitch, according to well-done research, managed to procure this little item to celebrate your anniversary." Georgi popped open the box, and Marissa's hands went to her face.

Georgi continued, "This is a fancy seven-point-nine carat pink emerald-cut diamond. Mitch went to see the jeweler, Mr. Orlando, in Stonington Borough, to have it sized for you. He wanted it to be a secret."

The room gasped. Marissa put on the ring, and tears rolled down her cheeks. Her daughter and friends gathered around her. She composed herself and said, "My heavy heart has been filled with love. I want all of you to know that I will wear this ring proudly, knowing Mitch helped solve this wine business delirium. Thank you all for your love and kindness." The room clapped loudly. A dry eye was hard to find. Drinks were poured, and hugs were shared all around.

Roxanne and Sam asked Detective Morrison to join them in a quiet corner. Sam wondered, "Did you find out more about Morelli's operation, Dan?"

"Yes, I did. Thanks to Mitch and Lester, we have the details that revealed the crime conglomerate. The FBI has connected at least a half dozen murders of vineyard owners worldwide to Morelli. And you'll find this interesting, Roxanne," Morrison added. "In most cases, the deaths were not suspicious but tipped off by poisonous plant derivatives. We learned that digitalis was used to create a heart attack in Lester Williamson's death. Jimson weed was used in others to create a quick death when it was added to food or a drink. And water hemlock was confirmed to have finished off Charlie Brass. We only knew that one because the assassin brazenly displayed it on him.

"It will take some time to fully investigate the twenty years Morelli had been investing in and buying out vineyards. The FBI and CIA are working with Interpol to determine the size of the operation. It is expected that, eventually, the families of the vineyards will regain their ownership and be fully reimbursed by Morelli's wealthy holdings."

Roxanne anxiously asked, "What about the killer, Silver? Who was he, and is he gone for good?"

Morrison looked at Sam, then quietly said, "Roxanne, you're lucky to be alive, dear. He was a really bad guy. Think of a James Bond gone wrong."

"Or maybe like Jason Statham," Roxanne said, smiling.

"She likes him!" Sam said with a sideways glance and raised eyebrow.

Morrison added, "Silver has a permanent home in jail and depending on who charges him first, he could get the death penalty."

Roxanne whispered, "Good! He deserves whatever he gets." Feeling fully relieved from danger, she took a deep breath and excused herself. "I need some fresh air. I'll be outside on the deck."

The men decided to visit the bar for another drink. Both Sam and Dan ordered a beer, and Jack Peabody joined them.

Jack nudged Dan. "Hey, boss, I think there is a woman here who knows you. She looks something like the long-legged beauty on your Safe Harbor beer bottle, but she's a brunette."

Dan glanced in the direction Jack was referring to. The long-legged beauty caught his eye and moved toward him. Somewhat taken aback, Dan watched this divine looking woman in a formfitting skirt, a draping blouse, and high-heeled, heading straight for him. He turned to see who was behind him because she certainly had to be approaching someone else. Jack and Sam leaned away as they saw that her target was Dan.

"Well hello, Detective. What a mighty fine job you did catching that devilish man," she congratulated him.

Dan stared at her, wondering where he could have met someone like her and not remember.

"Excuse me," he said, "but do I know you?"

"I think the only thing you could possibly remember," she said with a smile, "are my eyes or my voice."

Jack and Sam held their breath like teenage boys at their first dance.

Dan looked into her eyes directly as she said, "Don't worry, Detective. This happens all the time when you're the angel of death."

Suddenly, those golden-brown eyes and tone of voice were familiar, and Dan realized who she was. "Dr. Angela Storm, you certainly caught me by surprise."

She gently laughed, amused at another charade in her profession of wearing scrubs, hairnets, and medical masks. Sam and Jack both took a swig of beer and inched away, wondering if Dan Morrison had finally met his match.

***

On the deck of the Vinho Verde, the umbrellas were up, and a fresh breeze wafted as the setting sun cast a glow upon the water. Georgi joined Roxanne, putting his arm around her. "Well, my dear, it's been a blast, but I'm hanging up my PI shoes."

"Oh, are those the ones you left at the bottom of Long Island Sound?" she teased him.

Georgi frowned. "Those were my midnight-blue, leather lace-up Santonis."

"I don't know what those are!" she exclaimed.

"All you need to know is that they're Italian, and thankfully, they were insured," he said smiling.

"I think I still have a lot to learn from you," Roxanne quipped.

He raised his glass. "Thanks to you, I learned how to have brass cojones!"

She chuckled. "Well, thanks to you, we solved this together and bonded in ways I don't care to repeat." They clinked their glasses, sipped their pear wine, and watched the peachy sunset hues brush the buildings. As the golden glow of colors glinted off the windows from across the Thames, a warm summer breeze gently lifted the tablecloths around them.

"Fresh breezes, Roxanne, fresh breezes," Georgi sang.

All their cares seemed to drift away upon that breeze like a colorful hot-air balloon floating aimlessly into the ethers, suspending all concerns. They both exhaled a long happy sigh, lingering in the moment. A peaceful luxury as this was worth savoring as long as possible.

THE END

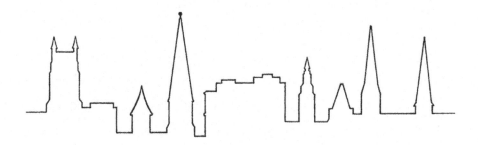

Months later...

At eight a.m. on a Friday morning, Georgi was sweeping the front sidewalk of the Vinho Verde Wine Bar. His dance music played from the exterior speakers, and the young wine sommelier swung the broom around like a partner. Bending back in a dramatic final move, Georgi's upward glance captured something odd on the third-floor balcony of the popular Hygienic Art Gallery.

Turning so he could achieve a better view of the curiosity, Georgi suddenly let out a bloodcurdling scream and wildly raced up and down Bank Street, not knowing what he should do.

The beautiful Marilyn Maroney, wearing a daring pinup girl dress, had been pierced dead. Her curvy form was in an awkward backbend position, draped over her recently installed art sculpture. Marilyn had been impaled. Her blood was dripping down her arm, creating a dark pool on the sidewalk below. Her lovely face was frozen in the horror of her last moment alive.

***

Keep watch for the next grand adventure of Roxanne and Georgi with the familiar cast and a few new characters. Discover the popular art communities of New London and Mystic, observe the twisted intricacies of a mad plot, and an art dilemma of the highest order in the City of Steeples.

Available Now:

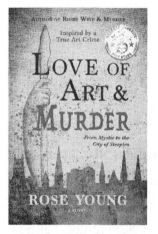

For the latest information and author talk schedule visit my social sites:

Facebook: @RoseYoungAuthor,

Instagram: @RoseYoungAuthor, and www.RoseYoungAuthor.com

You can sign up for my Mystery Fan VIP List for updates.

Acknowledgments

Thank you to New London's local businesses for inspiring my story: Thames River Greenery's Fred Argilagos's advice and allegories of wine, spirits, and cigars; Muddy Waters Café; Washington Street Coffee House; Captain Scott's Lobster Dock; Tony D's Fine Italian Restaurant; Sarge's Comics; Harbour Towers; Dev's American Bistro; HIVE Skate Shop; Hygienic Art Gallery; Whaling City Boxing; Cross Sound Ferry and Captain Matthew Dawley. Last, but not least, The New London Beautification Committee for your inspiration by making the city beautiful with flower gardens for us all to enjoy.

Thank you to local historian Sally Ryan and her classes at the New London Library and to the staffs at New London's Maritime Society's Customs House, The Olde Town Mill Historical Society, The Groton Monument Museum at Fort Griswold, The Coast Guard Academy's Museum, and to New London's, *The Day* Newspaper, for inspiring me with local stories and fabulous photography of Southeastern Connecticut.

With great gratitude and humble appreciation to my 2021 Editor, Heather Doughty of HBDEdits.com; and to my colleagues, encouraging friends, readers, and initial editing team: Editor Terrie Scott, Henry Koster, Firefighter Bob Lawton, Paula Anderson, Deonn Bunnell, Lisa Gray, Paula Michaud, Ann and Fire Chief Ron Samul, Ryan Torkelson, Lana Westgate, cover design Illustrator Cindy Samul, and Paul Maisano for the Italian translation.

A special thank-you to my dear friend and filmmaker, Joanne LaRiccia, aka Jojo. She gave enthusiastic support continuously and manifested my book trailer video.

Roses, Wine & Murder - Book Trailer Video:
YouTube – Roses, Wine & Murder Mystery
Vimeo Link - https://vimeo.com/238502114

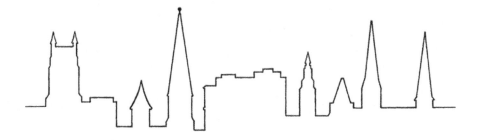

History books that inspired the story:
Wicked Plants by Amy Stewart
Griswold Point by Wick Griswold
Homegrown Terror: Benedict Arnold and the Burning of New London by Eric D. Lehman
History of Connecticut Wine: Vineyard in Your Backyard by Eric D. Lehman and Amy Nawrocki

Wine, Food, and Winemaking books that inspired the story:
First Steps in Winemaking by C.J.J. Berry
Oldman's Brave New World of Wine by Mark Oldman
Wine, Food & Friends and *The Wine Bible* by Karen MacNeil
The Winemaker Cooks by Christine Hanna
Wine Lover's Cookbook by Sid Goldstein
The Vintner's Apprentice by Eric Miller
Matching Wine with Food by Le Cordon Bleu

Music that enhanced the mood in storytelling:
Ch. 17: 'I Will Survive' sung by Gloria Gaynor
Ch. 21: 'Take Me to Church' by Hozier
Ch. 22: 'Despacito' sung by Luis Fonsi & Daddy Yankee
Ch. 38: 'Cruisin'' by Smokey Robinson
Ch. 40: 'Into the Mystic' by Van Morrison
Ch. 45: 'Summer in the City' sung by Lovin' Spoonful
Ch. 46: 'Riders on the Storm' by The Doors
Ch. 47: 'Mercy' sung by Shawn Mendes
Ch. 48: 'Safe and Sound' by Capital Cities

About the Author

Photo by Jojo LaRiccia ©2017

Rose Young grew up in the wilds of Maine and moved to Boston to attend New England School of Art & Design. Her profession in landscape garden design brought her to volunteer for a day at a city garden in New London, Connecticut, USA. This is where the story, ***Roses, Wine & Murder*** was born. Rose surrounds herself with nature, family, and friends in Southeastern Connecticut.

www.RoseYoungAuthor.com

Facebook: @RoseYoungAuthor

Instagram: @RoseYoungAuthor

Email: BestBooksPublish@gmail.com

Sign up for my <u>Mystery Fan VIP List</u> on my website!

Thank you for reading my book!

If you enjoyed the story, <u>please leave a review</u> on your favorite book site, or see my website for links.

Thank you! Rose

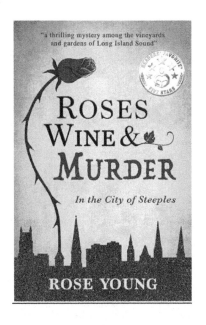

Roses, Wine & Murder - Book Trailer Video:
YouTube: Roses Wine & Murder Mystery

www.RoseYoungAuthor.com

Facebook: @RoseYoungAuthor

Instagram: @RoseYoungAuthor

Join my <u>Mystery Fan VIP List</u> on my website for special updates!

Email Rose at: BestBooksPublish@gmail.com

Made in United States
North Haven, CT
20 January 2024

47690073R00174